EYES

He knew the boy and the girl would be going into the lobby, so he crawled through the ducts to the grate just above the doors. He pressed his face hard against the thin bars to get the scent of her hair. It was exciting. He moaned softly and inhaled.

He moved forward, squirming and twisting his body as he slithered through the ducts, his lips dry, his tongue moving spasmodically in between his teeth. The boy and the girl were moving deeper and deeper into the hotel. He felt as if he had dropped the building around them and closed them tightly into his world. . . .

Books by Andrew Neiderman

BRAINCHILD
PIN
SOMEONE'S WATCHING

Published by POCKET BOOKS

ANDREW NEIDERMAN

SOMEONE'S WATCHING

PUBLISHED BY POCKET BOOKS NEW YORK

Distributed in Canada by PaperJacks Ltd., a Licensee
of the trademarks of Simon & Schuster, a division of
Gulf+Western Corporation.

Another *Original* publication of POCKET BOOKS

POCKET BOOKS, a Simon & Schuster division of
GULF & WESTERN CORPORATION
1230 Avenue of the Americas, New York, N.Y. 10020
In Canada distributed by PaperJacks Ltd.,
330 Steelcase Road, Markham, Ontario.

ISBN: 0-671-42831-4

First Pocket Books printing March, 1983

10 9 8 7 6 5 4 3 2 1

POCKET and colophon are registered trademarks
of Simon & Schuster.

Printed in Canada

ACKNOWLEDGMENTS

Ann Patty, an editor with the creative powers of a Muse; Pat Capon, for her insight and concern.

For my mother,
whose proud gypsy eyes
filled me with the dream.

Preface

Marty stood by his window and stared into the darkness below. He was looking for some movement, some confirmation of the terror and dread he sensed once again. He was afraid to lie back and close his eyes unless he was so heavy with fatigue that he knew he would fall asleep quickly. Being alone and thinking had become terrible. The moment his eyelids closed, all of his childhood nightmares returned.

As a little boy, he had often been cast into loneliness and darkness. After a while he had learned to subdue the tears by turning his fear into hate: hatred for his mother who had overdosed on heroin and left him at the mercy of an alcoholic father, hatred for the forces that had put him into this position, and hatred for his own genes, which made him resemble the parents he had come to despise. He had reached a point where he rarely cried, where he defied shadows and found nothing threatening in the sounds of the night. Now it had all changed. Once again fear had taken hold, and he had not found a way to defeat it.

With the moon so full and bright, he could see far into the white birch and maple trees behind the house. The moonlight made the bark of the birch glisten. When he looked to the right, he could see the old country road, its chipped and cracked macadam liquefied by the lunar rays. It seemed to flow past his house like a quiet river with an almost imperceptible movement. All around the house and across the street, the shadows of trees merged and then parted into elongated and distorted night fingers as the wind lifted and dropped the branches with a hypnotizing regularity. Although he could not see it, Marty raised his eyes and looked in the direction of the hotel.

The thought of it quickened his heartbeat and filled him with a sense of guilt. It was as though the hotel beckoned, drew him to its caverns of dark hallways, its dining room frozen in time, the tables set for imaginary guests. Despite its dangers, the hotel had become another world for him, a place where he could forget who he was.

He turned from the window and started downstairs. He moved as one in a trance but paused to be sure Judy didn't hear him. She wouldn't understand; she couldn't go back. Satisfied that she was still asleep, he continued on, walking softly down the stairs, avoiding the steps that creaked the loudest, until he was out the door. Once on the porch, he hesitated, and then, no longer in control of himself, he followed the beckoning shadows up the old road toward the hotel.

Where they lived, so far out of town, there were no streetlights. The closest house was more than a mile the other way toward town. There was always a heavy darkness about the house at night, and once he left the small reach of the single yellow-bulb porch light, he was totally dependent upon the moon. If there were no moon, it was next to impossible to see anyone, even if the person was standing beside him.

On warm summer nights the bats would dive toward the glow of the porch light and then pull away with miraculous maneuvers. Often he wouldn't see them; he would just hear them or feel the breeze created by their vampire wings.

He turned around quickly and headed back toward the house, afraid of the faces that would come out of the night—faces that in his youth had eyes filled with fireflies and mouths that twisted and turned in gleeful smiles, becoming even more distorted until they turned into liquid and poured themselves into the black earth.

He continued to study the darkness from his bedroom window, moving his gaze back from the road, along the edge of the forest, and to the yard. The feeling was stronger than ever. It was so strong that he turned to look at Judy to see if she had sensed it too and risen from her sleep. But she hadn't. He was happy about that. Since they had returned from the hotel, she had trouble sleeping. Now all he would have to do is tell her about the dark shadows out there and what he thought it meant. She would have endless nightmares.

Maybe death is a punishment after all, he thought, *and when evil people die, their spirits linger here on earth in torment.*

3

He thought again about the hotel. They had only gone in a few rooms, but at night, behind a hundred or so closed doors, perhaps the evil ones were left to their own nightmares, forced to relive their terrible actions. He shivered with the thought that someday his spirit would be locked in one of those rooms.

He had been left alone so much in his life that he had come to believe that there was always something there beside himself. It protected him only as long as he did what he knew in his heart was right. Now he felt as though he had lost the protection. So much of what had just happened remained confusing for him. Judy had once implied that they were committing one of the worst sins of all by violating someone else's dreams. At the time he had hoped she was wrong, but he was no longer very sure.

It was that fear that woke him at night, that brought him to the window to stand and search the darkness. It wasn't over; it hadn't ended yet, and what lingered draped his house with a tension that both he and Judy felt. At times they would stop talking and look at each other as though both had heard the same creak in the wood or felt the same breeze between them. Had they brought the spirits of the hotel back with them?

They were tied to each other by more than a growing affection. They shared the same primeval fear that made ancient men and women huddle beside one another in the darkest recesses of their sanctuaries. They tried not to speak about it, terrified that they might break the fragile shell protecting them from the past.

But each time Marty stood by his window at night, he remained longer and longer. There was something out there, someone watching the house, looking up at the windows. He was sure of it. Only the morning sun would bring him any relief. He longed for it.

1

Frank never exactly told him that he was going to remarry. Their conversations were rarely long or involved. For as long as Marty could remember, he was fending for himself. When he was very little, after his mother died, his mother's sister came to live with them for a while. She cooked and cleaned, but it got so she couldn't get along with Frank. While she was there, he felt some security, even more than he had felt with his mother. His aunt didn't drink or take drugs and she made him aware of cleanliness and nutrition. Much of what he was able to do for himself afterward was directly related to what she had taught him.

He never forgot the day she left, because after she had, he was struck with the realization that it was just going to be him and Frank. He was quickly initiated to what their lifestyle would be. Frank was fired from Mendy's Body Shop that afternoon. It had been his fourth job in three months. He had gone to work late, had been fired, and had headed to a bar immediately afterward. When he finally came home, he was in no condition to prepare supper or clean up.

They lived in an old two-story farmhouse that Marty's grandfather had originally left to Marty's Uncle Harry because Uncle Harry was older and a lot more reliable than Frank. Frank got the house when Harry's 30-30 rifle accidentally went off while he was hunting deer two weeks before the season had even begun. The bullet went up through his chin and entered his brain. The bullet didn't emerge, and some of the old-timers used to laugh and say, "I knew Harry had a whole lotta shit between his ears." Marty heard his father tell that story dozens of times, laughing hysterically each time.

"Your aunt left?" his father had demanded when he came home that day. She had announced that she was going at breakfast, but Frank had ignored her.

"Yes," Marty said. Whenever he remembered the scene, he recalled his voice sounding tiny.

His father had flopped into the worn easy chair, practically snapping the spindly wooden legs. Marty was afraid of him. He had seen him drunk many times before, and each time he turned belligerent and often violent. Marty stared at the old Emerson black-and-white television set, its picture snowy because all they had was a partial roof antenna. They lived in the resort area of the Catskill Mountains near a village called Woodridge, almost a hundred miles from New York City and the major networks. He was lucky to get three channels.

"Son of a bitch," his father had muttered, his eyes closed. Then he opened them quickly and sat up, his face raw and red from the alcohol he had consumed. "She leave anything to eat, 'fore she went?"

"I dunno."

"You don't know? What the hell you been doin' since you got back from school, watchin' television the whole time?"

"No," Marty had said, practically swallowing his tongue. Frank had stretched, then savagely kicked the Emerson on its side. Marty had winced and sat back, folding his arms across his stomach. He tried to prepare himself for Frank's approaching rage.

His father had always appeared giantlike to him; even now, eighteen years old, standing six feet one and weighing a solid one eighty, he felt small beside Frank. Marty knew he was powerful with his long hands and thick forearms. He handled the six-pound short-handle sledgehammer the way most men handled an ordinary hammer.

"See what there is to eat," Frank had commanded. Marty had obediently slipped off the couch and gone into the kitchen. He found a plate of cold chicken in the refrigerator and a pot of stringbeans beside it. When he told Frank, Frank told him to warm up all of it. At the age of eight, Marty had prepared his first meal. From then on it was catch as catch can. At times Frank brought in a woman to live with him. Sometimes they would cook and clean; sometimes they wouldn't do much more than Frank.

In school and in the community Marty and Frank were classified as "Scoopers" or "Stump-jumpers," terms used to describe low-class uneducated white stock who usually got by on handyman's wages or very menial laborer's pay. The first time another boy called him a Scooper, Marty got into a fight. He fought so hard and so frantically that even though the boy was much bigger than he was, Marty beat him down. Afterward, when he got off the school bus and walked the half mile down the side road to home, he cried, not because of the pain from the bruises and scrapes, but because of a deeper pain within.

For a long time he didn't understand the reason for such pain. He had little to be proud of, working barely up to average in school. He sensed there was little expectation that he would do much more and he knew that was because of Frank and the way they lived. He was quickly relegated to that clump of nonentities every school system endures, either because there is little interest in motivating them or priorities in budgets and teacher efforts demand that they be sacrificed.

But the deeper pain he felt came from a discovery about himself. While it was true that many of his friends fit the mold teachers and the system put them in, he began to feel that it wasn't the right mold for him. It took almost no effort at all for him to do the bare minimum of schoolwork, and he had questions, questions very few others seemed to have. He hid his intellectual curiosity from his friends because he was afraid of appearing different. Being a so-called Scooper was isolation enough. So when Frank decided he should quit school at sixteen to help him run their own body shop by the house, he didn't offer much resistance. And no one at school made any great effort to keep him there.

They got by with the shop. Sometimes Marty left to be a busboy or waiter in the area hotels and sometimes Frank took on part-time employment at one of the bigger garages. The heavy muscular labor built Marty into a broad-shouldered, firm young man. On a few occasions Frank tried to get him to join him on drinking sprees, but Marty refused. Of course, Frank would become more antagonistic because of that, but Marty tried to ignore it. He kept to himself as much as he could and their relationship became more and more strained. When Frank told him that Elaine Collins and her daughter, Judy, would be moving in, he had mixed feelings.

He was surprised to learn that Frank was going to marry Elaine. That kind of thing never mattered very much to Frank. Apparently it mattered to Elaine. Marty was encouraged by that. He had seen her only a few times before and didn't see anything special about her, except that she was more attractive than Frank's usual women. He had never seen Judy, so he was very curious about her when Frank brought them both over to look at the house. Frank told him that she was only about fifteen. "But she don't look like no fifteen-year-old," he added. Marty should have sensed something from that remark and from the look in Frank's eyes.

He was working on Bill Stanley's pickup truck when Frank drove up with them. The truck was battered badly when Stanley's kid rolled it failing to negotiate a turn. Marty stood up and waited while they all got out of Frank's car.

"Shoulda had that fender beat out by now," was Frank's opening remark. He headed directly for the house, leaving the introductions to Elaine.

At first he thought Judy was homely-looking. Her shoulder-length hair was a shade darker than light brown, but it hung loose and looked unbrushed. She wore an oversized, faded, blue cotton blouse that bunched up around the waist of her dark blue skirt and ballooned a little under her arms. He couldn't understand why Frank had made that remark about her. Later, when he saw her in more form-fitting clothes and her hair washed and brushed, he would see Frank's point. She had the full figure of a seventeen- or eighteen-year-old.

He wiped his hands on a rag and walked toward them. Judy looked at him and then quickly averted her gaze. He sensed her shyness and withdrawal and figured that along with her looks, she added up to a zero.

"Meet Marty," Elaine said. Judy looked up, but she didn't say anything. She just stood there playing with the collar of her blouse.

"Hi," he said. He caught something interesting in her eyes that made him look at her a little more intently.

"She's shy," Elaine said and then turned on her with a much harsher tone of voice. "I want you to get to know your stepbrother good, honey. He can tell you all about the school and the kids . . ."

"I haven't been in school for two years," he began, but Elaine wasn't interested. He looked more closely at the two women. Judy had inherited Elaine's slight facial features: a small, slightly up-turned nose; soft, light blue eyes; and a gentle mouth with an almost imperceptible, but cute, puffed upper lip. They both had high cheekbones, but Elaine's face was swollen and rounded from the excess weight she carried. Although her figure was starting to get away from her, it was easy to see that she had always had a nice one. He noticed that she had poor teeth, but all of Frank's women had poor teeth.

"You stay out here and talk to Marty," she said. "I'll go in and look over the house with Frank. Your father's hoping I won't come up with any ideas that cost money," she told him. Marty wanted to say, "If you did, it wouldn't matter because he doesn't have any." But he just smiled and nodded. Both he and Judy watched her walk to the house. There was a long, embarrassing pause between them. He looked at Bill Stanley's pickup truck. "Come over here," he said. "What grade you in?"

"Supposed to be in ninth," she said. He looked up quickly. She kept her arms folded just under her breasts and looked off at the forest across the road. He saw the way the breeze lifted strands of her hair from her temples and noticed the patch of freckles about the bridge of her nose.

Girls had always been a mystery to him. He had never been as successful with them as most of his friends were. For one thing, he was too particular. His two buddies, Buzzy and Tony, always accused him of messing up double dates and spoiling things for them. When they tried to fix him up, they paired him with the "easy" girls, girls anyone could go with. On occasion, when they pleaded with him desperately, he would do it just so they would be successful.

But he hated these forced dates. He felt like his father then. Frank could go with any woman; it didn't matter if she was short, tall, fat, skinny, had teeth, or didn't have teeth. He didn't make love to a woman, he made love to women, the gender. Marty had no greater fear than the fear that he would eventually become like his father.

But when it came to the girls he admired, the girls he thought were special, he found it almost impossible to get to know them. He never had to get to know the "easy" girls; they shoved their bodies at him, pressed their lips to his with more vigor than he had, and hungered for some animal satisfaction that terrified him with its ferocity. It was as though they were out to steal his manhood, drain him of his sex. He was afraid of them.

He wasn't afraid of the "special" girls; he was confused by them, by the things they laughed at, the way they turned a phrase or said hello. He had trouble beginning a conversation, finding common ground. He could say anything he wanted to the "easy" girls—it didn't matter; it didn't count. But with the other girls, first impressions were important because he wanted them to like him. He was afraid they would never like him. There wasn't much to like, as far as he could see. The bottom line was that he lacked the confidence because he didn't believe in himself. As he studied his new stepsister it struck him that they might have more in common than he first imagined.

"What do you mean, 'supposed'?" he asked. She turned to him with a weak smile on her face.

"I failed some subjects and they put me in an eighth-grade homeroom."

"Oh. Well, that doesn't matter. You'll catch up." She just shrugged. He rapped at the fender with his rubber hammer for a few moments. "Where do you live now?"

"In an apartment outside of Liberty."

"The school bus doesn't come down here. The drivers always made me walk to that corner of the main road." He indicated it with the hammer. She looked in the direction and nodded. "I mean, it's not a big deal . . ."

"No."

"What subjects did you fail?"

"Social studies and math."

"Math? That was always my best," he said. "I can help you with that." He turned back to the fender, and she took that moment to stare at him.

Ever since her mother told her she'd be marrying Frank O'Neil, Judy was terrified. But she was even more afraid to voice any opposition. She believed her mother blamed her for the breakup of her first marriage. Judy's remembrance of her father was clouded with memories of the terrible, often violent fights between him and her mother. The arguments always seemed to turn on the mutual accusations concerning who was more responsible for Judy's birth and the subsequent drain on their finances. She was nearly ten when he finally just upped and deserted them. After that, Judy felt that her mother resented her even more. She had to get a full-time job and give up the house they were renting. Gradually her mother lost concern for her good looks, gained weight, and became less selective about men.

However, for Judy, Frank O'Neil was the most gruesome of all. When he was drunk, there was a raw, animal lust in his eyes that frightened her. She hated the way he looked at her and laughed, his lips drooling with beer, his large hands opening and closing as though he were massaging an invisible breast. Usually she would flee to her room and lock the door. But just last week she had closed the door and forgotten to lock it.

She was lying in bed reading, occasionally listening to their laughter and movement. She heard them walk past her room to her mother's bedroom, and although she tried to ignore it, she couldn't help but hear their wild lovemaking. Afterward she heard Frank make his way to the bathroom, which was just past her bedroom. She heard the toilet flush and then, a few moments later, her door swung open and he stood there, totally naked, an idiotic smile on his face. Before she could scream, he laughed and said, "Oops, wrong room." She wanted to tell her mother about it after Frank left, but when she looked in on her, Elaine was already snoring.

Now she was worried about moving into the same house with such a man. She had wondered what kind of a son he could have and she was already surprised. Where Frank's features were chiseled and hard, Marty's were graceful and well proportioned. He was actually very good-looking. There was nothing of his father's madness in his face; there was a calm air about him that put her at some ease. Although his long, light brown hair didn't have the slick look of professional styling, it was neat and attractive.

"It's quiet around here," she said. He stopped working again.

"Well, there's nobody nearby. It's even like this in the summer because the hotels and bungalow colonies down the road have gone out of business. You'll get used to it, though."

"I don't mind it," she said, a stronger smile on her face. Once again Marty got the feeling that they might have a lot in common. He threw the hammer down.

"Come on," he said. "I'll show you around the house too. You'll have a nice, roomy bedroom."

When they walked into the house, they heard Elaine and Frank in the kitchen. There was the sound of beer cans being popped. Judy looked at the living room. She was taken aback by the deer's head on the wall above the fireplace. The large, glassy eyes were so sad-looking.

"My uncle Harry got that one."

"How terrible."

"Yeah, well, the deer got him back," he said, remembering the hunting accident. She looked at him quizzically, but he started toward the stairs. "The bedrooms are all upstairs. Watch the bannister. It's a bit shaky." She followed him up. He stopped by the first room on the right and pushed the door open. "This is my room. Nothin' much to it." She hesitated about looking in, but he didn't seem to care if she saw the clothes strewn about or the unmade bed. "Yours will be the one right across the way here," he said and opened that door. She followed him in. There was a nice double-size brass bed. Now it had only a naked mattress on it. There were two unmatching dressers, one a light walnut, the other a dark mahogany, both quite chipped and scratched. The longer one had a dusty wall mirror above it. There was one large wall closet to the right. She noted that there weren't any curtains on the windows, only faded yellow window shades. The room had a hard oak floor that looked as though it hadn't been washed in a decade.

"There's work to be done here," she said, and he laughed.

"Well, it's been a while since a woman's hand was felt on this house, a woman that cared, that is. You have any furniture to bring?"

"No, our apartment came with it."

"Just as well. The bed ain't bad," he said, sitting down hard on the mattress. He bounced a little and the dust began to rise. "Oops."

"Needs some work." They both laughed, then looked at each other, smiles frozen on their faces. *Maybe it won't be so bad,* she thought.

He felt a little excitement, and for the first time he wondered what it would be like to have a sister.

Two days later Frank and Elaine were married by the justice of the peace in Woodridge. It was a quick ceremony, taking a little more than five minutes. Besides the judge and his wife, Marty and Judy were the only people there. Frank wanted it that way, acting as though he were ashamed of it all. Marty didn't understand why, but he felt embarrassed. He looked at Judy and saw a simple, quiet smile on her face. Someone who looked at her quickly might interpret it as an empty, mindless look, but he realized it was the look she wore when she was trying to understand something or someone. *Actually,* he mused during the wedding ceremony, *Judy is rather cute.*

There wasn't to be any honeymoon. Neither Frank nor Elaine had the money for it. They did want to be alone, so they settled for a trip to a new bar Elaine had been to in Middletown. They were to have dinner there and be home "sometime before mornin'. Don't wait up."

"And don't get too friendly with your stepsister," Frank warned him, smiling lustfully. Marty could only look away, sure that Judy had heard the remark. Because of the remark and because of his own shyness, he was grateful when Tony Martin came over to the house not long after Frank and Elaine left. Tony wanted him to work on his car. He couldn't understand why Marty was so eager to comply.

They worked on tuning the engine and adjusting the carburetor until nearly eleven. Judy came out to watch, but she grew bored with their car talk and went into the house to watch television, poor as the reception was. Tony came in with Marty afterward and they drank beer and ate cheese sandwiches. Judy offered to make them, but Marty went right to it. She grew tired and went to sleep before Tony left.

In the morning their so-called new life began. Elaine worked as a cashier in the Jamesway chain department store in Monticello. Her shifts varied from week to week, morning to afternoon or afternoon to evening. Judy had a hard time starting in school, transferring at the tail end of the year, and her difficulty with math intensified.

One afternoon, when she returned from school, Marty asked her how it was going and she showed him a failed math test.

"Got a retest on this stuff tomorrow."

"How to find interest on a loan. It's just simple multiplication. Come up to my room after supper and I'll help you with it."

"Thanks," she said, her face lighting up. Her excitement made him think. Was she that eager to do well in math? He watched her run into the house, unaware that Frank had stopped working to observe the scene.

"Gettin' to know her real good, ain'tcha?" he asked when Marty turned back to the car.

"No."

"Gonna be some cockteaser," Frank said. "Already is," he added, looking toward the doorway. Marty hit the dent in the car door harder and Frank laughed madly. That laugh always reminded Marty of Jack Palance in *Shane*. He studied his father for a moment and for the first time experienced a sense of fear, fear not for himself, but for Judy.

Their dinners were usually uneventful. When Elaine was on the late shift at the department store,

Judy prepared the meal. Most of the time Frank wolfed down his food and went off to meet some of his drinking buddies. Occasionally he went back to work on a car. A number of times he didn't show up at all and Marty and Judy ate by themselves.

Lately, though, Marty noticed a change coming over Frank. He took longer to eat his meal, sat quietly and listened to their conversations, and leered at Judy. Marty saw the way his eyes moved as Judy went about the kitchen. He sensed that something was building in Frank, something ugly and explosive.

When Elaine was there, as she was for this particular evening, Frank was less obvious about his interest in Judy. He concentrated more on finishing his meal and getting out of the house. After dinner Marty went up to his room to read *Brainchild,* the new paperback he had bought at George's Luncheonette in Sandburg. He kept all his books well hidden in his room and didn't let Frank see him bring them into the house. Reading infuriated Frank, who was always disdainful of anything educational. He ridiculed Marty's interest, saying that reading made him soft and flaky, "like those damn fags who hang around the community college."

Marty left the doorway open deliberately, in anticipation of Judy's arrival. When she finished the dishes, she came upstairs, got her books, and appeared in his doorway. She tapped on the jamb and he looked up.

"Come on in."

She hadn't gone into his room since the first day he showed it to her. Even though there wasn't much to it, she looked about curiously. There was a single, pinewood frame bed, a light maple dresser that obviously didn't match, and a tall cabinet he used for a closet. A *Playboy* centerfold of last year's Miss August was pinned haphazardly above his dresser. The sight of it made her pause. He saw the object of her gaze and laughed.

"One of Frank's presents. Let's see the work."

She walked farther in. There was no place for her to sit but beside him on his bed. He opened the textbook and looked at the pages she had singled out with a piece of blue ribbon. "Okay," he said, ripping a piece of paper from her notebook, "let's go over it." She leaned toward him, conscious of the warmth and scent of his body. Her heart beat faster when his face nearly touched hers. Although he was talking and working, she was barely listening. When it came time for her to try the example, she put the decimal point in the wrong place. Patiently he explained it again. This time she listened hard and did it right.

"Thanks a lot," she said. "You're smart."

"I'm nothing special."

"You ever fail anything?"

"No, but I came close. This stuff's easy if you take your time reading about it."

She sat there for a moment, trying to think of something else to say and prolong her stay in his room, but before she could start a topic, they heard the phone ring and then Elaine called out to him.

"Probably Tony," he said, starting out. "I told him to call me if he wanted to go to a movie tonight."

"Oh." He left her and she got up from his bed slowly to stare at the girl in the *Playboy* centerfold. The woman's body had such rich, creamy flesh tones. She wondered if that was her real skin color or if they tinted her somehow. Was this the kind of woman Marty admired?

She went back to her own room to finish her work. Not long after, he was knocking on her door.

"Elaine told me to tell you she's going shopping with Madeline White."

"Oh. You're going to the movies?"

"Yeah," he said, pulling his faded and grease-stained T-shirt over his head. He seemed oblivious to the way she was staring at his muscular chest and shoulders. "I'm going to take the '68 Plymouth Frank got from Charlie Gordon as payment for the work he did on his wife's car. It has no plates or insurance, but I'm drivin' it only to the outskirts of Woodridge. Tony'll pick me up there."

"Is . . . is your father still here?"

"Frank? Yeah, but he'll probably be goin' off somewhere," he said. He was about to turn away from her when he caught a look in her face. "Why?"

"No reason."

"No," he said, moving farther into the room, "there's a reason." She closed her book and turned away from him. He looked behind him and advanced until he was at the foot of her bed. "Tell me."

"I . . . just don't feel comfortable alone with him. Please don't say anything," she added quickly. He stood there looking at her, holding his T-shirt, his arms frozen in air.

"Did something happen between you two?" Her silence confirmed it. "Tell me."

"Promise you won't say anything."

"Okay, I promise."

She told him about the incident at her apartment when Frank walked into her room naked.

"Why didn't you ever tell your mother?"

"I was going to, but . . ."

"But what?"

"She seems happy with him. I didn't want to do anything to break it up. Especially after what happened with my father." She looked as though she would cry.

"Has he done anything since you moved here?" Her hesitation made him repeat the question more firmly.

"He's pinched me a few times. Nothing terrible."

"That's terrible enough," he said. "He's an animal."

"I'm sorry," she said. "I mean, he's your father and . . ."

"Don't worry about it." He smiled at her. "You oughta brush your hair down. You have nice hair, but you've got to take better care of it."

"I know." She ran her fingers through the strands.

"Don't worry about Frank. He never comes home early. I'm sure he'll leave soon. If he doesn't, I won't go."

"Oh, I didn't mean for you . . ."

"That's all right. It's not important." He just stood there, his shirt in his hands, looking serious.

"How come you always call him Frank? Did you ever call him Dad?"

"Can't remember calling him anything but Frank." He thought for a moment and then said, "That's probably because I never liked thinking of him as my dad." He shrugged and left the room.

Judy stood up and went to the mirror above the dresser. She stared at herself for a few moments and then took a brush to her hair. As she stroked it she thought about the way he looked at her when he was explaining the math. *He has such nice eyes,* she thought.

She blinked her eyes and studied herself in the mirror again. Her face was flushed. She unbuttoned her blouse slowly to reveal the tops of her breasts and leaned over, pressing her arms against the sides of her body. It deepened the cleavage. The action made her giddy. Afterward, when she stood up straight again, she realized that her skin was too pale. She looked nothing like the *Playboy* model pinned on Marty's wall. As soon as she could, she thought, she'd put on her old bikini and go out to the backyard to work up a good tan.

2

       Marty was ambivalent about his feelings toward Judy. On the one hand, he was aware of Frank's obscene thoughts and expectations that Marty would have some sort of relationship with his stepsister. "Hell, you can thank me for it," he said. "I brought her around here."

Marty never reacted to that; he tried to ignore it as much as he could. His father had a way of distorting and polluting everything. The more he remarked about Judy, the more Marty hated him for it and the harder it was for him to admit his true feelings. The truth was that he had begun to find her attractive. As time went by, Marty found it more and more difficult to put thoughts of his new stepsister out of his mind, despite all his attempts to do so.

He'd be riding along with some of his friends or banging out a dent in a car, or even be talking with another girl, and suddenly he'd see Judy smiling up at him, Judy serving supper, Judy coming to him with her homework questions, Judy walking down the road after getting off the school bus.

He was aware, too, that some of his offhand comments had taken effect. She had begun to wear nicer clothes, clothes that fit her a lot better. Elaine brought home seconds from the department store—dresses, slacks, and blouses that had minor imperfections, all of which were Judy's size. Sometimes the manager of the store just gave things to her, she said, but Marty had the feeling she was stealing. Once in a while she claimed she bought something because the manager sold it under cost.

Whatever the truth about the clothes, Judy was taking much better care of her hair. One day he complimented her on it and her face took on a glow that made him blush. She hung around him a lot more than usual that day. He was embarrassed by the attention and afraid that Frank would notice it and make another dirty remark.

None of this had any positive effect on her schoolwork, however. As the school year drew to an end, it became increasingly evident that she was going to fail some subjects. Even so, he stayed up late two nights in a row studying and reviewing with her in preparation for her finals.

Frank's reaction to all this changed from disdainful smiles and sarcastic comments to the sort of outright belligerence that usually followed one of his drinking sprees. Marty became concerned. In a roundabout way he tried to warn Judy about it.

"You've got to expect Frank to get pretty nasty sometimes," he told her, "especially after a bad drunk. I don't think I've ever met anyone who could drink as much beer as he can."

"I never saw anyone drink as much. Was he always this way?"

"For as long as I can remember. It got so I used to hate it whenever he said, 'I'm just gonna stop for a beer.' Especially when I was little and I had to wait around those dingy bars. A few times he got so drunk he forgot I was with him and left me there."

"No."

"Yeah. I remember the first time that happened. I was terrified because no one seemed to notice or care. I hated to cry, but it was the only way I could get anyone's attention. I remember this woman who took me home. God, I'll never forget her."

"Why?"

"She was so drunk she nearly drove us off the road three or four times. And every time she stopped for a light or a stop sign, she'd reach over and pull me to her to hug me. She smelled from onions and stale beer. To this day I can't stand that combination. My stomach churned so much, I almost threw up on her."

"Ugh."

"Yeah, ugh. Turned out she was one of Frank's women. I had a vague memory of her being at the house. He brought so many around: fat, very thin, short with wide hips, all ugly women. It never seemed to matter to him, especially when he was drunk."

"I'm just surprised he doesn't have a beer belly."

"Yeah, well, the alcohol's probably eating away his insides."

"He's not much of an eater. I never saw him eat breakfast or lunch."

"He's strong, though, especially when he's drunk. I remember once," Marty said, smiling, "when he came out of the River Tavern in Woodbourne and found a '70 Volks Bug parked too close to our car. He lifted the front end of that thing right off the ground and pushed it away as though it were a wheelbarrow. The owner had to be surprised as hell when he found his car on someone's lawn." He laughed and then his expression became intense. "When he gets violent, though, his face changes horribly. He can scare someone just with the look in his eyes."

"I know." Judy's voice was barely more than a whisper. Marty's eyes became glassy. He had a far-off look and she imagined that he was recalling times when Frank was terrible. She felt sorry for him. Whatever hardships she had endured suddenly seemed pale and insignificant compared to living with Frank.

"Anyway," he said, snapping out of it, "whenever you see Frank boozed up, avoid him." She nodded, but he sensed that it wasn't going to be enough.

As her appearance improved Marty noticed that Frank began to pay her more and more attention. He would stop working on a car and wipe his hands as he watched her walk up the road and into the house, mesmerized by the movement of her hips and the slight bounce of her breasts. Sometimes, in the house, he would stand in her way and smile at her until she moved around him. Once Marty caught him reaching out to pinch her ass. He didn't say anything, but their eyes locked. Frank gave one of his chilling, insane laughs and moved on.

Marty wanted to warn Judy more about his father. He was just unsure of how to go about it. It annoyed him that Elaine was either blind to what was happening or didn't care. When they both got drunk on weekends, she was just as slobbering and moronic as Frank was. Nevertheless, Marty blamed himself afterward for not forcing her to face the facts.

It was the week after Judy had taken her finals. Even though she would have to repeat social studies and science, Judy was ecstatic over the fact that she had passed math. She credited it entirely to Marty's tutoring. Even Elaine was impressed and listened with interest when he explained why Judy should repeat the courses in summer school. Frank thought that would be stupid.

"She needs to work. We need the money. Didn't you say you could get her a job in Jamesway too?"

"I can, but maybe she could do both. We'll fix up the hours. The manager will work with me. I think Marty's right."

"Marty's got a big fuckin' mouth," Frank said. "He oughta keep his ideas to hisself," he added and slapped Marty on the back of his head as he walked out of the kitchen. Marty suppressed his rage. Judy felt sorry for him, but she didn't express any pity. He was red with embarrassment that it had happened in front of her. Later, as a way of consoling him, she told him she agreed: she should go to summer school and she would try her best.

"It's going to be different now. I never really cared about school, but I think I could do better if I tried."

"Sure you can. People are always putting you down," he said, glaring in Frank's direction.

"I don't understand why you quit school," she said and then regretted it immediately when she saw the pain it brought to his eyes.

"Because I was an idiot," he said. "Because Frank

28

made me," he added in a lower tone of voice. "This body shop was going to be our big thing, you know. Some big thing. Anyway, if I didn't quit, he would have made life miserable for me, even more miserable than he makes it now."

She was quiet for a few moments because she saw that tears had come into his eyes. He had that far-off look again. She wished she could reach out and touch his face.

"I never really thanked you for helping me so much," she said.

"Forget it."

"I've never been so friendly with a boy." He looked up sharply. "I mean, I've known boys, but I've never studied school stuff with them."

"Meet any boys you like here?"

"Not really."

"Not really? What's that mean?" He smiled, waiting. She twirled a strand of her hair around her right forefinger.

"The boys in my classes are so immature. I mean, there are some who are good-looking, but they're babies. Half of them are still flipping baseball cards as their chief entertainment."

He laughed. "What about the girls?"

"I like Linda Minarsky. She was in all of my classes. She keeps to herself a lot, just like me."

"I knew her brother Mike. He joined the army."

"She said you did. You used to spend a lot of time together."

"Been diggin' around about me, huh?" She blushed. "That's all right, as long as you don't find out about my great crimes." When she looked at him again, their eyes locked. For a moment they did nothing but smile at each other. Judy felt something pass between them and went to bed that night thinking about it.

The next morning everyone went his own way. Elaine had the early shift at the department store. Before she left, she promised Judy that she would try to work out something with the manager.

"They have everyone hired for the summer, but I'll see if I can get him to squeeze you in a shift."

Both Frank and Marty had breakfast early, before either Judy or her mother got up. Just as Judy came down, Marty was on his way out of the house.

"I gotta get some parts over in Monticello. Frank's in the car. I'm dropping him off in Hurleyville so he can pick up a car he's been promising to work on for weeks. I've dropped him off twice before and both times he went to Fred's Bar and Grill and forgot about the car."

"See you later then."

"Yeah." He paused at the door and turned back. "Maybe I'll get some time off later and take you over to Kaplan's Lake for a dip. It's going to be a hot one and that's where all the local kids go."

"Great," Judy replied. He left quickly, as if his invitation embarrassed him.

She ate a light breakfast, deciding that she should go on some kind of diet. Compared to the model's thighs in the *Playboy* centerfold, hers were already too wide. She planned to start exercising. The bright sun promised a good day to get a suntan. She decided to get a blanket and one of the *Modern Romance* magazines Elaine had brought back from the store, the kind with the front cover ripped off so the store could get credit, and go out to the back-yard. She ran upstairs and dug her bikini out of the pile of yet unpacked clothing. When she put it on, she was shocked.

She hadn't realized how much she had developed since last summer. Her breasts ballooned out of the flimsy top. The bottom seemed more abbreviated than she remembered it to be. The bathing suit was much too revealing to ever be worn in public, but considering she was going to stay by her own house, well hidden from the lightly traveled road, and considering that she was out to get a great tan . . . she decided she would wear it.

She scooped up the blanket and the magazine and moved quietly out the back door. It was a very sunny day with practically no clouds in the sky. Those that were there seemed painted against the blue, everything was so still. There wasn't even the slightest breeze. She spread out the blanket and began by lying on her back, her eyes closed, facing the sun. A warm glow quickly formed around her and she nearly fell asleep.

Her skin had become hot to the touch. Even in the bright sun, she could see the redness on her legs and stomach, so she turned over on her stomach and rested her face on her arms for a few moments. Then she reached back and unclipped her bikini top so there wouldn't be any streaks across her tan. She propped herself on her elbows and began to thumb through the magazine.

Frank had no idea she was back there when he came home. He drove right up to the body shop. He had converted the detached garage into his workplace. There was nothing neat or attractive about what he had done. He had taken out all the lawn and garden equipment he had stored in there and simply left the machinery beside the building, along with hoses, old tires, pieces of furniture, and rusty car parts. Both the house and the detached garage were in desperate need of a paint job. The one window in the garage had been broken and never replaced.

Despite the junkyard appearance of the yard, Frank was occasionally able to use some section of a door or piece of a car interior left to the side or behind the body shop. This was how he had come to spot Judy in the backyard.

It was already proving to be one of the hottest days of the year, so Frank had stopped at the New York Bar and Grill in town and spent nearly two hours drinking beer, cooling off, and talking with the owners. He took a six-pack with him on the way out and was carrying one of the cans in his hand when he came around the back corner of his body shop and set eyes on Judy propped up on her blanket. He froze in his steps and barely made a sound.

The bottom of her bikini didn't quite cover the separation of her buttocks. That, and the revelation of her breasts, stirred him quickly into a frenzy. His eyes widened; his mouth watered. His instant erection put terrible pressure against his tight old jeans. He squeezed the nearly empty beer can, silently crushing the sides together with his powerful fingers.

His lust for her had been growing ever since she had moved into the house. Every time she took a shower, he thought about her naked behind that old wooden door. Sometimes, when she walked past him in the hall or in a doorway, he'd get a whiff of her hair and grind his teeth in a smile. Elaine swore that Judy was a virgin. He didn't think it was true, but even so, he fantasized pushing himself into her, tearing at her innocence. After he fucked her, he thought, she'd never be satisfied with those pimply-faced peckerheads in school. She'd always want a man.

All of this came to mind now as he watched her. Judy was engrossed in a story that was an amazing coincidence. It was about this teenage girl who had become infatuated with her own college-age brother. References to her incestuous thoughts were subtly woven through the narrative. She had just reached the part where the older brother, realizing what was happening, had begun a deeply emotional and moving discussion with her.

Frank was glad Judy didn't hear him. He was only a couple of feet from her now and he held his breath. His fingers worked the button on his jeans and moved the zipper down in near silence. His fingers caught the top of his underwear as he slipped the pants down off his hips, revealing his enormous erection. In an instant he was at her.

When Judy suddenly felt hands clutching at her breasts, sweeping the bikini top away, she screamed with shock. The weight of his body sent her flat against the blanket, crushing her cheek into the material. She felt the cloth burn her skin with the friction.

As soon as he said, "Quiet," she knew who it was and what he was about to do. The knowledge sent her into a wild panic, but she was unable to move his body from her or get her arms around enough to grasp and scratch at him. His fingers squeezed her nipples so hard that she screamed in pain and fright. When she felt his right hand moving her bathing suit bottom down, she flared out wildly and tried kicking back, but he pushed her head down so firmly with his left hand that she was afraid he would actually smother her to death. She understood that she was

33

completely helpless under him. His strength was too great. He was separating her legs at will. To resist simply increased her agony.

When Marty returned home with the parts, he saw Frank's car and looked for him in the body shop. He was surprised that there were no sounds of work coming from there. He knew Frank was supposed to have Sam Cohen's Cutlass ready by the weekend. He had just walked in and out of the body shop when he heard Judy's first scream.

Without setting eyes on the scene, Marty knew what was happening. Instinctively he took hold of an old coal shovel left against the side of the body shop, held it across his body like a rifle, and charged around the building.

Frank had made his clumsy and gruesome entry, thrusting at Judy and then twisting her body roughly to bring himself the most satisfaction. Her arms moved back toward him weakly. She was trying to push herself off the blanket as well.

Marty didn't shout or call. In a blinding rage he charged forward, lifting the shovel as high as he could. Without hesitation, he brought it down with all his might. The spoon of it caught Frank smack on the back of his head. His hands flew up by reflex, but he never turned around. He just fell to the side. Blood streamed out of the gash and drew a quick line down his neck, disappearing under his shirt. His whole body shuddered and then went still.

Judy went flat against the blanket. Now free of his weight, but not fully realizing what happened, her screams intensified.

Frozen by the sight of Frank's crumpled body and the blood running down his neck, Marty stared down at him. He had known all along what Frank was capable of doing and he felt partially responsible. All of the fear of his father had turned into hate. Marty had begun to fantasize about his relationship with Judy. He saw them growing closer, developing a romance that was pure and good. Now Frank had destroyed and polluted that dream forever. And he had destroyed Frank.

Marty didn't move his arms or turn his head until Judy began to sob uncontrollably. Her convulsions frightened him. He dropped the shovel and pulled the sides of the blanket over her.

She spun around to strike out and saw that it was him. Her eyes, wild with fear, changed when she spotted Frank's crumpled form beside her. She looked up at Marty and clutched the blanket to her bosom. It had all happened so quickly—and in front of him! His eyes were wide with excitement, his face flushed, his chest heaving. She looked from him to Frank and back to him again. Her sobbing continued in spasmodic jerks. She couldn't stop it.

"Judy, I . . ." He stepped toward her and she screamed. The piercing, shrill sound made him close his eyes and then look at her in amazement. She pushed herself backward on the ground, clutching at the blanket.

"DON'T TOUCH ME!"

He didn't move. He tried to soften the expression on his face so that she would know he meant her no harm, but she continued to scramble back and away from him. *She's in shock*, he thought. *She doesn't know what she's doing.* Her hair was disheveled, her face red with pain and fear. She looked wild, mad.

"Judy . . ."

She made a guttural sound that turned into a whimper. He wanted to embrace her, to comfort her, but she wouldn't let him near her. He decided to just wait. She looked at Frank's body, squeezed the blanket even more tightly around herself, and stood up. Then, moving to the side and away, she ran toward the house. He just watched her rush inside.

For a moment the silence terrified him. He looked down at Frank's body again. What had he done? Why didn't he just pull him off? Why did he hit him so hard? Why was the blood still coming? He started to kneel down to touch him and then stopped in mid-action. What if Frank awoke? *He'd turn on me and kill me,* Marty thought. Now that his rage had subsided, his fear of his father returned. He stood up and backed away. He turned and walked quickly toward the house. As he opened the back door he looked back at Frank's body. He still hadn't moved. He thought about Judy and rushed into the house.

"Judy?" He realized she had gone upstairs. The door to her room was closed. He stood there listening for a moment and then tapped on it gently. There was no response. "Judy?" He tapped again, waited, and then tried the handle. "Judy? Are you all right?" She didn't reply. "Can I come in?" Without waiting for an answer, he opened the door wider and looked in. She was in her bed, her blankets pulled close to her face. "You okay?"

Although she was looking right at him, he wasn't sure she realized he was there. She looked tiny and fragile, her eyes still wide with fear, but more glassy. Her whole expression was strange. She looked more like someone in a trance. When he stepped closer, she shuddered.

"Judy." She looked at him more definitely now, her eyes blinking with recognition and awareness.

"I . . . can't stop . . . shaking," she said.

"Neither can I." He embraced himself for emphasis.

"Oh, God!" She buried her face in the blanket.

"It's all right," he said. "It'll be all right." He drew closer and touched her hand. She lowered the blanket and shook her head.

"I feel dirty all over."

"I know."

She saw sincere empathy in his eyes and relaxed a bit. For a few fleeting seconds she wondered how he saw her now, what she had become in his eyes after he had witnessed such a horrible scene. The realization of her nudity outside and her nudity now under the blanket brought a flush to her cheeks. Her body had been exposed in the ugliest way possible. What did she have left? The sound of a creak somewhere in the house drove these thoughts away and her fear returned. She saw it spread over Marty's face too. They were both still, listening hard, their hearts beating madly.

He went to her window, which faced the backyard. Frank hadn't moved, but the sight of him renewed Marty's terror.

"Is he coming in?"

"No. I think . . . I think I might have killed him." Judy digested his words, feeling both relieved and frightened. "If he's just hurt bad, he'll kill us both when he's able to. You don't know his temper." He looked about stupidly. "Listen," he said, "listen. We've got to get out of here."

"What do you mean? I don't want to go to the police. They'd make me tell it all and . . ."

"No, I mean hide out, get away."

"Where?"

"I'm not sure right now. Get some things together quickly." He moved mechanically, his whole body feeling numb. It was as if he were moving on air. He went to his room to pack some shirts and pants, socks and underwear, in his old gym bag. The panic that had set in made him feel like two people, one standing over the other and rushing him, driving him into action, while the other moved in a daze, nearly neutralized by what had just happened. His concept of time had been lost too. His discovery of Frank's attack on Judy and his subsequent reaction to it took only a few minutes, but he had the feeling that hours had gone by. It was nearly too late to get away.

Without any idea where they were going, he rushed down to the kitchen, found a small carton, and filled it with canned goods, a jar of peanut butter, the rest of the bread, a few bottles of soda, and half a dozen oranges. When he went back to Judy's room, she was dressed but moving very slowly, in a state of confusion. She had a small suitcase opened and had put in some underwear and a few blouses. Now she was just looking around the room.

"Don't you know what else to take?"

"I'm not sure."

"Take another pair of jeans. Hurry." He went back to his room to get his bag. Then he went downstairs and put it with the carton of food. He ran into the kitchen and looked out at the backyard. Frank was in the same crumpled position. He hadn't moved a muscle. The sight of him intensified Marty's panic. Could he have killed him, murdered his own father? He bit his lower lip so hard he tasted blood. With the thought of death came the memory of his mother's casket being lowered into the grave. His child's imagination at the time envisioned her waking up inside, and he'd thought he'd heard scratching on the inside of the lid. How many times had he woken up from nightmares in which he heard the same sound of scratching. In the beginning he would scream her name and cry. If Frank heard him, he would tell him to shut up and go to sleep. Most of the time no one heard him. As he considered Frank's body out there, he wondered what terrible nightmares he would have now.

He rushed to the front of the house and began to shout for Judy to hurry. She came hesitantly to the top of the stairs, her suitcase in her right hand.

"Quickly." He picked up his stuff and opened the front door. She came down the stairs like a sleepwalker and stood beside him. The moment he stepped outside, he paused in total confusion. Where were they going? How were they going? Did he really know why they were going?

It was true that he was afraid of Frank, but it was also true that he was afraid of what he had done. Even though it seemed clear that he was protecting Judy, he didn't think he could ever face the questions. "Why did you hit him with a shovel? Why so hard? Did you try to pull him off first?" He screamed back at his thoughts: *I didn't mean it; I didn't mean it to be such a blow.*

None of that mattered now. What mattered was to get out, get away. He looked at Frank's car. The idea of taking it occurred to him, but now the thought of touching anything that was Frank's was too repulsive. He didn't want to sit where Frank had sat, touch what Frank had touched. He decided to take the plateless '68 Plymouth. They weren't going to go toward traffic and people anyway, he thought.

"Come on." He took Judy's hand and she let herself be led to the car. "Get in."

"Where will we go?"

"I have an idea," he said.

She looked back at the house. For a few moments she felt panic rising again because she was outside of her room, but the house also represented Frank. It was Frank's home and if she remained in it, she would certainly be victimized by him. Despite her confusion and hesitation, she was driven enough by that fear to want to go. She got in beside Marty and put her suitcase in the backseat with his things and the carton of food. He started the car and backed out quickly, not even looking back at the house.

His mind was working like mad. He didn't go up the old country road much anymore, but when he was younger, he used to pay an occasional visit to an abandoned bungalow colony a few miles away. It still had some remnants of its seasonal occupants: old toys, discarded barbecue stoves, old clothing, household utensils.

But there was someplace even better. The abandoned bungalow colony was just another reminder of the declining Catskills resort world. Many of the mountain roads were no longer used much because the bungalow colonies and small hotels had gone bankrupt. Farther up this road was a hotel that he had occasionally looked at but never approached. One of his few rational thoughts at the moment was the possibility of going there. It was the perfect hiding place. At least for the time being, he thought.

For a while they drove along in silence, both just beginning to emerge from the traumatic events. Their bodies settled down cautiously; their breathing became more regular. With the softening of tension came the full realization that they were together, fleeing.

As Judy looked at him she thought about his reactions to it all and realized that he was a victim of the same violence. He had been as frightened and as confused as she, but through it all he had thought about her, worried about her. She felt a new warmth for him and realized that what they shared in common now had already begun to draw them closer.

For the time being she pushed down the memory of being violated. It was only by doing so that she was able to think clearly. She knew she could never destroy the memory of what happened, but right now she felt that the memory could destroy her.

Marty permitted himself a comforting smile. She pressed her lips together and looked ahead. They were both still quite afraid. They moved forward and stared at the unknown, like people moving from one nightmare into another.

3

"Where are we?" Judy asked when Marty turned the car into the hotel driveway. They hadn't seen a person or another car along the way.

"We're at an old hotel. It went out of business a few years ago." He pointed to a large sign on the right. Tall grass and untrimmed tree branches covered some of it, but WELCOME TO LEVINE'S MOUNTAIN HOUSE was still visible.

Marty got out of the car and walked to the rear to look back down the country road. His heart began to beat fast again as he imagined Frank becoming conscious, realizing what had happened, and starting after them. Any moment his car would come tearing down the road, with Frank clinging madly to the steering wheel, blood dripping behind his head and splattering his shirt collar, his teeth clenched, his eyes riveted in their direction with hateful determination. Marty listened hard for the sound of a car engine.

"What is it?" Judy asked, getting out.

"I just wanted to be sure we weren't being followed."

She looked back too. Instead of the tension lessening as they traveled farther away from the house and Frank, it had intensified. She looked at the hotel again and felt a cold chill travel through her body.

"This place looks creepy," she said.

Marty turned and walked up beside her. "That's what I like about it. I've only been by it a few times, but I never forgot it. Once or twice before, when I considered running away, I thought about coming here and using it as a hideaway. No one would ever think of looking for us here. We'll be safe."

"Safe?" She didn't mean to have such a harsh tone of voice, but in her mind it was already too late for it to be safe, at least for her. He seemed to sense her meaning and looked away.

"I never saw anyone crumple like he did," he said. "Except in the movies, of course."

"It was terrible."

"You know, lots of times I've wished something really bad would happen to Frank. I used to wonder why he wasn't punished for some of the bad things he did to other people. I mean, he suffered pain, got sick, had headaches, banged his fingers, scratched his arms and hands while working; but nothing bad ever happened to him when I thought it should.

"And then," he said with a short laugh, "I'd feel guilty for wanting it and imagine God was going to punish me for having such thoughts. Now . . ." He looked away quickly, ashamed of the tears that had formed in his eyes. The mixture of fear and sorrow had left him emotionally exhausted. He wanted to stop himself from thinking.

He studied the hotel and saw some small sticks that had fallen from nearby trees onto the cracked and pitted driveway. Many were crushed by the weight of an automobile and there was the outline of tread in some spots.

"Someone's probably been parking here. They couldn't find a better place for it."

"Parking?"

"You know, after a date. They probably came up here to neck and . . . to neck," he said. Judy bit her lower lip as though to hold back tears and looked down. "Everything else looks perfect," he added quickly.

Perfect, she thought and considered the front lawn of what once had been a popular Catskills resort. She couldn't understand what he meant by "perfect." The gloomy main building looked lost and forgotten. If anything, it looked to her like the haunted houses described in books and seen in movies. There was something threatening about the overgrown and uncared-for grounds. The bushes that lined the drive grew wild and invaded one another. The tall grass could be cut for hay, and the areas reserved for planted flowers were filled with weeds. There was an air of death about the place.

A number of those large, uncomfortable wooden lawn chairs with the sharply slanted seats and the heavy, wide arms were overturned and broken. The gazebo to the right had a portion of its railing sliced off and there were weeds growing out from under its webbed bottom and through its wooden floor.

But nothing gave the place the feeling of death as much as the four great weeping willow trees that bowed over the lawn, their thin, tearlike limbs touching the grass. From Marty and Judy's perspective they formed an eerie veil hiding the building from the road.

"I don't like this place," Judy said.

"We're not buying it, don't worry." He tried to get her to smile, but she just shook her head. "I know it doesn't look so great, but that's why other people wouldn't bother with it. Frank wouldn't think of it," he added, using his best selling point.

"But maybe somebody's here."

"Look at it. Does it look like somebody's here? Naw, no one's been here for years. Let's drive up the rest of the way," he added quickly. He realized that if they delayed and discussed too much, they would end up undecided, and Marty really had no other sensible ideas for any kind of escape. He was sure Judy hadn't any, either. He went back to the car, but she didn't follow. "Come on," he said. "We want to get settled before it gets too dark."

She moved reluctantly and got back in beside him. Even though she was still quite afraid, she felt secure when she was near him. He seemed sure of himself now. Slowly they continued up the driveway.

The main building of Levine's Mountain House looked like it once held between three and four hundred guests. It was typical of old Catskills hotels in its mixture of styles. The middle section had obviously been built first. Five stories high, it had a modified Queen Anne roof with four eyebrow windows just above the fifth story. The facing of the entire building, additions and all, was done in the gray-white stucco that hotel owners put on the outside of their structures to give the impression of fireproofing.

The long, wide front porch looked like an afterthought; the style of its columns and railings indicated a different builder from the builder who had done the main portion of the structure. Levine's Mountain House had a history similar to most of the smaller hotels and even some of the larger ones in the region. The central portion of the main building had been started as a farmhouse. Gradually, as more and more boarders were taken in, the building was expanded into a tourist house and eventually became a small hotel. One could almost describe the history of the place from the way additions were tacked on, each section growing as the resort area grew, as more tourists came up and more things were done to make their vacations enjoyable.

A smaller but large building to the left still had the word CASINO inscribed above the large double doors. This was where the hotel staged its evening entertainments, where it held its daycamp on rainy days, and where it ran its bingo games or its lectures and auctions for the guests.

As they got closer to the buildings, Judy drew closer to Marty. The ominous feeling she'd had when she'd first seen the hotel grew as they moved nearer. Although it wasn't that tall, the main building seemed to loom above them; the eyebrow windows became squinting eyes. Instinctively she took hold of his right arm. Frank's attack on her had made the whole world threatening. Danger was everywhere. A shadow was no longer just a shadow, and every crooked branch on every tree made Nature grotesque, threatening.

"I'll tell you something," Marty said, "this place is different from the others."

"Why?"

"Windows aren't smashed out. There's plenty of peeling paint, but this place looks better preserved than most."

"Maybe someone comes around here once in a while to keep it together."

"Naw," he said after a moment's consideration. "What for?"

"It's probably all locked up."

"Maybe, but there'll be a way in through a window or up the fire escape. I've crashed these places before."

He hit his brakes quickly because a doe and a fawn had sprung out from the right and run across the driveway. They both stopped on the lawn and looked at the car.

"How beautiful," Judy said. Marty tapped the horn lightly and they shot off across the grass to disappear in the wooded area on the other side of the hotel property. The sound of the horn sent a swarm of birds up and out of the eaves of the main building. They circled in the air and then dove back toward the roof, disappearing in the nests they had built in crevices.

Marty turned off the driveway and went to the right, moving the car slowly through the tall grass and bushes until he reached a flat area that he believed had once been the hotel's parking lot for guests. The car was well hidden from the road.

"We'll leave it here," he said, turning off the engine. "Grab your stuff." He reached back and took his old gym bag and lifted the carton of food.

Judy didn't move. The reality of what they were

47

doing finally occurred to her. Everything was happening too fast.

"You really think we should go in there?"

He paused and looked at the building as though he were considering it for the first time. Maybe they shouldn't have run away; maybe he should have forced her to go to the police. But she was in such a terrible state of mind, and what if Frank was dead? He wasn't thinking so clearly himself back there. It just seemed right to get away as quickly as possible. But what were they going to do once they hid in the hotel? How long would they be able to stay there? What would they do afterward?

"I don't know," he said. "I don't know. I just know we have to do something, and that something isn't going back to the house to face Frank and Elaine. Is it?"

"No."

"Grab your stuff," he said again and got out of the car. She came up beside him, holding her suitcase close to her body. They looked at each other and then started toward the hotel.

The tall shadow in the attic stirred in the darkness, as if waking from a long sleep. He was in the corner, dozing just out of reach of the ray of light that came in through the eyebrow windows. There had been a sound, vaguely familiar at first and then recognizable. It roused enough interest for him to lift his hulking form from the floor, and for a few moments he just stood there concentrating on the noises. Then, crouching and turning his shoulders in to take the posture that had been his for so long, he made his way quickly to the one open attic window and peered out.

Strands of his long hair fell over his face, blocking his vision. He pushed them back quickly, almost clawing himself with his uncut, jagged fingernails. When he saw that the car had stopped and a boy and girl got out, his breathing quickened and became so loud it annoyed him. It interfered with his ability to hear what was going on.

When they got back into the car and continued up the driveway, he pulled back quickly, afraid they would see him. No one must ever see him, he chanted to himself. It had the power of a commandment. Even so, he was excited, more excited than he had been in a long time. He couldn't help but peer out again.

They had parked their car where all the guests used to park theirs, and were walking toward the hotel. Soon they disappeared beneath him. He turned sharply and looked about the room. There were things to do, things he could do without being seen. He started to make a mental list. He picked up all the family albums he had been looking at earlier and put them back in the carton.

Still on his hands and knees, he crawled to the drop ladder. Once again he got a splinter in the palm of his left hand. "Stu . . . pid," he muttered and stopped to pick it out of his skin. He saw a squirrel sitting in the far corner of the attic. It must have come in the open window, he thought. He wondered if he could catch it and squeeze its head off. When he started toward it, the animal jetted back out through the window and was gone.

He started to laugh aloud but stuffed his hand against his mouth quickly. No noise, he thought. Mustn't make noise. If he made a disturbance, he could be locked in the basement again and then he would never be able to get to the girl. "Shh," he said to himself.

He began to descend the ladder to the top floor of the hotel's main building, moving with unnatural silence for someone of his size. That gave him a sense of pride. He could move through the building as quietly as the mice. He could stay in the shadows for as long as he wanted and watch people for hours without them knowing he was there. He had done it many times before, and he had seen many things, some he could remember and some he had long forgotten.

He stopped and listened just before his feet touched the floor. The front door had been opened. He sensed it; he felt the vibration in the building. His heart beat wildly. The girl was almost in the building. He stepped to the floor eagerly and pushed the ladder up toward the ceiling. The springs took it the rest of the way, softly snapping it into place.

"Good," he said. "Shh."

He crouched down again and turned his shoulders in. His hair draped off his head and hung below his chin. Then he scurried down the steps of the hotel stairway and disappeared into the darkest reaches of the building.

When Marty and Judy got to the long cement front steps, they paused and looked around. There wasn't a sound from the road or from the hotel grounds, yet they both sensed something.

"You think the front door will be open?" she asked. She was hoping it wouldn't be and that they would have to go somewhere else.

"Only one way to find out," he said and moved up

the steps. He hesitated a moment and then turned the big brass knob. There was a click and the door opened. A whiff of hot, musty air came out at him. He looked at her and shrugged. She continued to look up at him, waiting with her suitcase held tightly to her chest.

He thought she looked so small and helpless, and for a moment he forgot why they were there and what they had gone through. She stood there watching him, almost as if they had come to a real hotel together and she was waiting to see if there were any vacancies. He opened the door farther, surprised that it didn't squeak more.

"Couldn't we get into trouble for trespassing?" she called.

"What kind of trouble is that compared to the trouble we're already in?" he said. "Come on." She moved up the stairs slowly, looking around. Despite the hotel's desolation, she couldn't put aside the feeling that they were violating someone's privacy. She half expected someone to shout at them.

Marty turned and stepped into the hotel lobby. All the Catskills resorts he had ever been in had the same basic design. Levine's Mountain House, being a smaller hotel, wasn't as plush as some of the bigger ones. There was only one large oval rug in the middle of the planked oak floor. He was surprised that the furniture wasn't covered and that there was so much of it still here.

There were some small couches and big soft chairs arranged around the room. To the immediate left was the check-in desk. The wall within it was covered with open post boxes still containing room keys. He could see the chains and tabs hanging out. The attention bell was on the counter, as were a long pad, pens, and a pile of postcards.

"You know," he said, "this place probably doesn't look much different from the days when it was open. Look at all this stuff. It's amazing no one's crashed this place."

"The paintings are still on the walls," Judy said, coming farther in. "Are they valuable?" Her curiosity pushed her uneasiness aside for the moment. She hadn't been in a Catskills resort before, deserted or not deserted.

"No," Marty answered. Most of the paintings were common country scenes he had seen at other hotels. There were portraits of horses, some people he assumed were hotel family, and pictures of fruit. Above the check-in desk was a large picture of an old farmhouse. He guessed that it was a picture of the original Mountain House.

Judy came beside him and for a moment they listened to the silence. There was a religious atmosphere in the stillness, and they both felt as though they had moved through time, violated some boundary. Without realizing it, they lowered their voices until they were practically whispering. Marty put the carton of food on one of the couches and dropped his gym bag softly beside it while Judy lowered her small suitcase to the floor, taking care not to make much sound.

"Maybe they're getting ready to open this place again," she said.

"No," he said, looking about and shaking his head. "By now there would be a lot more activity around here. Look at how overgrown the front lawn is. They would have gardeners, carpenters, and painters all over the place by now. Besides," he continued, "what would bring this hotel back and not the others?"

Just then they heard a loud creak in the wall down the corridor to their right. Both of them turned quickly toward it, but the sound wasn't followed by anything. Nevertheless, Judy hugged herself as though she had just felt a terrible chill.

"We could sleep right in the lobby if we had to," Marty said, but his voice didn't sound as confident as before. He wondered now if they were capable of doing it, of hiding out here until . . . until what? He chastised himself for his own cowardice. How did he expect her to be brave if he sounded indefinite? Damn it, he thought, there's nothing here but a deserted old hotel. He had to change the mood and do it quickly or she would run right out and he'd have to follow.

"First," he said, moving toward the main desk, "we have to check in."

"Huh?"

He saw that the counter was dusty, but the pad looked clean. He thought it was odd, but he hopped over the counter and slapped his hand down on it.

"Can we help you, madam?"

"Stop it, Marty." She looked around as though she were afraid someone would hear them.

"Why? You have to check in."

He looked down at the shelves under the counter. There was all sorts of stuff there: more pads and postcards, hotel stationery, additional room keys, packs of playing cards, a few checker games, one game of Chinese checkers, business cards announcing taxicab service to the city, a Short Line bus schedule, a flashlight, and little boxes filled with odds and ends like safety pins, buttons, pencils, rubbing alcohol.

"I don't know if I want to stay here, Marty," she said.

"Just look at all this," he replied, ignoring her. She was still embracing herself tightly. He saw the telephone on the wall and reached up quickly and brought the receiver to his ear. Even though there was no dial tone, the sound wasn't at all like a dead phone. Then he noticed that the intercom button had been pressed and the system was still in operation.

"Amazing," he mumbled.

"Marty, this place scares me," she said, speaking in a loud whisper now. He nodded, came around the counter, and sat down on the couch near her. "I know you're trying to do the right thing, but . . ."

"There aren't exactly a thousand places for us to go," he said in a quiet, matter-of-fact tone. She bit her lower lip and sat beside him. "All I'm looking for is some breathing space, a chance to think."

"I know." She swallowed hard, forcing the revolting memory back.

"If only I didn't hit him so hard," he said. She looked at him. His face had grown soft again, his eyes watery. For the first time, she realized what sort of a commitment he had made for her. He could have just stood by and yelled or even pretended he didn't see it happening and go away. Now he might be his father's murderer.

"You had to," she said. She touched his hand. He nodded but continued to have that far-off look. "And anyway," she said, "I could never go back to that house and live in it with Frank."

He turned to her, anxious to believe that Frank was still alive. The realization hit them both almost at the same time. They couldn't go back now, even if they wanted to, and they had nowhere to go. He looked around the hotel with a new perspective. It would have to be their sanctuary. Whatever fears they had, they would have to subdue. She seemed to know that, too, because her expression changed and she looked at the lobby as though she were finally considering it.

"You're right," she said. "We'll stay here. How long will we stay here?"

He smiled. It was as though she were two people. "I don't know. I just didn't want to be there when it was all discovered."

"Me neither." She realized that he had taken her hand. She squeezed his more firmly.

"We just need a little time. Well," he said, standing up. Immediately she stood beside him. "Let's go see what the rooms are like on the first floor. We're going to need a safer spot."

She nodded and followed him across the lobby.

It filled him with excitement and pleasure to know they couldn't see him watching them.

A long time ago people had come and put the big chutes in the building. They called it . . . air conditioning. When the hotel closed after the Jewish holidays, he'd discovered a large opening in the ducts in the basement, but he didn't tell anyone about it. Instead he crawled in.

It was the best thing he could have ever done. As he moved along the maze, he discovered that he could go to almost any part of the hotel and see and hear whatever he wanted without being seen. No one could get mad at him for that. He did what they wanted: he didn't let anyone see him and he stayed out of everyone's way.

Of course, now that he was a lot bigger, it was a lot harder for him to crawl through the ducts. But they were still the best way to travel unseen. In the summer, when the cold air was traveling through it, he wore two or three shirts and two pairs of pants. He wore gloves, too, so his hands wouldn't get all black and sooty, and if he wrapped two old flannel shirts around his knees, they didn't get sore from the crawling. Now he had large calluses on his kneecaps.

He knew that the boy and the girl would be going into the lobby, so he went directly to the card room and entered the ducts through that grate. Then he crawled over to the grate that was just above the doors to the dining room. From this place he could look out at them as they entered the hotel.

He pressed his face hard against the thin bars to catch the scent of her hair. It was exciting to smell a pretty girl's hair, and this girl *was* pretty. "Pretty girl," he whispered. "Pretty girl." He moaned softly and inhaled, but he smelled only the musty dampness of the hotel.

When they began to talk, he turned his head around and pressed his ear to the grate, but he couldn't hear all the words. That made him angry, and a small guttural sound began at the base of his throat and rolled over the top of his mouth. He clenched his teeth so hard it hurt his gums.

As soon as they started toward the first floor of rooms, he moved. They weren't going to get away from him. There were two ducts that faced out on that corridor. He scurried back, taking care not to bang his feet against the metal and send a hollow reverberation down the length of the ducts. Sometimes, when he got too excited and moved too quickly, he would do that. It sounded like slow thunder, the kind that moved along bruised clouds in an angry summer sky threatening rain.

But he could barely control himself. This was the first time he had a chance to spy on anyone in the hotel for a long time. In fact, he couldn't even remember when he did it last. That kind of memory was vague.

He stopped crawling because his pants got caught. That happened more and more now. He was really too big for this. He reached back and got his cuff loose. It had caught itself on a popped-up bolt. He started to pound it with his fist and then remembered the boy and the girl and stopped. He would just remember it was there and be careful.

It was always dark in the ducts now, even in the daytime, but he had traveled through them so much over the years that he had learned his way from the feel. He recognized certain cracks and crevices and bumps. He knew turns and seams.

He slowed down when he heard their voices below. When he looked through the grate, he caught sight of the girl. She was standing just before him now. He could see her eyes and her cheeks and the way she looked about nervously. *Girl's got a nice face. Just touch her once,* he thought. *Just smell her hair.*

He pulled back as she looked up at the grate, his heart beating rapidly. Had she seen him? Their voices were muffled. The boy was still speaking softly. He leaned forward again. They were continuing down the corridor. She hadn't seen him, but he had to be a lot more careful.

He closed his eyes, trembling. He could hear Jake's snarling voice. "Remember. Keep out of sight of the guests. I don't want to hear one complaint about you, understand? Damn it, do you understand?"

He nodded frantically, then opened his eyes and realized that he was in the duct and Jake wasn't near him. "Not see me," he said as though promising an invisible partner. "Promise." He leaned back and raised his hand as though taking an oath.

It was a promise he felt he could keep. After all, he had kept it for years and years.

He moved forward, squirming and twisting his body as he slithered through the ducts, traveling between the walls like a large rodent, his eyebrows gray with dust, his lips dry, and his tongue moving spasmodically between his teeth. They were moving deeper and deeper into the hotel. The building was surrounding them and closing them tightly into his world.

4

Marty figured that most of the rooms would look the same. Even so, they went down the corridor, opening doors and looking in. None of the beds in the rooms had any linen on them, although they all had pillows. He thought they should try to find two adjoining rooms.

"I don't want to sleep alone in any room," Judy said, emphatically. "This place is too creepy for me to be by myself."

He looked at her and for the first time really considered what it meant for them to be alone together. He would share a room with her, maybe . . . even a bed. Although her request was innocent enough, his thoughts followed a different path. He felt guilty doing it, but the fantasy was there. He was ashamed of the sexual thoughts that came to his mind and looked away quickly because he was afraid she could read it in his face. But she didn't see any of that. She just went on about being afraid.

"Okay," he said. "Let's look at some of these others."

Finally one of the rooms they looked at had two single beds instead of the typical double. All of the rooms had the same basic decor: a thin, nylon rug, a very plain wood dresser with a large mirror, two wall closets, and a small nightstand by the bed. The room with the two single beds had a soft chair in the corner and a standing lamp beside it. Marty tried the lamp, but of course there was no electricity.

"We'll stay in this one," he said and dropped his gym bag on the bed to the right. He started to take the food out of the carton he had brought and began to put it on the dresser. Judy tried the mattress on her bed, still holding on to her suitcase as she bounced gently. The springs rattled.

"Do you know what time it is?"

"No, I don't." He stopped unpacking. "You don't have a watch either. We're going to have to go by the position of the sun. Hungry?"

"Not really."

"Oh damn!"

"What?" Judy asked fearfully. She thought he cut his finger. Right now the image of blood was especially terrifying for her.

"I took all these canned goods, but I didn't take a can opener. We'll have to find the kitchen and see if there's still one there."

"I don't think I can eat anything."

He was going to say she would later, but considering what she had been through, he understood why she would have no appetite. He didn't really have

60

one either. He wanted to eat just so they'd have something to do. He knew it was important that they think of other things.

"Well, maybe we'll each just have an orange for now." He threw one to her before she could refuse, but she didn't start to peel hers until he started. "Ever been away from home before?"

"You mean by myself?"

"Yeah."

"When I was ten, I went to my grandmother's in Hoboken. That's in New Jersey."

"I know where it is," he said, smiling. "You never told me about your grandmother."

"You never asked me."

"Which grandmother?"

"Huh? My grandmother."

"No, I mean your father's mother or your mother's mother."

"Oh, my mother's. I never met my father's mother. Anyway, I went to see her a little while after my grandfather died. We went to the funeral and my grandmother made my mother promise to send me. I went on the bus, but I had to change buses in Mahwah. That's in—"

"I know, New Jersey. Hey, I've been around some." He bit into the orange and the juice squirted over his chin. She laughed as he wiped it off. "I even hitched to New York City once."

"You did?"

"Yeah, me and Buzzy Lipkowski did it one summer. As soon as we got over the George Washington Bridge, we started back. I was scared shit and so was he. We were both only fourteen at the time."

"Did you get into trouble?"

"No, nobody knew, and if they did, they probably wouldn't have cared. You sure an orange is going to be enough?"

She nodded and kept eating. He finished his and went to the window. The glass was very dusty and grimy, so he took a piece of orange peel and rubbed out a clear circle. The view revealed the unfilled swimming pool with its deck chairs piled under the extended roof of the large cabana. Although the grass was tall right up to the pool area, he could see long cracks in the cement walls of the pool. Grass and weeds were growing out of them. The red clay stones of the patio area were also cracked and peppered here and there with tall weeds. There was a lone metal deck chair to the rear of the patio.

Just to the right and beyond the pool was an overgrown baseball field. He could tell it was a baseball field because the chain-link backstop was still up, although it was quite rusty from years of no maintenance. It was easy for him to imagine all the excitement and activity here on a warm summer day.

There would be music at the pool and refreshments sold at the cabana. He could almost hear the squeals of children, the sound of splashing water, the loud laughter and conversation of the adults. Behind that would be the shouting of the men playing softball. Perhaps it would be the hotel staff team playing another hotel staff's team. He had seen all that before.

"This must've been some place once," he said without turning from the view.

"I never stayed in a hotel before. We stayed in a few motels."

"We never did. Frank never took me anywhere with him," he said. "He left me at home a lot."

"Really?"

"Sure," he said, turning. "I'd go to sleep and wake up in the morning to find he never came home that night. Some time during the morning or early afternoon, he'd come around."

"Wasn't he worried about you?"

"Worried?" He laughed bitterly. "A lot of my friends used to think I was a big deal because I stayed home alone so much." He looked back out the window. The sticky orange juice had made it somewhat blurred. "Little did they know how much I hated it. You can't imagine what it was like for a ten-year-old boy to be alone at night."

"I was alone at home many nights too."

"I bet." He looked at her again. She studied the room and then shrugged.

"What are we going to do here?"

"We'll see. Don't worry. We'll explore the place. There's got to be a lot to it and that'll keep our minds off things for a while. Hey," he said, considering her fully now, "are you . . . are you all right? I mean, physically? I should have asked you that before, but I didn't think of it."

"Yes," she said, barely audible.

"You have a bad bruise on your face, but . . . you're not bleeding anywhere or anything, are you?" She shook her head quickly.

"Good, because I didn't bring any medicine. Although, I'll tell you something. I bet we find plenty of that stuff around here too. I never seen a deserted place with so much left in it."

"I don't know much about deserted places," she said and he laughed. "What's so funny?"

"Just the way you said it . . . like deserted places is a subject or something. I happened to have broken into a few in my day," he said, rubbing his fingers on his chest in mock pride. "The mountains are full of joints like this, but most of them have been cleaned out by the owners or the banks."

"Banks?"

"Sure. They foreclose their mortgages. You know, they can't pay their loans, so they take over the hotels and the hotels go bankrupt. Then the banks try to sell them to make their money back, only a lot of 'em don't sell so they're just left deserted."

"Think that's what happened here?"

"No," he said thoughtfully. "I don't. This place is weird. It's like the guests left one day and the owners just closed up. I don't know. Whatever happened, it's good for us now."

"What if it gets cold at night?" she said, running her hand over the mattress.

"Maybe we'll find some blankets. We oughta start looking around before it gets too dark outside for us to see anything in here. I didn't bring any candles. Didn't think of it."

"It smells funny in here."

"The whole place'll be like that. The windows have been closed. Things are damp. It needs a good airing out." He tried the window. It was practically glued to its frame because it hadn't been opened for so long.

"Is it locked?"

"No," he said. He felt the muscles in his neck strain with the effort. He gave it his best, knowing she was watching him. "Damn." He pounded the frame carefully with his closed fist. Then he went at it again. It snapped free, but it didn't go up smoothly. It was a battle all the way.

"Lucky you're so strong."

"Yeah, well . . ." He slapped his hands together. His palms stung from the pressure he had put on them, but he didn't say anything about it. He closed his fists to hide the redness. "Yeah, we'll be all right." She stood up.

"Should we go look for the kitchen?" His show of strength and confidence encouraged her. She realized the hotel could be fun. She had often passed resorts like this, wishing she could enter them either as a guest or a worker.

There was always something glamorous about the bigger hotels with their dazzling lights, their crowds of people, their big-name entertainers advertised on billboards. A number of times she had ridden past them on weekend summer nights and seen the guests all dressed for dinner and the show. The women were beautiful and rich-looking in their gowns and high heels. The men were debonair and mysterious in their sleek suits and ties.

She would look at her mother and think, *We'll never go to a place like this.* Her mother's idea of entertainment and excitement was the bowling alley or the drive-in movie. They ate popcorn and Popsicles while rich little girls her age got dressed in beautiful clothes and sat in elegant lobbies. Later they would be permitted to stay up and watch famous entertainers or go to the hotel's teen room and dance to discotheque.

Even though this hotel was much smaller and older, it was still a mountain resort. There would be things to see and think about. Maybe even things to try.

"I don't expect the kitchen will be hard to find," Marty said. "It should be right off the dining room."

"Where's that?"

"I think those big doors at the rear of the lobby open to it. We'll leave our stuff here and go exploring." He started out.

The twilight had already begun to cast long dark shadows down the corridor. Their footsteps echoed in the emptiness in the building. Even their voices reverberated. Judy felt as though they were on the verge of entering another dimension. It reminded her of a science fiction television show she had seen once.

She couldn't help looking behind them. Maybe it was silly, but she felt as though there was something else there, some presence close by them. She didn't want to say anything about it to Marty. He seemed completely satisfied with it all. The feeling passed quickly and she forgot about it. Marty had stopped to open a door.

"What is it?"

"This looks like a closet door. Maybe some of the bedding was left behind. There's usually a linen closet in every corridor."

"You know a lot about hotels."

"Worked in 'em. You get to know stuff."

He pulled on the door. It wasn't locked, but it was stuck. "The wood expands and contracts with the change in weather," he explained. He pulled, kicked, and banged on it until it broke free of the jamb and opened abruptly. He nearly fell back on his behind. "I'll be damned!" he exclaimed.

"What?"

"Look. It's full." She stepped in front of him. "There's enough linen in there for every room in the corridor. I don't get it." He reached in and took out some sheets, bringing them to his face and then to hers. "They don't even smell that bad."

"Here are some pillowcases," she said, stepping farther into the closet.

"There are blankets there on the floor. I had a feeling we'd find some of this stuff, but not this much. Let's get what we need to our room first and then go look for the kitchen."

They gathered what they wanted and then headed back quickly, behaving as though they had discovered gold.

"I'll make the beds," she said cheerfully. "You can go look for a can opener."

"You sure?" He was surprised that she decided she could stay by herself.

"Yes. Just don't take too long."

"Oh, I won't. I can't. We don't have that much daylight left. If you finish before I come back, meet me in the lobby."

"Okay."

"Hey," he said, turning back in the doorway, "maybe I'll find some candles so we can have some light."

"Oh, I hope you do. Candlelight is fun."

He laughed and ran down the corridor, thinking that there was something delightfully fresh about her, about the way she asked questions and got excited about the simplest things.

But before he reached the end of the corridor, he felt guilty about feeling so good and being so happy. There was something sick about it, considering what had happened and what he had done. Why didn't he feel more grief and more guilt? What he felt was more fear than sorrow.

He stopped running and walked slowly as he reached the lobby. It seemed as though the world he had known was put on hold the moment he and Judy had entered the hotel. Was there something mystical about this place? It was sort of frozen in time. What had happened here? What was happening?

He moved on, far more intrigued now by thoughts of what might lie behind every closed door.

She wasn't that far away and she was alone. If the grate weren't there, if the duct weren't so narrow and he weren't so big, he could stretch forward and reach out to touch her. His frustration made him push up against the roof of the duct until the muscles in his legs ached.

When she worked on the other bed, he couldn't see her. He twisted and turned and arched his neck, but it did no good. He even turned over on his back to get a different angle, but she was still out of sight. And he had to be so careful about the way he moved so he could avoid the slightest sound.

One thing puzzled him: Guests didn't make their own beds. Why was this girl making beds? Maybe she wasn't a guest. Who was she and who was that boy with her? Maybe his grandfather knew.

The girl suddenly appeared again. She went to the window and looked out. She stood there for a while and then went to one of the beds and sat down again. She closed her eyes as though she were very tired. He could see her face well and noticed that she had a bruise on her left cheek. It reminded him of the times Jake had beaten and bruised him. Then he would go down to his hiding place in the basement.

There was a small room in the old part of the foundation, the part under the original house. The room had been used for storing potatoes and things. A long time ago it had been closed up and forgotten, but he dug an opening out of the fieldstone foundation. There was no light in the room, but he didn't mind the dark. No one knew he went in there. Sometimes he heard movements near him and once he reached out and touched something furry. It was a rat. It didn't bother him and he didn't bother it.

He would hear Jake pounding the cement walls with a stick and calling his name. When Jake couldn't find him, he'd curse and threaten. But he never made a sound and finally Jake would give up. Sometimes Jake'd forget he was after him, and sometimes he wouldn't and catch him later.

The memory of all that made him angry now. The guttural noise began in his throat again and started to travel up through his mouth, but he remembered that he had to be very quiet, so he swallowed hard and kept it down.

When he looked back at the girl, he saw that she had unbuttoned her blouse to look at her left shoulder. He was surprised at the sight of black and blue marks on it. What had happened to her? Maybe the boy did it, he thought. If he did . . . bad boy. He'd squeeze him like a squirrel and pop his head.

The girl leaned forward a little and he pushed his head against the top of the duct to get a better view, but he couldn't see much. When she straightened up, she was buttoning her blouse. A moment later she stood up and walked out of the room. He heard the echo of her footsteps as she started down the corridor.

After a moment he worked his way back to the main artery and backed his way down to the first grate in the hall. She was already past that and heading for the lobby. By the time he reached the lobby openings, she had already gone across the room to the dining room doors. He stopped and listened as hard as he could to the sound of her footsteps and the sounds the boy was making in the kitchen. His eyes widened with satisfaction.

They could go nowhere in the hotel without him knowing it, and whenever he wanted to, he could slip out of the walls and be right beside them.

Marty had run down to the dining room doors quickly, not wanting to leave Judy alone too long. The two sliding doors moved along their rollers with surprising ease. He stepped in and looked over the dining room. It was a nice size room, capable of seating over three hundred. Just about all the chairs were up on their tables with their seats face down.

As he walked farther in, he saw that the busboy's station to his immediate right had some trays on it. The station was a little cabinet with a silverware drawer and a small countertop. There was enough room at the station for a busboy to keep a pot of coffee and a pot of hot water for tea. Marty opened the drawers and was surprised to see silverware neatly arranged within. It wasn't valuable silverware, but still he thought it was strange that the owners or foreclosers would leave it there. He found a small pile of neatly folded cloth napkins in the drawer as well.

Although it was a nice size room, he could imagine that with a crowd of people in it and the waiters and busboys rushing about, it must've seemed cluttered and very noisy. However, the room had a homey decor: soft dark pinewood paneling, pretty flower print curtains on the windows, and a checkered light brown and white tile floor. Many of the hotels he had worked in had more of a cafeteria appearance. This room had personality to it.

In fact, he noticed as he looked around that there was a definite family touch to the Mountain House. It had its own identity. So many of the big hotels in the Catskills had become factories for enjoyment. Most were corporations with a hotel bureaucracy as large and impersonal as in any urban business, and had the decor to match.

He moved across the dining room to the doorway that was obviously the entrance to the kitchen. He went through the swinging doors and confronted a wide room with everything left quite neat and orderly. To his left were the stoves. There were still some large pots on them, but he could see that the pots were clean. There was a long serving counter in front of the stoves. Waiters would slap their trays on it and shout their orders to the chefs, who would respond or fail to respond in proportion to how well they liked an individual waiter or busboy.

In the short time he worked at hotels, Marty saw a number of fights in the kitchens. He quickly learned to be on his toes, because he could be outsmarted or outmaneuvered by another busboy or waiter. There was a subtle competition going on in the kitchen, because everyone was trying to give his people the best possible service so he could get the best tips.

Directly across from the doors were the large refrigerators and freezers. All still had shiny aluminum doors and looked as though they had just recently been scrubbed and polished. To the right were the utility cabinets. He was sure he'd find a can opener there. Beyond the cabinets was another doorway that he imagined led out to the storerooms and the stockrooms. The dishwashers and dryers were to his immediate right. One of the dryers had its tray out, which was half filled with dishes and silverware. The sight of that gave him his first strong feeling that they might not be alone here.

How could that be, though? he thought. Why would anyone stay in an old deserted hotel? It didn't make sense. No, this was just the way things were left, he told himself, and yet . . . yet something was very strange here. He didn't want to talk about it too much. Judy was frightened enough as it was.

He went to the cabinets, and as he suspected, everything he could ever want was still there. He took a hand can opener, but it occurred to him that they might just as easily come down here to eat what they had. It would be better than eating in the room all the time.

Before he left the kitchen, he went to the entrance to the stockroom and peered inside. What he saw shocked him: the shelves were full of goods. He didn't know how much was still edible, but there was all sorts of stuff: cans of soup, boxes of noodles, seasonings, boxes of matzos, flour, sugar, salt, all kinds of cereals. He opened a box of soup crackers and tasted one. It was stale, but it still had some flavor. He decided to take one with him to show Judy.

When he turned and looked back at the sinks from this perspective, he saw a glass with a spoon in it and the remnants of what looked to be tea. He walked over to lift the glass out of the sink and smell it. It *was* tea and it couldn't have been there for months or years. He spun around suddenly, as though expecting to see someone standing behind him. There was no one there.

Still his heart beat quickly. He should have realized it the moment he stepped into the lobby of the hotel—someone must come around here periodically to take care of this place. It had to be that, he told himself. Nothing else made any sense. After all . . .

"Marty."

Judy's voice jolted him. He looked at the glass and then dumped its remaining contents into the sink. If he told her what he had found, she'd leave immediately.

"Coming," he called back. He rushed out and met her in the dining room.

"Wow," she said, surveying the room. The only thing she could compare it to was the school cafeteria, and this seemed twice as big. For a moment she wished it were filled with people just so she could see the excitement, hear the noise, and be part of it. He saw the admiration in her face.

"It's nice, but it's really one of the smaller ones."

"Smaller?"

"Sure. Can you imagine what it's like to work in a dining room that feeds two thousand people?" She just shook her head. "Hey," he said, remembering the box in his hand, "there are still some supplies left in the storerooms. Stale stuff, most of it, but we might be able to use some. Try this," he said, offering her a soup cracker. She took one gingerly.

"It's all right."

"We could live here for weeks if we had to," he said. The excitement in his face was infectious, especially when she looked about the dining room.

"I have the beds ready," Judy said. "You didn't find any candles?"

"Oh yeah, candles. Wait a minute," he said. "There have to be some holiday candles." He started back to the kitchen before she could say another word. When he appeared again, he held up a box of candles and matches in his right hand. "Come on," he said, stopping by one of the busboy stations to take out some silverware, "we'll have our peanut butter sandwiches by candlelight."

She laughed and then stopped, startled at the happy sound in her voice. It was this place, she thought. It had different effects on her. She wasn't sure she liked that, but for the moment it seemed okay.

"Let's go," he repeated, and she followed him out of the dining room, neither of them aware of the eyes that studied them, jealous of the laughter that lingered in their wake.

5

The flickering candle washed her face in a soft yellow light. The darkness that had fallen quickly around them now seemed to serve as an insulation between them and the world. They stayed within the confines of the small flame. As soon as Marty had touched the match to the wick, a magical moment began. Judy was hypnotized by the glow in his eyes. Neither of them spoke much above a whisper. The candle cast their silhouettes against the far wall. Judy imagined that separate parts of them had been driven from their bodies by the light and now waited and watched outside the flame-lit circle. Was it the better or the worse part of them?

It was as though they had just met for a first date. They had trouble thinking of things to say. The intimate moment they now shared made them both nervous. It was hard to look directly at each other.

They both felt emotionally exhausted, as though the events of the day had carried over weeks.

Marty felt so confused. He had rescued Judy from the grip of a gruesome, vicious experience, and in doing so, he had taken on the role of protector. It was he, after all, who had brought her here. He was older, wiser, stronger. She was gradually developing a trust in him. He felt it; he wanted it.

And yet now, as a few times before, he felt a more intense attraction to her. He looked at her and saw how the glow of the candle made her face soft and golden, and despite his desire to ignore it, the knowledge that she was dependent upon him turned into something sexual.

For most of his life he had cared for no one but himself. He was responsible for nothing else. He didn't have a dog or a cat; he had few possessions to service or maintain. And now he had another human being under his care, a female who was becoming more attractive to him every moment. He nearly surrendered to the voice that said, "You want her; you want her like Frank wanted her."

No matter how good we are, evil thoughts come into our minds, he told himself, *and we are good or bad only in relation to how quickly and firmly we subdue them.* For him his moral strength lay within the comparison to Frank. Nothing could turn him off faster. If he were to love her, if he were to want her, it would have to be in a way that was totally different from Frank's way. Right now he was afraid that the bottom line was that there was no other way, that when you got right down to it, men and women wanted only what they could take from each other, and all the candlelight, all the music, and all the poetry didn't disguise that truth. After all, aside from what he had seen in the movies and read in books, his view of the relationship between men and women had been on only one level: Frank's level, Frank's way. He tried not to think about it.

For Judy the candlelight, the darkness, and the warm silence between herself and Marty all helped her keep the memory of the day's events at a distance. She tried to think of this as only an adventure. She'd often fantasized running away, being alone, traveling. Now it was really happening. It was scary, but it was also exciting, and after all, it was happening with him.

He had grown so in her eyes from what he had done at the house, how he had handled it afterward. How brave he had been. The darkness outside their room was frightening, but between it and her was Marty, and his strength made her feel secure. An ugly thing had happened, a thing so terrible that she drove it down in her mind with all her strength. But out of this ugly thing, something beautiful had begun. Her childish fantasies of the last few weeks seemed to become possibilities.

And even though what happened to her was the most dreaded violation of her sex, she felt that it had pushed her into womanhood, that it had made adult demands on her and forced her to think like a grownup. She felt more capable, though still upset. And sitting here with Marty, she couldn't help but feel excited, but in a warm and comfortable sort of way.

Marty had put the candle on a dish on the nightstand between their twin beds. They sat on her bed and he unscrewed the top of the peanut butter jar. Looking for something to do with her hands, she seized the package of bread and untied the end. She handed him a piece and he smeared the peanut butter on it and folded it. Then he gave it back to her. They didn't speak, but every action seemed to mean something, as if they were participating in a religious ritual.

"I never had a more romantic meal," he said. She smiled and he thought she looked angelic.

To Marty this was the quiet after the storm. The electricity in their bodies, the tension of the day's events, had not ended. The lightning still lingered. That was why they were so intense about their ceremonial little supper.

"Peanut butter has suddenly become delicious," she said.

They ate slowly, watching each other, drawn to each other's every move.

"It's also nutritious," Marty said. She giggled. "It is."

"I believe you. It just sounds silly."

"What I mean is, we're not going to starve," he said with a note of pride. "Even if we didn't have this stuff, I could hunt."

"Oh, I wouldn't want that. I don't want you to kill anything."

He stopped chewing and thought about Frank. He couldn't help it, couldn't help the rush of images: the stream of blood, the folded body, the damn clunk of that shovel. He kept hearing it and hearing it, as though the sound had followed them up the road to the hotel.

Judy saw the look on his face and leaned forward.

"We don't have to hunt though. You said so yourself—this place has all sorts of food left in it."

He nodded, but his expression didn't change. In

his mind he could see Frank rising from the ground, embarrassed and furious that they had left him with his pants down, enraged when he reached back and felt the blood on his neck. He pictured him running with a lunatic frenzy to dig Uncle Harry's 30-30 out of the closet. Even now he was hovering by the hotel, attracted to their window by the Halloween glow of one candle. As soon as one of them stood up . . .

He nearly put the candle out. Her smile changed to confusion as he held his hands near the flame. She saw the expression of terror come into his face. "What's wrong?"

"Nothing, I . . . nothing." He settled back. "I was just thinking about Frank and what a lousy hunter he is. A good hunter shoots to kill, aims for the heart so the animal is in a minimum of pain. But when I went out with Frank once, he shot the deer anywhere he could, and when the animal fell, he let it struggle in agony for a while before he walked up to it and finished the job. It was horrible. It made no sound, but I could hear its silent scream in my mind and see the pain and fear in its eyes."

"That gives me the chills," she said, hugging herself.

"Me too. I never went with him after that. He tried to force me to go a few times. I actually had to run away from home to keep him from dragging me along."

"Why did he want you to go so much?"

"To beat the bush, chase the deer his way. I was always afraid he would shoot me by mistake. That kind of stupidity runs in my family."

"You're not stupid."

"I'm always afraid that I will be. You can't help it," he said, widening his eyes, "when you have relatives like I have."

"You must have some good relatives."

"Yeah, well, if I do, I don't know them."

"Your mother . . ."

"No," he said quickly, "she wasn't much better than Frank."

She saw his reluctance to say anything more about her so she held back any questions. The topic of conversation had taken something out of the mood. The sandwich had become heavy; she found herself forcing the last bite.

"Don't make anymore for me," she said as he reached for another piece of bread.

"I haven't got that much of an appetite either." He covered the jar and tied up the package of bread. She watched him put everything back in the carton.

"If he was all right," she said, "and went looking for us, my mother would know. She would stop him."

"Maybe. She went in late today. I don't think she's even home yet."

"But she'd see we were all gone."

"I doubt that she'd call the police or anything, and if she did, what do you think they would do?"

"I don't know."

"I'll tell you. The local police know about Frank. In fact, he's got a county-wide reputation. He's been picked up by the state police in our area, as well as local cops a number of times. Either for drunken driving or fights or just being a general nuisance. If Elaine called them, they'd promise to look and then just make some calls to the bars."

"But if she told them we were gone too . . ."

"They'd think he just took us along on one of his binges. Try not to think about it. At least tonight." He looked around the dimly lit room. "You did a nice job on these beds. No one would know this place isn't open for business."

"Did I?"

"Yeah."

"I don't think I'm tired enough to sleep yet," she said, bouncing herself on the bed.

"Neither am I. Too much has happened for me to go to sleep early. I don't think I'd sleep anyway. I'd probably just stare up at the ceiling with my eyes wide open, thinking."

"Me too." They were quiet for a moment. "You want to play something?" she asked.

"Like what? What could you play in a dark room?"

"Twenty questions," she said. He laughed and sat on his bed. "No, really. Here's how it works. I'll go first. Whoever goes picks a topic and gives one clue. Every time you ask for another clue, it costs you five questions. If you don't get it by twenty, I get a point and keep going."

"All right," he said, lying back on his bed and folding his arms across his chest. "Go ahead. What's your topic?" The candlelight danced on the ceiling. It kept the darkness just outside the opened doorway. He had thought about closing the door, but then thought, what would be the point of that? They couldn't lock it without a key. And if someone was actually still living in this hotel, they would have thrown them out by now. There was probably just a caretaker who visited the place occasionally. They weren't going to stay here that long so it didn't matter. "Well?"

"Let me think a minute. Oh, I know, TV stars."
She giggled after she said it.

"No soap opera people. That would be unfair."

"No soap opera," she said, turning on her side
and leaning on her elbow. "Here's my first clue:
They take very good care of his coat."

"His coat? His coat. Oh, I know," he said.
"Columbo the nutty detective. He had that raggy-
looking coat he always wore." Marty was proud
about how quickly he had guessed the answer.

"Nope."

"Huh? His coat? That's the clue?"

"You want another one? If you do, that's five
more questions."

"Wait a minute, wait a minute." He thought for a
while, but nothing sensible came to him. "This is
stupid," he said. "All right, give me another clue."

"His most famous words spoken on television
have to do with a tree."

"A tree? Damn." He figured the best thing to do
was to just go through his memory of the *TV Guide*,
thinking about what was on Monday, Tuesday . . .
concentrating on what he thought would be the
programs she would watch. He took five more
guesses, but she said they were all wrong. He
couldn't relate a coat and a tree. He tried creating
words out of maple and oak, hickory and pine.
Finally he had to ask for another clue and he had
four questions left.

"He can't write his own autograph. Someone has
to do it for him."

"A crippled star?"

"That's a question, you lose."

"All right, I lose. What TV star worries about his

coat, has famous words related to a tree, and can't write his own autograph?"

"Lassie."

"Lassie? You mean the dog?"

"Sure. They have to take good care of his coat of hair. His most famous words are 'bark, bark, bark,' and that's got to do with a tree, and he can't write, so he can't write his autograph."

"Well, I'll be damned." He thought about it and then started to laugh. "Who told you that one?"

"I made it up once when I was playing with Ethel Green. She's really good at it."

He laughed again, then encouraged her to tell him about her old girlfriends. She talked quickly at first, and then slowly, softly. He had never seen her so talkative, but he guessed that she was trying to forget her fears. Neither of them was anxious to close his eyes.

The candle burned down until it barely threw any light. The encroaching darkness made them both feel colder and they crawled under their blankets. When Judy had exhausted her topics of conversation, he began. He tried to remember some of the silly games he played with his friends when he was in school, but after a while everything he said sounded forced.

Although they both dreaded the silence that would come between them, simple fatigue took hold. There wasn't much silence anyway. Wood creaked, there were strange echoes in the hotel's corridor, owls moaned nearby, and two stray cats battled near their window. Every sound started them talking again.

Finally the candle died out completely. Marty

listened to Judy's breathing, then realized that she was subduing sobs.

"Hey," he whispered.

"What?"

"You've got nothing to worry about with me around."

"I know."

"I mean I know you've had a really bad day and this is a tough thing we're doing, but it's going to come out all right. You'll see." She was quiet for a while and then she called out his name.

"What?" Marty asked.

"What you did back at the house . . . I know it was terrible, but thank you. I'm glad you did it."

"I'm glad, too, but I'm also sorry."

He heard her rustle in the bed. Something was there in the darkness between them. He sensed it, even though he couldn't see clearly. Slowly, hesitantly, they both reached out and found each other's hands. She squeezed and held on to his gently. They remained that way for a while, in silence. Then he let go.

"Good night," he said.

"Good night."

A sound came from far off, deep in the hotel. He thought it sounded like a door slamming. He listened hard but heard nothing else. Then he hoped for sleep, thinking he would need all the energy he could muster when morning came. Despite the show of strength he was putting on for Judy, he could feel his own childhood fears threatening to surface. They were like little animals in the darkest recesses of his memory, nudged by the shadows in the hotel, by the sounds in the darkness, by the mystery of a place that seemed frozen in time. There was something here, something that both attracted and terrorized him. It challenged his courage, but he knew that if he turned and ran from this place, the flimsy foundation that kept Judy from crumpling would give way. He sensed that what would follow could be worse than anything else.

He had never seen or heard anything as exciting as this. He lay frozen in the ducts the whole time, not leaving even when he felt he had to go to the bathroom. He simply urinated in his pants, afraid that if he peed on the duct, the tinkle against the metal would alert them to his being in the wall. If only he could get closer, know more, see more. He was determined to do just that, but the ducts weren't going to be good enough. This was special.

It would be like following the daycamp around. Under no circumstances, absolutely no circumstances, Jake had said, was he ever to join in any of the daycamp activities. "God help you if any of those counselors see you around those children," Jake had warned.

Nobody knew it, but he had found a way to be near them when they were in the casino: He'd climb up in the fake ceiling and look down. Of course, it was easy to follow in the bushes when the counselors took them to the lake.

He was very anxious to get near this girl. The boy might not like it, he thought. The boy might get mad, like Jake. What if he did? The boy wasn't as big as Jake. He wouldn't be afraid of the boy. The boy wanted no one else near the girl. They were having too much fun. They were laughing in bed and they were talking.

Then their voices got very low and he had to strain

to hear. It made him very unhappy. He curled his fingers around the small bars in the grate and silently bent them. Of course, he was too far away to do anything, but he worked his hand through anyway. It was too dark for them to see it, but he liked the feeling of reaching out for her. He even imagined stroking her hair, touching her face. It felt like . . . felt like . . . he didn't want to think about whom it felt like.

Her name went through his mind like an electric jolt and he pulled his hand back. For a few moments he was frightened. He even thought he heard someone coming after him, crawling through the duct. He listened. Maybe it was just a rat. Sometimes rats got in there, although they didn't like it. It was easier for them to just run over the floors.

Even so, there was something, something in the darkness. It was coming just because he thought of her. He was never to think of her. If he didn't think of her, he didn't feel bad or afraid. The girl made him think of her, this girl sleeping in the dark. For a few moments he was confused about the girl. Was she good or bad? Should he like her or not? He wasn't sure now; he wasn't sure.

He backed away from the grate ever so slowly, hardly breathing for fear he'd make a sound. When he was far enough away, he curled up in a ball and for a while just lay there, terrified of the darkness before him and the darkness behind him. Why did he have to think of her? Everything was so good up till then.

He waited and listened. After a while he regained his confidence and straightened his body out again. Then he began to work his way back through the ducts.

Their candle had gone out. He listened keenly and was sure he heard their regular breathing. They were asleep. He began his retreat, moving with the agility of a sleek cat. Although he was big, he was able to twist and turn his body with incredible grace. He could slide through openings that seemed barely wide enough for his legs. He had lived within the shadows so long that he became one of them, molding and changing his form at will.

Sometimes he could stand so still in a room that even his grandfather would walk right past him without noticing him. He knew how to merge with corners and become one with the silence. On cold nights, when the world outside raged with angry winds and wet snow and rain, he could draw the blanket of darkness around him and find warmth in the sound of his own heartbeat.

He had become a thing unto himself, clawing at the bad memories, cowering from the haunting fears, fleeing from the sounds of voices of the people who were no longer there. He didn't feel safe that often and it was very rare when he was happy.

Now, he knew only that it was time to sleep. In the morning he would think more about the girl and the boy. He would get up early and watch everything they did. Then he would decide what he would do with them.

Consciousness returned to Frank in the form of a pinhole of light that grew larger and larger until the twilight took shape around him. He blinked his eyes and focused on a blade of grass. Almost immediately a fierce throbbing began at the base of his skull. He groaned and reached back to touch the area. At first he couldn't manipulate his arm properly. His body shuddered and his arm fluttered feebly. Finally he was able to direct his hand to his head, and the feel of the warm blood shocked him into awareness.

It wasn't until he sat up that he realized his pants and underwear were down between his ankles and knees. Little red ants were crawling all over his naked thighs and buttocks. There were even some moving within his pubic hair. He groaned and braced himself on one arm. The moment he did so, it felt like there were knives at the back of his head. Never had he felt such sharp pain. Despite that, he slapped at the ants and scrubbed them off his body as best he could.

He turned over to brace himself on his hands and began to vomit. His stomach strained with the pain as beer began to rise in his throat and acid burned the roof of his mouth. When it was over, he remained in the same position to catch his breath. It was then that he saw the top of Judy's bathing suit and began to remember what happened.

"Son of a bitch," he said and struggled to pull his pants and underpants up. Then he stood up to buckle his belt. He couldn't believe the dizziness he experienced when he did so. He had been drunk many times in his life, but it was nothing compared to this. He staggered about until he regained his balance. Then he gathered up the pieces of Judy's bathing suit, determined to shove it down her throat. He had other plans for Marty.

He had to brace himself against the house as he made his way to the back door. The waning afternoon sun left a coolness behind and he shivered and embraced himself, the bathing suit dangling from his hands.

"Fuckin' cocksuckers," he muttered. His anger gave him renewed strength and he continued toward the door. He practically fell inside when he opened it, but caught hold of the back of a kitchen chair and steadied himself. He looked around and listened. He saw no one, heard no one. What if they went to the police? he thought. What time was it? The wall clock swam in and out of focus because of his dizziness. What time did he come home? What time did he. . . . *No*, he thought, *it's been too long. If they went to the cops, they'd be here by now. Besides, what could they prove? It'd be their word against mine.*

They're upstairs, he thought, *hiding. Maybe they're together, screwin'.* That ungrateful bastard . . . he was eager to beat the son of a bitch to a pulp. He wondered if he had the strength right now. He could barely keep on his feet.

"Fuckin' shit." It was one thing to be hit from behind—he'd been hit from behind before. But by his own son! Didn't he feed and clothe the son of a bitch for years? He sat down and tried to catch his breath and stop the room from spinning. Gradually it stopped.

He seized a bread knife from the counter and started through the kitchen, steadying himself against the walls as he went along to the foot of the stairway. Once there, he took hold of the shaky bannister, mumbling curses as he pulled himself up.

For a moment he just stood looking into Marty's empty room. Then he screamed "BASTARD!" and lunged forward, driving the knife into Marty's pillow and jerking it down until he had made a long slit in it. He grabbed the pillow and wildly ripped it apart, sending the feathers floating around him, over himself, on the bed, and down to the floor.

Still enraged, he lifted the knife high above his head, dreaming of Marty's body sprawled beneath him, and plunged it deeply into the mattress, its silver edge disappearing into the guts of the bedding. He did this repeatedly until the bed was in shreds. He was exhausted from the effort and collapsed face forward on the bed.

For a few moments he just lay there, wheezing and gasping, able to think only of curses and oaths. His rage had brought on nausea and dizziness. He was just able to make his way to his own bedroom and collapse on his bed, where he immediately fell into a deep sleep.

When Elaine came home and discovered him, she assumed he had gone on a drunk again and simply passed out because of it. She gasped at the sight of blood on his pillow though and woke him to ask about it. His mind was clear enough for him to concoct a story.

"I found the son of a bitch stealin' from me," he told her. "I asked Curtis Ingber for the money he owed me on the flatbed truck and he said he give it to Marty last week. When I asked him about it, he lied and said he ain't got it. Then, when I said I'd bring him down to confront Curtis, he hit me with a shovel when I turned my head. Him and that cockteaser of yours ran off somewheres."

"I can't believe it."

"Well, believe it, damn you." He sat on the bed, his face still sickly white.

"You'd better go to a doctor anyhow."

"Fuck the doctor. Just bandage me up."

"I think you need stitches, Frank. You might even have a concussion."

"I ain't got no concussion," he said, but then reconsidered. "Ah, shit. Drive me up to the hospital emergency room then. I ain't goin' to none of these local doctors."

He had been to the emergency room a number of times before, after fights or after stupid accidents. There would be less questions because they knew him up there.

As they drove off, Elaine repeated her disbelief.

"I just can't believe they'd run off like that."

"Believe it,' he said, his eyes closed. "He took that old Plymouth. It don't even have plates. They probably got it parked off some side road. Wouldn't surprise me if they're plannin' on hidin' out in it a while."

"Marty just don't strike me as the type . . ."

"Yeah, well, he struck me. That's why we're goin' up to the hospital."

He peered at her through a slightly opened left eye. She just shook her head and drove on. He was satisfied that he had covered up the episode well enough for the time being.

The emergency room doctor confirmed his concussion. When he asked for an explanation, Frank created a story about his falling backward off some scaffolding. The doctor was skeptical, but when he looked at Elaine, she confirmed it. She didn't see any point in "airing out the dirty linen."

Frank needed stitches and the doctor wanted him admitted for observation, but he refused to stay at the hospital. In the end the doctor told him to go home and stay quiet for a few days.

Both of them half expected the kids to be there when they returned, but the house was dark and the Plymouth was still gone. Frank knew that Marty couldn't go far in a car without plates. He would have to stay off the main roads. Probably went to one of his buddies to hide out until things got cooled down, Frank thought.

Elaine wondered aloud if they shouldn't call the police, but he disagreed.

"They'll only wanna know the whole story. Might be forced to have my own son arrested," he added. She saw the logic in that and decided he was right: they would wait a day or so and see if the kids returned on their own.

"I wonder how he talked Judy into goin' off with him."

"Shit, you're as blind as a bat sometimes."

"What'dya mean?"

"I seen 'em pawin' over each other all the time."

"Really?" Elaine considered the possibility. "Maybe you're right," she said, thinking how Marty and Judy had grown closer. "And all that time they had to be alone," she added, thinking aloud.

"Right," Frank said, satisfied that he had done a good job of covering his ass. "I'd better rest like the doctor said." Elaine nodded and watched him walk off.

She looked out only twice that night before going to sleep. Neither time did she see anything. Frank was already snoring away when she went up to bed.

She listened to the old house creak in the wind, shrugged, and thought, *Oh well, they're big enough to take care of themselves, and if all that Frank said was true, they don't deserve me worryin' myself sick over 'em.*

It didn't take her long to fall asleep.

6

The cool morning air woke Marty. From the low position of the sun, he guessed that it wasn't more than six or six thirty. The moment he opened his eyes, he saw Judy directly across from him, her face closed tightly in sleep, her body folded in the fetal position, her hands clutching the thin blanket under her chin.

He didn't stir or speak. His brain gradually focused in on yesterday's events and he realized the significance of what had happened and what they were doing.

What were they doing? The increasingly bright light of morning was forcing him to face reality. After he had struck Frank, all he could think of was flight. He feared being there if Frank was all right, and he feared being there if he wasn't. But what were they to do now? Should they stay away another day? Could he ever go back?

And what about Judy? He had taken on quite a responsibility when he brought her along. He wondered if it wasn't partly because of his own fears and the need not to flee alone. He did feel sorry for her, so much so that it would have been difficult to just run off and leave her there sobbing in bed. And what if Frank had come to and taken out his rage on her? No, he was right to bring her along.

It was just that now, as he looked at her, he realized how fragile she was. She looked so small and innocent, so vulnerable. He turned over on his back and looked up at the ceiling. Images of the rape scene played before him. The violent eroticism aroused him even though he fought against it. He hated that part of himself that wanted to linger on Judy's nudity, Judy's helplessness.

Frank's genes were at work in him, he thought. He would always have to be on guard against that. After all, he was Frank's son and a strain of that viciousness ran in his blood. There were times when he'd had too many drinks, and, catching sight of himself reflected in a window or in a mirror, he'd thought he'd seen the Frank in him coming out. It had always sobered him up immediately.

It was the old Dr. Jekyll and Mr. Hyde story. He never told anyone about it, because he was sure the person would laugh at him, but he had this fear that if he ever tried to do anything intelligent with his life, the Frank in him would ruin it. Even when he simply dreamed, a part of him ridiculed him. It made him insecure, and maybe just as vulnerable as someone like Judy.

He sat up in the bed and brushed back his hair. It was going to be the kind of day where it would be warmer outside than in. His stomach rumbled with hunger. Neither he nor Judy had eaten that much the day before. He spun around to find his shoes and spotted something on the room's doorway floor. It was a sheet of paper.

Judy moaned and turned on her back. Her eyelids opened and closed and then flickered. He smiled at her confusion.

"Morning."

"Oh."

"Once we fell asleep, I guess we both slept pretty well."

She rubbed her cheeks. The bruised one throbbed with pain and she winced. That brought back the full, ugly memory. It hadn't been a dream; it hadn't been a nightmare. She closed her eyes to shut it out, but that only produced Frank's gruesome face: his eyes wide with excitement, his lips wet and drooling, his nostrils puffed like a bull's. His unshaven face with its sharply drawn jawbone resembled a work cut in granite. She felt like lifting her hands and pounding the air before her to drive away the haunting images.

"Are you all right?" Marty asked.

"Huh? Yeah. Any idea what time it is?" She sat up too.

"Not exactly. Just that it's early." He slipped into his shoes and stood up. He went to the doorway and picked up the paper.

"What's that?"

"A hotel menu, breakfast menu," he said and laughed.

"How did it get there?"

"I suppose it was always here. We didn't see it in the dark."

"But it was light when we came to the room."

He thought about it and shrugged.

"We just missed it, I guess. Or maybe a breeze blew it down the hall. I don't think anyone would leave us a breakfast menu, do you?"

"No."

"I'm hungry though. Let's take some of those oranges and squeeze some juice in the kitchen. We can make coffee."

"There's no milk."

"I saw some of that dairy substitute. Most of the hotels that keep kosher kitchens have that stuff so the guests can enjoy coffee the way they like it, even when they have a meat meal."

"Really?" She got up, found her shoes, and brushed back her hair with the brush from her pocketbook. He watched her for a moment.

"Sure. They even keep separate dishes: dishes for meat, dishes for dairy. I'll show you when we get down there."

"I'd like to wash up and go to the bathroom. Think there's one working?"

"The water's running in the kitchen. Probably the bathrooms nearby work. Actually," he said as they started down the hall, "that surprises me."

"Why?"

"Well, a deserted place like this would have to have its water pipes drained or they could freeze and burst in the winter. Maybe just certain pipes are working. The bathrooms in the guests' rooms aren't working."

"Let me see that menu," she said. He handed it to her as they walked. "Wish some of this was there."

"Me too."

As soon as they stepped into the lobby, he sensed something different. He stopped to look around. She waited quizzically by his side. He didn't want to say anything that might frighten her, and yet . . . someone else had been there very recently. He felt it. Had he hung that intercom up again? Did he leave those cards in so neat a pile? Was the bell in the middle of the counter or to the side?

"What's wrong?"

"Nothing. I just can't get over how much good stuff is left in this place," he added quickly. She relaxed. "C'mon."

They walked through the dining room quickly; but quietly, but before he opened the kitchen door, he spun around. Judy had turned over those goblets on that front table. He remembered that for sure. Now they were all upside down again and neatly arranged. Someone was looking after this place, keeping everything ready. But why?

"Did you hear something?"

He didn't reply. He looked at the kitchen door for a moment and then, hesitantly, with some trepidation, he pushed it open. There, sitting at one of the long tables, eating eggs and drinking tea, was an elderly-looking man. The moment he set eyes on them, his face broke out in a wide smile. He sat back with a look of relief and happiness. Neither Marty nor Judy moved.

"Is that you?" he said. He waved his long, bony right forefinger. "You gave us quite a scare," he said. "Your mama's lookin' all over for you. And with the season about to start. Not a nice thing, Sylvia. Not a nice thing."

"Sylvia?" Judy said.

Marty shrugged. "I think he's talking to you."

"Let's get out of here."

"Wait a minute."

"Come, come," he said and gestured emphatically. "Eat some breakfast."

Judy slipped her hand into Marty's as he stepped forward. The door closed behind them. Marty looked about, wondering if anyone else was there. Apparently the old man was alone. He was dressed in a shabby-looking dark blue sports jacket and a pair of unpressed light blue pants. His black shoes were old and scuffed. There were spots of white paint on them. The elasticity of his socks was gone and they hung in small folds just above his ankles. He was unshaven and his very thin white hair looked as though it had been trimmed by a novice barber. He slapped his hands together as they drew closer. The action stopped Judy in her tracks.

"So," he said, "who's this? Who's this? A new waiter?"

"Yes," Marty said. "I'm a waiter."

"Marty," Judy whispered. He jiggled her hand.

"Good, good. It's never too early to start," the old man said, tightening his face with seriousness. "Sylvia can tell you. And we don't have to wait for my wife to come to give orders. I can tell you where to start.

"But first," he said, "you've got to eat, and you mustn't think because you eat in the kitchen that your food isn't as good as the guests'. You get the same food at Levine's Mountain House, right, Sylvia?"

"Say right," Marty whispered.

"No."

"I'm sure your food's always good here," Marty said, and then he turned to whisper to Judy. "I'm really hungry. Let's get some of that."

"Marty!"

"Always, always." The old man got up and started toward the stoves.

"You should finish eating first," Marty said.

"I'm finished. How much do I eat? Sit down. Sylvia, get some dishes and cups and silverware."

"Do it," Marty said in a loud whisper.

"I don't know where any of that is."

"The dishes are in that room there. Those are the dairy dishes I was telling you about. You'll see cups on the lower shelves. Silverware is in those drawers," he said, pointing. She hesitated. "Go on." Reluctantly she moved to the storage room.

Marty watched the old man crack some eggs over a pan. He beat them slowly with a large fork and then poured in a little milk. *If he owns this place,* Marty thought, *he must be Mr. Levine.* Marty moved to the table and pulled out a seat.

"Expecting a big season this year, Mr. Levine?"

"Oh, sure, sure. You call me Pop," he said, waving his big fork. "Everyone calls me Pop. Only, my wife likes to be called Mrs. Levine."

"My name's Marty."

The old man nodded as though he already knew.

Judy came out with the plates and cups and set them on the table. She looked at the old man nervously and then turned to Marty and stamped her foot silently, gesturing that they should leave now. He smiled and shook his head.

"Sylvia works the children's dining room," the old man said without taking his eyes off the pan. "She does a good job too."

"Oh, that can be hard sometimes," Marty said.

"Children's dining room?" Judy asked.

"Waitress," Marty said.

"We got a lotta work to be done, a lotta work,"

Pop said. He turned and waved his fork at them. "We'll start with the silverware first."

"What's he mean?" Judy whispered.

"Polishing."

"We'll start right after breakfast. Mrs. Levine might inspect this kitchen any time," the old man warned. "We are proud of being spic and span. Sylvia," he said, turning to Judy, "I noticed the back fire exit window has a lotta dust. Maybe you can clean it before your mother sees it." He stared and waited, so Judy nodded. When she turned to Marty, he was smiling widely. "Good," Pop said and looked at Marty. "You're earning money for college, I suppose?"

"That's right."

"Well, if you're courteous, you work hard, and remember that the hotel has a reputation to maintain, you'll make a lotta money. Levine's Mountain House has put a lot of students through college, right, Sylvia?"

Marty turned to her.

"Right," she said. "This is silly," she whispered when the old man turned away.

"Okay," he said, scraping the eggs into the dishes Judy brought out. "Eat, eat. You'll need your strength. We got a lotta work to do."

Marty picked up his fork quickly and dug in. Judy eased her way into her seat. She was reluctant to participate in the deception, but the aroma of the eggs and fresh coffee was enticing. She followed Marty's lead. The old man poured their coffee and took his seat. He watched them for a while, a wide smile on his face.

"This is very good," Marty said.

"Listen, I've been cooking a long time. Of course,

Mrs. Levine is the best cook in the mountains. In the early days, boarders came to our farmhouse just because of her cooking."

"Where is Mrs. Levine?" Marty asked. The old man's eyes grew smaller as though his mind had to focus very hard on the answer.

"She's downstairs," he said in a much lower voice, almost a whisper. "She's not feeling well. That's why we've got to start to work, so when she comes up, she'll be happily surprised. She thinks nothing can be done unless she's supervising."

"You run this whole place with just your wife?" Marty asked.

"What's so hard to believe? We worked harder in the old days when we didn't have so many machines. Sylvia was just a baby."

"Is that right?" Marty smiled at Judy, who just shook her head.

"As soon as you're finished, you go to the main lobby. Two doors down from the main desk you'll see a little room where we keep some staff clothing. Find something that fits," Pop said, "but don't take too long. The sooner we get started, the sooner we get done."

"No one but your wife and you are here now?"

"There'll be a lotta people here soon."

"Oh yeah, I know, I know." Marty finished his coffee and stood up. "Okay," he said, "let's get to it." Judy rose slowly.

"Start in the children's dining room," Pop said.

"Gotcha." He nodded at Judy and they started out of the kitchen.

"What are we going to do?" she whispered as they left the kitchen.

"Just what the old man said."

She grabbed his arm to stop him. "You can't be serious. That old man is crazy."

"Oh, he's just senile. He's harmless, can't you see? This situation is perfect!"

"But he thinks I'm his daughter."

"So? We'll humor him. I'll pretend I'm a waiter and you'll be his daughter or whoever he wants you to be. What's the harm? In the meantime, we'll have food and a safe place to stay."

She studied his expression. He looked as though he was really enjoying the situation. She was afraid, afraid they were getting themselves into deeper trouble.

"I don't know if I like this."

His expression soured. It was as though she had slapped him.

"Are you ready to go back and possibly face Frank?"

"No, but . . ."

"Then I say let's take advantage of this," he said, gesturing widely with both arms. She saw how enthusiastic he was and her opposition began to fade.

"What about the old man's wife? She could call the police or something? They both can't be senile, can they?"

"She sounds like she's an invalid. Maybe she doesn't even exist. In any case, whatever he tells her, she'll probably think it's just part of his senility."

"How come people left him here all by himself if he's so senile?" she asked, searching for a final argument.

"I don't know. Look," he said, taking a softer, more reasonable tone, "until something happens to make it difficult for us, let's hang in, okay?"

She could see how much it meant to him and she also saw the opportunity they had to make it into a safe hideaway. There were worse places to go, and if they kept running, they might be discovered. She had no idea where to run to anyway. She was totally dependent on Marty's ingenuity.

Besides her confidence in him, though, she had to admit she enjoyed being with him this way: alone, tied together by a mutual fear. She had fantasized about a relationship and now, even though the circumstances that caused it were horrible, her dream was turning into reality.

She didn't say anything else, so Marty continued across the dining room, back to the lobby to find the staff clothing room. She followed but couldn't help looking back continually. He found the room quickly. There were many white shirts on hangers and a few pairs of black pants. Judy found some waitress uniforms and Marty even located some black shoes. She sifted through the rack until she found a uniform that might fit her. She held it up against her.

"Looks like it's your size. Put it on," Marty said.

"Should I?" His excitement was beginning to affect her.

"Of course." He held up a pair of black pants and a shirt. "I'm going to put these on. The old man'll really think we work here after this. It's perfect."

"You keep saying everything's perfect. I don't see what's so perfect," she said. She couldn't help sounding annoyed. She was feeling quite frightened by all this, and he was acting as if it were all a game.

"I keep telling you—for the time being it is!"

"Well, I'm scared. My mother's probably looking all over for me by now. She probably called the police."

"Somehow I doubt it," he said.

She thought for a moment. He was probably right. Going to the police would be the last thing Elaine would do, and only after more time had passed. Unless, of course, Frank was hurt very bad, so bad he . . .

"Just put that on," Marty said. "You change in here. I'll change in the lobby." He walked out before she could say anything else.

For a moment she just stood there holding the uniform. Then she thought, *What difference will it make anyway?* She'd put it on and play this game if Marty thought it was the best thing to do. She had to depend on him now. He seemed to know what he was doing. He did handle the old man well.

When she stepped out, they confronted each other in the staff uniforms. Her uniform fit perfectly. The pants were a trifle too long on him, but his shoes fit well.

"You look like you could go right to work," he said. She did feel like a professional. "And you told me you wanted to work in one of the hotels."

"Yeah, but a real one."

"This is a real one."

"It's not in business. You know what I mean."

"So you'll have a dress rehearsal." He laughed. "Now let's see, where was the children's dining room?"

"I still can't believe we're doing this."

"It has to be right off the main dining room. Probably through that side door. C'mon," he said, "let's see."

Judy caught her reflected image in one of the lobby windows. She looked good. It was a silly thing to do, but still. . . . She raised her arm and turned her palm up flat, pretending to hold a tray. That made her laugh to herself. *Oh well,* she thought, *at least this will keep our minds off what happened yesterday, and it's what Marty wants to do.* He looked so good in his outfit too.

"Are you coming?" he said, turning at the doorway to the dining room.

"Yes," she said and walked gracefully as though she were carrying a tray full of dishes.

So they were workers. Why did they sleep in a guest room? If Jake knew that. . . . Maybe Jake said they could until people came.

Did his grandfather call the girl Sylvia? Sylvia was his mother's name. She had the same color hair his mother had, too, and the same light skin. Was she as tall as his mother was? He couldn't remember. He had to keep looking at her picture or he'd forget what she looked like.

Jake didn't know, but he had taken his favorite picture of her to the basement. It was the one where she was just a girl, like this girl. In the picture his mother was sitting on a swinging love seat on the old farmhouse porch. She was smiling.

If Jake knew he had that picture, he'd be mad. *So what,* he thought. *I'm big, too, big as Jake, bigger than Jake.* But was he as strong as Jake? He had seen Jake lift many heavy things, things he couldn't even budge when he tried after Jake was gone.

That was a long time ago though. Now he went around and lifted all those things. Jake never lifted much anymore. He wasn't around much. When Jake did come, his heart would beat quickly and he would make little whimpering noises. Sometimes he'd break into a sweat or feel a chill down the back of his neck. "Hit me," he would mutter, "Jake hit me."

He wanted to do something to hurt Jake now, but he was afraid to go near him. He brought food, said a few things to his grandfather, and went away. He didn't know where he went, but he was glad he went.

A while back, he didn't know how long ago, he had met Jake. He hadn't seen him drive up or he would have remained inside. He had just come up from the basement thinking he would go into the woods to look at the deer. There were so many more of them since people had stopped coming to stay in the rooms.

He had just come out of the back door when Jake came around the corner of the building. The moment he saw Jake he began to stutter. He couldn't help that. He'd been doing it ever since the day at the lake.

Jake's eyes had widened and his mouth had twisted with rage. His hands closed into fists. He hadn't said anything, had just stood there looking fierce and terrible.

"No . . . no . . . no," he had said and pressed his body against the hotel wall as he made his way quickly to the corner. Then he ran down the left side of the hotel grounds and into the brush to disappear behind some trees. There he had crouched in fear and waited.

It had been hours before he could get the memory of Jake's blazing eyes and hate-filled face from his mind. Sometimes he'd look in the mirror to see if he could make the same scary face. He thought he could. *Be mad,* he thought. *Mad like Jake.* It made him feel stronger to do that.

If he had to, he could frighten somebody too. He could frighten the boy. He could make his eyes big and his mouth ugly and the boy would run away.

And then there would just be the girl. Just the girl and him in the hotel.

Good, he thought. That would be good.

7

"For my first job in a hotel, I was a busboy in a children's dining room," Marty said as they walked through the main dining room.

"Really?"

"Yeah. I was only fourteen and they wanted boys sixteen or older, but I was big for my age and it was easy for me to lie to the service manager. Actually Frank had gotten me the job because he worked on the manager's car and told the manager he had a sixteen-year-old son who needed something to do. I was afraid the manager had told Frank just how much money I would make, so I turned over all the money I made that first time. Later on I got smart and held back."

"Weren't you scared to start in the children's dining room?"

"No. That's the best place to start. Kids don't appreciate good service, but they don't recognize

very bad service either. It's good training ground."
He laughed.

"What's so funny?"

"I had a couple of little bastards to deal with. They
would deliberately spill things and ask for things they
never used, you know. So one time I fooled them. I
made believe I lost control and spilled two glasses of
milk all over them. I still made good tips though."

He opened the side door and as he expected, it
opened to a smaller dining room, obviously reserved
for children. There were only a dozen tables in it,
and all of the chairs were shorter and smaller.
Instead of paneling, there was old wallpaper with
Disney characters. The paper was faded and stained,
probably indelibly marked by food stains from pieces
of meals the kids had thrown about. He could see
where some kids had kicked in the Sheetrock.
Nevertheless the room was still pleasant.

Judy was watching him evaluate the children's
dining room, and he got the feeling she was waiting
for him to make some critical comments and offer
advice. For a moment he felt like the experienced
waiter in the Levine Mountain House who was
assigned to orientate new help. He paced about for a
few moments and then looked back at the door and
nodded.

"What?" she asked.

"The only bad thing about this," he replied, "is
the distance from the kitchen. You'd have to walk
through the main dining room to get here. Some
waiters won't like you moving in and out of their
tables. You have to find the route that's easiest and
least troublesome."

She studied him for a moment. He sounded and

looked so serious. His attitude didn't frighten her, but it should have. She looked about quizzically. She saw from the expression on his face that it was important to him that she go along with the fantasy.

"I should?"

She looked back through the door as though she were considering what he had just said.

"Okay," he said, taking down one of the chairs and setting it up by the table. "I'm a five-year-old brat and I'm hungry." He plopped into the seat and folded his arms. Then he kicked the table leg, and one of the chairs on the other side slid off and crashed to the floor. Immediately he let out a wail.

"What is it?"

"I'm hungry. What's for supper?"

"Supper? Oh, supper." She stepped closer. "Let's see, what do you want?"

"Bacon and eggs."

"Okay."

"No," he said, assuming his real voice. "You can't give him that. This is a kosher hotel. They don't have bacon here, and I told you before, they don't mix milk and dairy products with meat products."

"Oh, that's right." She assumed a stern posture. "Well then, you can't have bacon and eggs for supper, and I'm surprised at you for asking such a thing, young man."

"But . . ."

"You want me to go out there and tell your mother what you asked for? Well, do you?"

He looked up at her. She had her hands on her hips and her face screwed up like an old school-marm's, but he didn't laugh. Rather he was amazed at how quickly she could get into it.

"No," he said in a subdued tone of voice. "Well, then what can I have?" He made himself look as though he were about to cry.

"You can have mashed potatoes and peas. No, spinach, I mean, and hamburger."

"Ugh, spinach."

"And if you eat everything, you can have chocolate cake for dessert. But only if you eat everything," she emphasized.

"My mother said I don't have to eat spinach."

"I'll ask her on the way out to the kitchen. You better not be lying. Now behave yourself and remember, there are other people eating at this table with you."

"There are?" he said. "Well, they better get their own chairs off," he added and laughed. She laughed too. He pulled up a chair for her to sit on. "That was pretty good," he said. "You know, I bet you could get a job in the children's dining room at one of the hotels."

"You think so?"

"Why not?" He stared at her for a few moments. "You look good in that outfit."

"It's probably a little tight."

"No, I don't think so."

"You look good too."

"No, this shirt doesn't fit." He looked down and then raised his eyes to meet hers. They were close to each other now, looking at each other intently. A warmth came over him. He couldn't keep his eyes from the opened top of her uniform. The unbuttoned holes revealed the start of the rise in her bosom. The skin was a shade lighter there.

What she sensed in his gaze both frightened and

excited her. It was as though Frank's gruesome sexual attack had permanently stained all things male for her. She wanted her own arousal to be something clean and pure, but there was still an ache in her thighs from the way Frank had twisted her legs, and there was still a sting in her bruised cheek.

He saw the hesitation in her eyes and understood. He wanted to touch her in a comforting and reassuring way, but he recognized that it was too soon even for that. When he finally spoke, he resented the sound of his own voice.

"Judy, I . . ."

"So there you are," old man Levine said. He stood in the open doorway, the jar of silverware polish in one hand and two rags in the other. Marty and Judy simply stared at him. "I went to the lobby and couldn't find you." He looked at the children's dining room and shook his head. "So much work. The floor's got to be washed and waxed yet."

"Oh, yeah," Marty said, "yeah. We were just discussing that." The old man came farther in. "You have a nice place here, Pop."

"A nice place? You should have seen this place in its prime." He nodded at his own words as though someone else had said them. "It was the jewel of the Catskills. Everything so clean, so organized—the flowers blossoming, the hedges perfectly trim . . ."

"I can trim hedges," Marty said quickly, but the old man didn't hear him. He was lost in his reverie.

"There were always so many people in those days. We were always full up. At night the porch was filled with guests sitting in the chairs, talking and laughing. When the show started in the casino, we had a packed house."

"Maybe it will be packed here again this year," Judy said. She looked close to tears. Pop Levine shrugged.

"Many of my old friends don't come back. We get letters sometimes, telling us about this one passing away, that one passing away. It's not the same. My wife says it would be better if we didn't get any letters at all."

"Well," Marty said, breaking the heavy pause, "we have work to do."

"Right. Here's the polish. Start on the silverware in this room."

"C'mon," Marty said, handing Judy one of the rags the old man brought in.

"It's important," old man Levine said. "The parents come into the children's dining room to inspect. You want things to look good so you'll get good tips." He waved a warning finger at Marty. "My daughter can tell you."

"They'll look good," Judy said. She smiled warmly at him. The old man seemed relieved. They watched him walk out. "Now what are we going to do?" she asked as soon as he left.

"Polish the silver. You promised to do it," he said. He went to the service station and opened the top drawer to take out the silverware and organize it neatly on top. "I'll do the forks and knives," he said. "You do the spoons."

"Really?"

"Sure. I've done this many times before. I had a waiter once who bitched like crazy about it. No matter how I polished them, they weren't shiny enough. He was like a marine drill sergeant." She watched what he did and then imitated it. They worked quietly for a while. "We might get this place in such good shape they'll want to reopen it," Marty said.

"Who will?"

"I don't know. Whoever really runs this joint."

"It's pretty strange," Judy said, looking around. It was more than strange, she thought; it was eerie. She felt as if she had walked into someone's home and begun to live in it as though it were her own. That was all right, only there was an ever-present feeling that the person had never left, that the person was there, watching, waiting. For what? she wondered.

Was it some kind of trap? Had they been lured into the place, tempted, made comfortable and secure only to set them up for something horrible? All sorts of weird ideas ran through her mind. Perhaps this hotel was haunted by guests long dead. The idea made her shudder.

As she gazed around the room, something caught her eye. She turned abruptly and saw what she thought looked like fingers coming out of the grate. She dropped the silverware and screamed.

"What the hell—" Marty whirled around.

"There," she said, pointing toward the grate. "I saw fingers or snakes or . . ."

"Hey, hey, calm down," Marty said, walking to the grate. He peered through the thin bars. "There's nothing in here. C'mon."

"I saw it. I swear."

"Fingers or snakes, huh?" He stuck his own fingers in to demonstrate his skepticism. She grimaced but relaxed when he smiled.

"Let's get out of here, Marty. Please."

He turned on her roughly, his face flushing with anger. She stepped back.

"And go where? Back to the house? Did you ever think he might be waiting for us, looking for us?"

"But I thought maybe he's . . ."

"What if he isn't? What if he's okay? Do you wanna meet up with him on this back country road? What are we goin' to say? 'We're sorry'? 'Forget the whole thing'?"

"I don't know. I just feel . . . frightened."

"So do I. So what should we do, run? Look," he said in a much softer tone of voice, "let's look for some fun and get our minds off things for a while. We'll explore this place. There's a lot here we haven't seen yet. What do you say?" He took her hand. "Huh?"

"Okay."

"That's the spirit." He led her out of the children's dining room. They checked, but the old man wasn't anywhere in sight, so they went back through the lobby to their corridor. Marty had seen a door at the end of the hall. It led out to the pool.

The sidewalk that ran alongside the main building was cracked and chipped so badly that in some spots there was grass growing through. Much of the grass around the hotel was waist high, but the pathway to the pool was still sufficiently clear for them to follow it.

As soon as they drew close to the pool, they saw the remains of a shuffleboard court. The squares and numbers were still visible, but the cement had cracked and small weeds popped through the openings.

"Ever play shuffleboard?" he asked.

"No."

"Most of the older hotels have a court near the pool. You have these two long sticks with V-shaped hooks at the end, see." Judy couldn't get over how quickly he could lose himself in the place. "You shove the discs into the squares," he said, stepping onto the court. "If they don't touch a line, you get whatever points are marked in the square. Your opponent can try to knock out your disc if he wants to and you can do the same. Maybe they still have the sticks and discs in the cabana."

He went to look while she walked around the pool. It was a deep cement pool that must have been quite nice when it was kept up. The inside had been painted a light blue, and there was a wide black stripe painted on the bottom and the sides to warn swimmers that they were going into deeper waters. The sides of the pool had the depths painted on them. All of the numbers were faded. For landscaping they had used firebricks cemented into a flooring. Many of the bricks were chipped away and cracked. She was sure the whole thing had been pretty when it was first done.

"Too bad it's not filled," he called. "It's hot enough to swim today, huh?" She stopped on the little stairway to the children's section and sat on the top step. He watched her for a moment and then looked into the cabana.

He couldn't believe how much stuff was still in there: a badminton net with rackets and birdies, a couple of basketballs and some volleyballs, a volleyball net, a pile of deflated tire tubes that had probably been used for swimming games, the shuffleboard sticks and two piles of different-colored discs, a life jacket probably worn by the lifeguard, and a couple of horseshoe sets.

"Hey," he yelled. "You've got to come over here and see all this." Judy looked up but didn't move. "We have a great choice of games." She still didn't move, didn't even look up and acknowledge him. "What the hell . . ." he muttered and walked over to her. She was running her left forefinger along one of the cracks in the top step. He sat down beside her. "What's the matter?"

"I was just thinking about my mother. Maybe we should try to call her." She looked near tears.

"Oh." He looked out over the hotel grounds. "The only problem is Frank could answer or be right beside her." He pulled a long blade of grass out of a crack in the cement and held it in his teeth. Judy embraced her knees and brought them close to her body.

"Think she found out what Frank did to me?"

Marty was reluctant to talk about it. He had been grateful for the fact that she had been able to avoid thinking about it constantly. The image of the blood trickling down the back of Frank's neck appeared before him. He blinked hard to change the picture, but it lingered a while.

"I don't know," he finally said. He felt she would have waited all day for his answer. "It depends on whether or not he could talk and how much Elaine guessed."

"She was nearly raped once when she was a kid."

"Really? How come you never told me before?" She shrugged. "Who tried to do it?"

"Her uncle. He took her for a ride somewhere and stopped the car where there were no houses. She had to run all the way home."

"What happened to the uncle?"

"Nothin'. She said everyone thought she was exaggerating. He just never came around much anymore."

"Damn."

"Maybe people would think I was exaggerating if I said anything."

"No. People know what Frank's like. Who'd ever believe him?" Judy looked as though she was going to start crying any moment, so he tried to start a new conversation fast. "Must've been a nice place to swim."

"Yeah."

"It's really a big one. All of these old places have such big pools. You know what it would cost to build one like this today?"

He stood up and walked down the small stairway, pretending to step into cold water as he moved forward. He lifted his legs high and hugged himself. She laughed when he grimaced with imaginary pain. He pretended to shiver, clicking his teeth hard. She laughed again and he splashed her with imaginary water. She actually winced and then pretended to splash back. He went wild, as he would in a real water fight.

When she stepped back, he walked on until he reached the spot where the water would be above his head. Then he took a deep breath and held it as he kept going. He backed up and turned to face her with his cheeks puffed out. When she laughed again, he began to jump up and down, acting as though he were drowning.

"Help, help, help."

"You're so silly."

"Quickly, give me your hand. Give me your hand! You're going to let me drown?"

She got up and walked toward him until he could reach out and take her hand. He let her pull him forward to the area where they would be in more shallow water.

"Thank you," he said, "thank you, thank you. You saved my life." He embraced her, kissing her on the neck. She giggled and backed away.

"You're crazy."

"C'mon," he said, reddening, "let's try the shuffleboard now." He ran out of the pool.

"But I don't know how to play."

"I told you how. It'll be fun, especially with this court in such bad shape."

He went into the cabana and brought out the equipment and then demonstrated how to use it. They started the game, and Judy got interested. Just before they stopped, she looked up at the main building. Something in one of the back windows of the top floor caught her attention.

"Hey," he said, "you go. I said you go." She didn't move. He looked in the direction of her gaze. "What is it?"

"I don't know."

"What'dya mean, you don't know?"

"I saw someone."

"What?"

"It looked like someone peering out between those curtains in the third window from the right."

"So? It was probably the old man."

"No, it didn't look like him."

He put his stick down and walked up to her. Standing beside her, he studied the third window from the right.

"I don't see anything."

"He's not there now, but he was."

"Someone else? Besides the old man?" She nodded. "Can't be. That doesn't make any sense. Why wouldn't he have come out to talk to us and find out what we're doing here? It was probably the old man or no one."

"Those curtains weren't together; they were parted, Marty."

"So it was the old man," he insisted.

She stared at him. Why was he so determined to ignore her fears? Could it be that the hotel had charmed him in some way? She looked around at the grounds and the building and the old pool. There was no question that he saw something exciting in all this, something she didn't see. In a way—and this idea frightened her the most—Marty was like that old man. He was too nonchalant about it all. Why didn't he see the same dangers?

"I'm telling you," she said with as much calm as she could muster, "there was someone up there and it wasn't the old man."

"All right. It was a ghost, the ghost of a dead guest." Her eyes widened. "I'm just kidding, for crying out loud, don't look at me that way. Forget about it. Take your shot."

"I don't wanna play anymore," she said, dropping the shuffleboard stick.

"Jesus."

"Well, I can't help it, Marty."

He looked at her. She was crumpling fast, he thought. He wouldn't be able to keep all her fears away.

"Okay," he said, "okay. I'm tired of this too. Let's do something else."

"Like what?" It was getting so she was frightened by his every suggestion.

"We'll keep exploring. How about that building over there," he said, pointing to their right.

"What is it?"

"Probably help's quarters. It has that look about it."

"Help's quarters?"

"Sure." He smiled widely. "Where do you think the staff of the hotel sleeps in places like this? Not in the rooms of a main building. They'd be reserved for the guests. It would be a loss of money for the hotel to put staff up in any one of them. In fact, I've heard of overcrowded hotels talking guests into sleeping in the help's quarters."

"What are they like?"

"Usually pretty dumpy. Let's take a quick look," he said, starting in its direction. Once again he was enthusiastic about the place. She couldn't get his mind off it. She followed him, but periodically she shot a quick glance up at the top-floor window. The curtains didn't move and for a moment she wondered if Marty was right—she had simply imagined it.

"You know, in one of the hotels I worked in," he said, "a place called Chesters, the staff called their quarters the Dungeon. Not that it was that bad . . . it was just that the waiters and busboys slept in the basement of this main building."

"Where Mr. and Mrs. Levine now live," she said, looking at the bottom of the main building.

"Well, I expect their apartments are a lot nicer."

He led the way back to the cracked sidewalk and followed it around the very back of the main building. They could have cut through the grass, but it was so high and wild that even he was afraid of snakes.

The help's quarters was a small two-story A-frame building. There was no porch, just a small landing at the front door. The outside of the building was in desperate need of a paint job. Marty tried the door, but it was locked. It rattled on its hinges. He could have forced it open easily, but he didn't.

Judy looked through the windows. Most of them had plain white shades drawn down, but the shades on two front windows were raised about halfway. He stood beside her and peered in too. There was a small dresser and a single bedframe without a mattress in this room. The walls were bare, except for the graffiti and smudge marks.

"Now this looks more like the other deserted hotels I've seen," he said. "I guess they only keep up parts of the main building. I bet the old man rarely comes out here."

"I wouldn't want to stay here," Judy said. "Are all the help's quarters like this in all the hotels?"

"You don't spend much time in it anyway, just sleep actually, and maybe a card game. There was always a big card game going. I remember this one kid, Bernie Kaufman. He lost all the money he made for half of the summer in a night of card playing. I thought he was going to kill himself that night. The game went on and on until five in the morning."

"And then they went to work?"

"Had to be in the dining room an hour and a half later."

"You did that too?"

"No, I hated cards. Still do. And after what I saw

happen to this guy, I was too terrified to ever play. I think the other guys cheated him, although I never knew for sure. Imagine working like that for half a summer and then losing it all in one night."

"His parents must've killed him."

"He was working for college tuition too. I wonder what the upstairs is like here," he said and tried to open the window. It was locked.

"I've got to go to the bathroom anyway," Judy said. He nodded and they started back. They could just see a piece of the back road that ran past the front of the hotel. He heard the sound of a car and touched her arm.

"Down," he said. They crouched, but he was able to catch a glimpse of what he thought was a police patrol car as it went by. "Okay," he said, standing.

"Was it anything?"

"No," he said, but he hesitated so he could study the road for a few more moments. Instinctively she looked up at the third-floor window again. She was positive that the opening in the curtain was wider than before. Her heart began to beat quickly. "Come on," he said.

Reluctantly she followed him back into the main building of the old hotel.

The girl almost saw him; he was sure of it. But he liked looking at her. He saw the boy hug her in the pool and then kiss her. That boy was lucky. Maybe he could get the girl to like him, too, if he could just talk to her. She would smile at him and let him touch her hair. Then she would kiss him too.

Would she let him touch her hidden places? The very idea both terrified and excited him. Thinking about her hidden places made him want to touch himself. He didn't understand why that was, but he did it and it felt good. He had seen men and women touch each other in the hidden places, but he had never touched a girl that way.

What if this girl let this boy do it? he wondered. It could happen and he could see it happen. He made a fist with his right hand and drove it rhythmically against the palm of his left hand.

He didn't like this boy at all, he decided. He reminded him too much of other boys, boys who used to make fun of him. Why couldn't the girl have come here by herself? Why did she have to come here with him?

Still, something could happen to the boy, couldn't it? Maybe something heavy would fall on his head. He laughed and rocked back and forth on his buttocks as he embraced his legs and pulled them toward his body. Something could squash him like the boulder he used to squash the rabbit. He had carried that boulder up to the fifth floor and waited by the window near the end of the corridor. That big gray rabbit came to the same spot as always. When it was right below him, he had dropped the boulder and . . . splat.

He'd run down all the flights of stairs to rush out to see it. He couldn't believe how flat the rabbit's body was. Its eyes rolled out like marbles. Would the boy's eyes roll out like that? he wondered. Maybe. Splat. He laughed.

When Frank awoke late in the morning, Elaine had already left for work. At first the pain in the back of his head was a dull ache, but as he sat up and the dizziness returned, the pain sharpened and intensified, especially where the skin had been sewn together. He cursed and got out of bed, his physical agony reminding him of his need for vengeance.

He went as quickly as he could to Marty's and Judy's rooms, but a look into both revealed that neither had been in since he went to sleep. He went downstairs and drank some of the coffee Elaine had made. He had no appetite and he was even impatient with the time it took him to drink the coffee. He sat there strumming the table with his right hand and thought. Where would that bastard go? He settled on Jack Martin's kid.

Sure, he thought. Jack Martin worked as a security guard over at the Monticello Racetrack and then did the late-night shift at the Pines Hotel security gate in South Fallsburg. Barbara, his wife, waited on tables at the Wonder Bar in Old Falls until the wee hours. With neither of them home most of the night, it would be easy for those two bastards to sneak into the house. Tony Martin was one of Marty's steady buddies.

He looked up Martin's number in the phone book. If Jack answered, he would ask him to check it out. He'd tell him not to let the kids know he was asking. Then he'd go over there and he'd . . .

He'd handle Marty quickly, belting him right in the teeth. He would just walk over to him and drive a left uppercut into the kid's jaw. It might break a few teeth, but the kid deserved it. If the bastard didn't go right down, he'd punch him again—a one-two blow like he'd delivered on Mike Tooey over at the Hot-Cha Club last spring. That old son of a bitch went ass backwards over the patio railing and fell face down on the road.

After he finished off his bastard son, he would go after Judy. He'd tell her the whole thing was her fault. She'd been teasin' him and comin' on. What'd she expect? There was only one way to treat a cockteaser and that was to fuck her good and hard so she'd know what it was like to raise a man's flag. Then he'd give her another lesson. Afterward, neither of those two would say a damn thing because they'd be scared shitless of what else he would do.

His sexual fantasy drove him to move faster. He dialed Martin's number and waited. The phone rang and rang. He was about to hang up when he heard Jack Martin's tired voice.

"Fuck you," Martin said before he had even said a word, and hung up. Frank cursed and dialed again. Again it rang and rang. This time he spoke quickly as soon as Martin picked up the receiver.

"It's Frank O'Neil. I'm lookin' for my boy."

"You bastard."

"Come on, Jack."

"There ain't nobody here."

"How do you know? He run away with some money," he added quickly. "He and your boy . . ."

"Son of a bitch." Frank heard Jack put the receiver down. He heard his wife's muffled voice in the background. After a few moments Martin returned. "My son's asleep and there ain't nobody here. Now fuck off," he added and hung up.

Frank squeezed the receiver until his hand hurt. Then he bashed the phone back on its cradle. The anger and the effort brought a wave of pain into his head, which tightened around his temples like a vise. He grimaced, tears coming into his eyes.

Where the hell were they? he wondered. They had to come back soon and when they did . . . he grew tired just anticipating. *Take another nap,* he thought. *Rest up, so when they return, I'll have the strength.*

8

Marty waited in the lobby while Judy went to the bathroom. The old man wasn't in sight, but every once in a while he heard some sounds that seemed to be coming from upstairs. He imagined that the old man was up there doing something to get his hotel ready. Marty thought that Pop Levine's senility was keeping him alive. In his world of illusion, he had to be active and healthy. Thinking about it from that viewpoint, Marty realized that it would be tragic for the old man to be cured of his senility. Like the Lady of Shalott in the poem of the same name, a poem he had loved, the old man would die if he faced reality. Perhaps that was way why his people left him here. Here he would go on living; in an old-age home he would quickly die.

He got up from the small couch and looked out one of the front windows, peering at the road to see if the police car would return. There wasn't a soul out there, not a movement. He wondered how he would feel if the police did come for them. Would the story be in the newspapers? What would his old schoolteachers think? He could just hear it now, because he had heard it said about others (even others who had done far less than he had done): "He wasn't a particularly bright boy, but he didn't get into any serious trouble. I knew he had a bad home life, but none of us expected this."

What would his friends think? He envisioned Buzzy and Tony coming to visit him in prison. The scene brought a smile to his face because he figured they would say something stupid like, "You want us to help you escape or what?"

Then he thought about Elaine. What if she came looking for them? That might be a different story. Perhaps she didn't believe whatever tale Frank made up; perhaps they'd had a bad fight and she'd decided to take their side.

Actually the chances were better that no one would come looking for them. Everyone would just expect them to show up somewhere soon. The police would make only a small effort, especially the local yokels. They had their hands full as it was with an incoming summer population. They were certainly not going to run a door-to-door search because Frank O'Neil asked them to.

"Anything out there?" Judy said, coming in behind him.

"Nothin'. A dog could sleep out on that road and not move for days."

She sprawled on the small couch in front of him and folded her arms over her stomach. He sat down across from her in one of the big, soft chairs. They just looked at each other for a moment, and then she looked up at the ceiling. He slouched down farther and pressed the palms of his hands together.

He realized that she had come out of yesterday's violence a lot better than he'd expected. It also occurred to him that she might be in some sort of state of shock. Maybe in another day or two she would snap out of it and be a basket case or something.

"I never asked you. What was it like going to school up at Liberty?"

"It was okay."

"Did you have a lot of friends?"

"No."

"Any boyfriends?"

She looked at him to see if he was serious. "Nobody special this year."

"What'dya mean, 'nobody special'?"

"I didn't go steady or nothin'."

"What about last year?"

"I went with a boy named Tommy Wilson."

"What happened?" She shrugged. "Why did you break up with him?"

"He just started going with Debbie Cassidy."

"What did you do?"

"I took his picture out of my wallet and burned it on the electric stove. It caught fire and burned so fast it singed my fingers before I could drop it in the sink." He laughed. "Did you have any special girlfriend?"

"No."

"What about Diane Taylor?"

"Who told you about that?"

"Linda Minarsky."

"Boy, you two sure did a lot of talking about me."

He saw that she was waiting to hear, so he said, "We went together for a while and then she moved to California. I was in junior high. It wasn't anything."

"Ever write to her?"

"Nope. No point to it. She moved to California and I knew I wasn't ever going to see her again."

"Was she very pretty?"

"I'd say more like cute." He saw that made Judy happy. "She wrote poetry."

"I have no talent," Judy said quickly. "I can't do anything." She turned on her back again.

"Who told you that?"

"I just know it. No one has to tell me I haven't any."

"Sure you do. Everybody's got some talent. Look at me. I've got the talent to screw things up all the time."

"You don't screw things up."

"Yeah, well . . . I guess I'm good with my hands. When I wanna be, that is."

"I can't do anything. I can't sing; I can't paint; I can't write poems."

"How do you know you can't sing? Were you ever in the chorus?"

"I was going to take it last year, but . . ."

"But you didn't even try, I know. I'm sure you never tried out for a school musical."

"No. I was in a play in the seventh grade, a play in class," she said, "but it was a very small part."

"So what, you still did something. I bet you could sing very well if you tried."

"I can't."

"You never know until you try," he insisted. "Hey, don't you know there's a singer with your name?" She turned to him again. "Yeah, Judy

132

Collins. Hey, you've got a singer's name; maybe you'll be a singer."

"That's silly."

"Not any sillier than not trying or dreaming. Listen," he said, "at Levine's Mountain House, all of your fantasies come true."

She studied him standing there with his hands high, his head tilted back, and his eyes closed. He was just pretending for her right now, but she had this nagging suspicion that he believed what he was saying. Somehow he had developed the idea that this was a magical place. Or else—and this was an idea that was making her increasingly nervous—this place *was* magical.

"Marty," she said, intending to ask him about it. But before she could say anything, old man Levine appeared in the dining room doorway.

"I want you should set up a table in the dining room," he said. "I have to start taking my meals with my guests."

Judy and Marty looked at him and then at each other. He closed the door and disappeared in the dining room.

"Marty?"

"C'mon," he said. "I'll set up a table like he wants."

"You're kidding. Wait a minute. This is getting very weird, don't you think?"

"Harmless. Besides," he added, deliberately avoiding her concern again, "you should see how it's done. You said you wanted to work in a hotel someday."

"But what happens when no guests appear?"

He shrugged. "We'll change again and pretend to be guests. I don't know. C'mon."

When they entered the dining room, they saw Pop Levine at the far right corner table. He gestured that he wanted that table to be the one. Marty nodded and went into the kitchen to get a clean tablecloth and napkins. Judy waited in the doorway.

"Make four settings," Pop Levine said as Marty smoothed out the tablecloth. He set out place settings for four while the old man stood by like an inspecting general. "Good. Tonight the Bienstocks will sit with us."

"The Bienstocks?" Judy asked. Marty smiled widely at her.

"A wholesale butcher," Pop Levine said and then lowered his voice to a loud whisper, "from Brooklyn. Worth a million dollars easy."

"The owner's table is like the captain's table on a luxury liner," Marty explained. "It's an honor to be asked to sit here for a meal. Don't worry, Pop," he said, turning to the old man, "I'll be sure to give special service tonight."

"It's important," the old man said and raised his right forefinger. With his eyes wide and his head tilted, he looked comical. Marty had a hard time holding back a laugh. Judy just stared. The old man froze like that for a moment and then dropped his arm quickly. It was as though he could jump from one time period to another as quickly as people changed channels on their television sets. "It's time for lunch," he said. "Come, we'll have some borscht." He started for the kitchen.

"Borscht?" Judy whispered. "I never had it. What is it?"

"It's just beet soup," Marty said. They followed the old man into the kitchen.

"Ugh."

"It's not so bad. Why do you think they used to call this area the Borscht Belt?"

"The Borscht Belt," Pop Levine said, hearing only the last few words. He turned around.

"Why did they call it that?" Judy asked.

"You ask such a question? Sit, sit," he said, pointing to the table. He started for the refrigerator to his left, talking as he took out the jar of borscht and the container of sour cream. "Borscht has always been a staple food for Jewish families. My father told me it was invented in Russia, but my mother said Poland. Who knows?" He pulled his shoulders up and tilted his head. He brought the jar and container to the table and went for bowls and spoons. "When people first came up here, they brought their borscht kettles along, and the small boardinghouses and tourist houses that later became hotels all served borscht. So we became known as the Borscht Belt. My daughter should ask such a question," he repeated, looking at Judy and shaking his head.

"The young people. What do they know?" Marty said.

Pop Levine nodded and smiled. "No one likes to hear about the old days anymore," he said.

"I do," Marty said. "I think it's interesting."

The old man shook the jar to stir up the strips of beets and then opened it and poured some in each bowl. He went over to a drawer under one of the counters and came back with a loaf of rye bread.

"That looks fresh," Judy said. "How did he get that?"

"I don't know. Delivery boy maybe," Marty said

quickly. They watched him scoop sour cream into the borscht and then dip a piece of rye bread into it. The juice ran down the sides of his chin.

"Eat, eat," he said. Marty reached for the sour cream. Judy took half a tablespoon of borscht and tasted it. "We started here with only eight rooms," he said, gesturing widely. "Our boarders learned about us from word of mouth. You think we put our name in the papers in those days? Who had money for such things?"

"Word of mouth was enough?" Marty asked.

"It was enough, it was enough. Once a boarder learned about my wife's cooking . . . it was enough. Besides cooking, she entertained as well."

"What did she do?"

"She sang, she danced. I tried to tell jokes, but as a toomler, I was a big failure."

"A toomler? What's a toomler?"

"A toomler is a toomler. He toomles. He's a comic man, what you call it . . ."

"A comedian? He was on the stage?"

"No, not just on the stage. He walked around the hotel making people laugh, organizing games . . ."

"Oh. Did he wear something funny?"

"Sometimes. A crazy hat. You know," he said, thinking, "I don't have a toomler this year."

"Maybe Marty can be your toomler," Judy said. "He can be pretty funny when he wants to be."

"Get outta here. You're getting to be a wiseguy."

"We'll see," the old man said.

"I thought you had professional entertainment."

"Not right away. Lots of times the guests made their own fun. We had Topsy-Turvy nights."

"What's that?" Judy asked first.

"Men dressed as women and women dressed as

136

men. And don't forget the mock-marriages. Oy," he said, tapping the side of his head, "what a time that was. Two guests would act as bride and groom and one guest would be a rabbi. Such preparations you never saw at a real wedding. Sometimes," he said, leaning toward them, "the mock-marriages would become real ones. You know," he added, waving his spoon like a conductor waves his baton, "a family would work it so their daughter played the bride. I don't have to tell you what went on."

"Are there costumes?" Marty asked.

"Some stuff, still in the casino. Eat, eat," he said again. Marty passed the sour cream to Judy and took some bread.

"It's not bad," he said. She nodded. Then the three of them ate quietly for a while, Marty and Judy eyeing each other and then eyeing the old man.

Although Judy was still anxious, she was able to relax in the old man's presence. Despite his senility, she sensed that he was harmless, if not pitiful. She admired Marty and the way he spoke to him. Conversation came so easy to him and he always sounded so sincere. He had a great curiosity about things and asked his questions with interest. She could see that the old man felt good talking to him.

But Marty was more than a good audience, she thought. He controlled and directed things too. Sitting there and listening to him question the old man about the past, she forgot for the moment that the hotel was becoming strangely threatening to her. Pop Levine's descriptions and information made the hotel seem quaint and interesting. She wished she had been here when it was alive and vibrant.

And yet she also wondered if their invasion of the hotel and their humoring of the old man wasn't a more serious violation than the mere trespassing on private property. They were trespassing on private lives, and she and Marty, by play-acting in the old man's illusions, might be guilty of a great sin.

That was the thought that was making her afraid. How long could they carry on this way? Something was bound to happen. There was something here that could stop them. She felt certain of it, but she had no idea how to express this to Marty. He seemed to be enjoying himself far too much to pull back.

As for Marty, things did seem different. As he ate the borscht and listened to the old man's stories, he felt as though he had slipped into some time machine and traveled back through time. Now they were caught in Pop Levine's past. That's it, he thought, that's the feeling he had the moment they walked into the hotel.

It was as though they had crossed some boundary and entered a world where people cared about one another again. The old man's stories were warm and alive with humanity. He wished that he had grown up here and been the old man's grandson. He wondered if Judy could see that in him. He felt her eyes on him, but when he looked at her and forced himself back into the present, he sensed something else as well.

There was a small, almost indistinguishable nagging feeling in the back of his mind. Instinctively he turned and looked around. Of course there was no one there, but it made him think about Judy's continuous fears. He tried not to show his own anxiety. If he did that, she'd be out the front door in a flash. Stay calm, he thought, stay calm. He pushed the wild ideas aside.

* * *

He watched them eat. After they were finished, he would sneak down and get what he wanted. Only he had to be very careful about it today because he was pretty sure today was Jake's day. He usually came in the late afternoon, but it was better to be safe and stay out of sight.

It was no fun to eat with his grandfather anyway. "I want you should wash the floor in the card room," he would say. Or he would tell him to wash the windows on one of the floors of rooms. He would have to eat fast because his grandfather kept telling him to do things before the guests arrived.

But now two staff members had arrived. Something was happening. What would Jake do? Would Jake move in again? He couldn't remember how long it had been since Jake left. One day, long after the guests stopped coming, Jake packed most of his clothes and some other things into the back of the old pickup truck and left.

When he asked his grandfather about it, his grandfather said, "Jake doesn't want to stay here anymore. There are too many sad memories for him, he says."

"What about me?"

"What about you?"

"I'm not sad here, Gran . . . Grandpa."

"So. No one said you had to go. Do what you want."

"Are you go . . . going?"

"No. I'll stay here until the day I die."

"Me too."

His grandfather looked at him and nodded. Then he smiled widely and suddenly began to laugh like a madman. That frightened him and he ran down into the basement to hide.

He often found his grandfather sitting by himself in the lobby, crying. Sometimes he found him wandering about the hotel talking out loud as though there were people doing work. He would look around for the people. Where were they? he wondered. Sometimes his grandfather would tell him to go tell people things, people who were no longer there. He'd say, "Ask Mrs. Keppleman if the Kasofskys are comin' next weekend."

"Where is . . . is . . . she?"

"In her office, dummkopf."

"I didn't . . . didn't see her."

"So look for her. Can't you look for her? You forgot how to look for people?"

"I didn't forget."

He went to look. He looked everywhere, but he never found her. He never found anyone his grandfather told him to find. Where were they? Why couldn't he find them?

After a while he stopped looking. He'd pretend to look and then go do what he wanted. Sometimes he'd pretend to be people he always wanted to be: the man behind the main desk, the headwaiter, a bellhop. He even gave orders to imaginary people, like Jake would give them. Whenever he did that, he'd lift his shoulders and lower his chin to feel more like Jake.

One time Jake came to the hotel with a woman. As soon as he saw her, he became excited because he thought it might be his mother finally coming home. When he got a close look at her, he was disappointed. He was going to hide in the basement, but then he heard her say, "I'd like to see more of this place."

"It's too late already," Jake said. "I'm not

creepin' through this building. The electricity is on only in this section and downstairs."

"Where's the old man?"

"Who knows? Probably on the dead telephone talking to old guests calling for reservations." He laughed and she laughed.

"Why don't you just have him put away?"

"For what?"

"You wanna sell this place, don'tcha?"

"So? If I should ever get a buyer, which I sincerely doubt, then I'll think about it. Until then, he ain't hurtin' anyone. I'm doin' it for my wife's memory."

"Aw, that's sweet. But what if he dies here?"

"No better place for it. It's what he'd want."

"Maybe he's dead now. How would you know?"

"I'd know."

He pulled away from the grate. Grandpa might be dead, he thought; Grandpa might be dead. He frightened himself so much that he backed up clumsily and smacked his head against the ceiling of the chute. The metallic boom echoed through the guts of the hotel.

"What's that?" he heard the woman say. He didn't wait for Jake's reply. He slid back more carefully, but more quickly, and when he popped out into the card room, he scurried across the lobby and up the stairs to hide in the attic.

Afterward, when he was sure Jake and the woman had left, he came back down and went into the basement to his grandfather's room. He listened, but he heard nothing, so he opened the bedroom door and peeked in.

His grandfather was lying on his back, still dressed in one of his old sports jackets, a very creased pair of corduroy pants, a white shirt that had faded yellow around the collar and cuffs, and his old black shoes. He was so quiet he looked like he really might have died.

"Gran . . . Grandpa," he said. "Grandpa," he repeated, much louder. The old man's eyelids flickered and then opened.

"What? What is it?"

"I thought you were . . . were . . . dead," he said. The old man stared at him a moment.

"Go to sleep," he said.

"But Jake said . . ."

"You should go to sleep. I want you should vacuum out the lobby tomorrow."

"Okay," he said and backed out and closed the door softly. That woman shouldn't have said that, he thought. And Jake shouldn't have said what he said either. How would Jake know if his grandfather died? Dead things smell, he thought, remembering the cat that had been dead in the toolshed for days and days. That was what Jake meant.

As he watched the boy and the girl eating with his grandfather, he suddenly thought that maybe Jake had sent them to the hotel. Maybe Jake sent the boy here to check on him, to see if he was showing himself and frightening away guests.

He folded his legs against himself again and stared ahead. The boy looked like the kind Jake would like. He would have to watch him more closely to see if he took anything or changed anything.

And if he did . . . if he did . . .

9

Pop Levine's head snapped up as though someone had just said something important to him. Marty and Judy both stopped eating and stared at him.

"That's right," he said, "we've got to finish working on the pool. My God, we're so far behind."

"Huh?"

The old man didn't answer. He screwed the top tightly onto the borscht jar and covered the sour cream. Then he got up and began to take things back.

"We'll have to scrape down the pool for repainting," the old man finally said. "We do it every year. Come, come, I'll show you the tools and we'll get started. It should have been done already."

Marty took one more spoonful of borscht and stuffed the rest of the bread into his mouth. When he shrugged and stood up, Judy took the dishes and silverware to the sink. The old man started for the back door.

"I'll go with him," Marty said. "Meet us at the pool."

The old man pointed to a portable tool chest lying by the basement door. Marty picked it up and followed him outside. Although the old man shuffled instead of walked, he was able to move rather quickly when he had his mind on something specific. Marty smiled to himself as the old man looked back with impatience at Marty's slower pace.

"This is not easy, but it has to be done, it has to be done. For years I did it all by myself." The slight breeze lifted the long, thin gray hairs from his head. He squinted against the bright sunlight and rubbed his hands together in anticipation. Marty came up beside him. He looked back to be sure Judy hadn't appeared on the back landing yet.

"Tell me," he said, "who brings you the fresh food? You don't go to town yourself, do you?"

"No, no. We'll need to do some patching. We'll need to do some filling in."

"So how do you get the bread and the dairy? Do you have it delivered?" The old man shook his head. "Who brings it?"

"Jake brings it," he said, obviously impatient with the questioning.

"Who's Jake?"

"Jake's Jake. It's not important now. What's important is we get to the pool. Do you know what is today's date?"

"Right," Marty said and looked to the pool.

It was beyond repair, but somehow Pop didn't see it. Marty wondered if the pump that brought water into the pool even worked. He set the tool chest down and stared at the chipped paint and gaping seams. The old man knelt down, snapped off the clips, and threw the chest open. He pulled out the scrapers and went down the steps of the children's section into the depths of the pool. Marty followed reluctantly. He looked back at Judy, who was closing the back door behind her and starting toward them.

"Here's how it's done," Pop said. He went to the far left corner and demonstrated. Marty was amazed at the old man's energy. It was ironic how his body maintained its strength and health while his mind crumpled into senility. "Try it," he said, handing Marty the scraper.

Standing in that concrete pit on a hot, sunny day was like being in an outdoor steambath. The rays of the high sun reflected off every side and the bottom. The walls were hot to the touch. After only a few minutes of work Marty had to take off his shirt. The old man watched him until he was sure Marty had gotten the hang of it.

"Okay," he said, "that's good. I'll be back later. If anyone else is free, I'll get them to come out and help you."

"I hope someone else is free," Marty said, but Pop didn't hear him. He was already on his way back to the main building. The excitement of seeing real work done cheered and invigorated him.

Judy, who had been standing in a shady spot, went to the deep end of the pool and sat with her legs dangling over the sides. She unbuttoned the top of her waitress uniform and sat back, bracing herself with her hands. She closed her eyes and faced the sun.

"Enjoying your vacation at the Mountain House?" Marty asked. She looked down at him.

"Well, I don't know what you're doing."

"I told you, we're humoring him."

"This is really a great sun," she said.

"You wanna good tan? Come in here and do some of this. You'll get a good tan."

"Why is that better?"

"It's like being in the middle of a giant reflector, and there's no breeze," he said, holding his arms out. "I'm too low and the walls block it out."

She considered it for a moment and then got up and walked around to the pool ladder.

"You're right," she said, standing next to him. "Are you going to keep doing that?"

"A little. I'd like him to feel something's being done."

"Got another one of those tools?"

"Why?"

"I'll help."

"You can't do this. It's hard work."

"I can do it."

When she got angry and determined, her eyes shone with a brightness that changed her whole face. That soft, innocent look disappeared and she appeared aggressive, capable.

Her expression excited him. It made her violently pretty. He had a strong urge to lean forward and kiss her. He didn't think she saw any of this in him; she was too intent on convincing him that she could do what he could do. Embarrassed by his feelings, he laughed.

The delight she saw in his eyes confused her. She didn't understand what she had done to cause it. For a moment she lost track of her intent.

"Okay," he said, handing her the scraper the old

man had left on the side of the pool. "Here's one. Go to work."

She took it from him and began. He showed her that her small, jerky strokes were not as effective as careful, smooth ones. She watched the way he put his shoulders into it and did the same. He was really surprised at her effort and her results. She could do it. For a short while they were actually in some kind of competition with each other. Sweat beads broke out on her forehead; her uniform became soaked and clung to her back, but she worked on, pausing only to get a better angle here and there.

"Hey," he said, "wait a minute. What the hell are we doin'?"

"What'dya mean?"

"There's no point to all this work. I mean, I said I'd pretend to do it, do a little bit, but not really do it. So slow down." He reached for his shirt and wiped his face with it. She rubbed some of the chips of paint off her hands and wrists and then considered herself.

"Ugh," she said.

"Yeah."

"If I had my bathing suit and I could go swimming after this, I wouldn't mind it so much."

"Yeah, I'd still mind it." There was some shade in the deep end of the right corner, so he went there and sat down. She walked to the shallow end of the pool and looked toward the main building.

"I don't see him."

"He'll be back soon. He'll see what we did and he'll think there's hope for this."

"Is there?"

"No way. He sees what he wants to see."

147

Judy wanted to undo the rest of her waitress uniform buttons and shake the garment to get some air between her skin and the material, but she saw that Marty was looking at her, so she hesitated. She had been trying to avoid thinking about the rape scene, but whenever the memory successfully forced itself on her, she relived the embarrassment she'd felt.

Marty had been a gentleman about it, covering her as quickly as he could. He had been more concerned about what he had done to Frank. She was grateful that he hadn't mentioned one detail about how he found her. He was as anxious to avoid reliving the scene as she was, but for different reasons.

She wondered what it would be like if they ever really kissed or he ever saw her nude again. Would he always remember the rape scene? She was too self-conscious and too afraid to undo more than one additional button.

Even though she was very subtle about it, Marty sensed her modesty. If anything, that made her more attractive and more desirable. She was still innocent and fresh, shy and almost completely unaware of her own seductiveness. The rape hadn't changed her basic nature. She was very much the same wide-eyed girl who had come into his room for help with her homework. To be sure, Frank's vicious attack had shattered her view of things and might even have destroyed her capacity to love and make love, but her identity was intact.

He couldn't help staring at the way the sun hit her moist skin and made the top of her chest shine. What was revealed was tempting. It quickened his blood, made him conscious of a flush in his cheeks. He wanted her to undo the next button and the next. He caught himself in the middle of this fantasy and looked away from her.

"We need something to drink," Judy said. "I'll look in the big refrigerator in the kitchen."

"You will?" He was surprised at her courage and then wondered if he should let her go off alone. He looked at the hotel and thought about possible dangers, but she was already up and started. "Yell if there are any problems," he called. She waved and went on.

He went back to doing some scraping to relieve his frustration. He worked for what seemed to be a good fifteen minutes, fighting off thoughts about home and what must be going on. Then he stepped back to admire what he had done.

He was impressed with himself. As he considered what he had accomplished and what else had to be done around the hotel, he wondered if it could ever be brought back to the point where it might be opened again. The idea was crazy. It was as if the hotel had a spirit of its own and was trying to possess him so it could make him its slave.

"It's too late," he said to the grounds and the buildings. "Your day has passed. No one can bring back the past or change what's been."

He realized he was speaking out loud to buildings and grass. He looked down at his hands. They were shaking. What was he doing? What was going on in his head? Why did he do all this stupid work on the pool? He was just as crazy as the old man.

He flung the scraper against the opposite side of the pool. It rattled to a stop in the children's section. Then he scooped up his shirt and started to get out of the pool. Just as he reached the steps, he saw Judy appear with old man Levine. She was carrying a container of something and he was shuffling along beside her, talking incessantly and gesturing wildly toward various parts of the hotel.

"Shit," Marty said and located the scraper he had flung. He put his shirt down again and turned back to the area he had been working on before Judy left.

"Hi," she said, approaching. "I made lemonade. There was a can of mix."

"Is it cold?"

"Full of ice."

"Good work, good work," Pop Levine said. He came down the steps to inspect. Judy poured a cupful of lemonade and handed it to Marty, who downed it in one gulp and asked for more. "Now I'm going to check to see we have enough paint," the old man said.

"All these cracks'll have to be patched up," Marty said.

"Right, right, the cracks."

"Why are you teasing him so much?" Judy whispered.

"I want him to realize what a job this really is."

"You're not going to do any more work, are you?"

"No, no. Hey, Pop. There's a sign back by the main desk about using the rowboats. Where are these rowboats? Where's the lake?"

The smile left the old man's face. He turned and stared at them for a moment, blinking rapidly.

"No lake," he said. "No one goes to the lake."

"What'dya mean? I saw the sign."

"No. We don't use the lake anymore. No boats."

"But I saw—" Marty stopped when Judy put her hand on his shoulder.

"It's bothering him," she said.

"I wonder why."

The old man started back up the pool steps. Suddenly he looked very worn, tired and shaky. Marty guided him up. He paused at the top and looked back over the pool. Then he started toward the main building.

"Where you going, Pop?" Marty asked.

The old man stopped, looked back at them, and then looked to the right. "I have work," he said and walked on.

"What the . . . he's a strange old bird, all right." Marty looked in the direction the old man had turned to before heading back. There was the semblance of a path through the bushes just off to the left. "I bet the lake's off there somewhere."

Judy gazed at the bushes too. "He seemed frightened when you asked him about it."

"Probably just part of his senile ways. C'mon," Marty said, reaching down to scoop up his shirt again. "Let's follow that path and see where it takes us. If there is a lake and it's halfway decent, I might just jump in." He walked off quickly.

Judy hesitated, looked back at Pop Levine, who was almost at the main building, and then went after Marty, who was already at the beginning of the path.

When he saw them head out toward the lake, he experienced both terror and disappointment, for he was afraid to follow them. *Can't go,* he thought, and the image of Miriam's body bouncing gently on the lake's bottom came back to him. The sound of her name in his mind seared his brain, and he pressed his palms hard against his temples. Now he couldn't stop the memories.

She was on the dock, stamping her foot, her two

golden curls bouncing against her head. He was in a rowboat. He had gotten into it as soon as the daycamp kids left.

"Eric," she demanded. "Boat. Take me. Eric."

"No."

She started to cry very loud. He thought Jake was sure to hear and come out to the lake and see him rowing.

"Stop it!"

"Take me then. Boat."

"Okay," he said. He remembered how his eyes grew so small that he almost couldn't see her. He rowed toward the dock. She looked happy, tugging on her skirt, standing there and waiting. "You're bad," he said when she got into the boat. "Jake be mad."

"Row me."

He looked down the path first to be sure no one was coming. Then he dipped the oars into the water and pushed the boat away from the dock. She squealed with excitement.

"There," she said, pointing, "and there. Go there."

"No," he said. She put her hands on her hips and made a face. He knew she would start crying again, but he put the oars up on the boat and folded his arms. The boat just drifted. Miriam stood up to stamp her foot.

"Row!" she commanded. He shook his head. "Eric row. ROW." He was mad at her. Jake and his mother took her rowing sometimes. Even his grandfather took her, but no one took him.

She began to stamp her foot. She climbed up on the seat and stamped it and started to cry. He got scared again. He grabbed hold of both sides of the boat and rocked it. He did it very hard and she slipped on the seat. In a moment she fell to the right and went over the side of the boat into the water. He stopped rocking the boat and just sat there for a few seconds. He was happy she couldn't scream and he was happy she fell in. Then he thought he would get into trouble because she got her dress wet. He stood up and made his way to her side.

When he knelt down and looked over into the water, he saw her bouncing lightly on the bottom of the lake, her hair floating, the little curls out, and her mouth wide open. He thought she might still be shouting. A fish was swimming very close to her.

He reached down through the water and took hold of her hair, but he thought it might hurt her to pull her up that way so he let go. Instead, he sat on the edge of the boat and lowered himself into the water until he could get his feet hooked under her arms. Then he lifted her that way. It was harder than he expected, considering how small Miriam was, but she finally came up. Her eyes were closed now and her beautiful hairdo was ruined. He knew how hard his mother worked on that. She never worked on his.

"Miriam," he said and shook her by squeezing his legs together. Her head swung from side to side and some water came out of her mouth, but she didn't speak or open her eyes. "Miriam?" He didn't like it. Something was very wrong now. "Wake up, Miriam." His legs were getting very tired, so he leaned forward until he could get his hand on the shoulder of her dress. When he opened his legs to release her, he was able to hold her up. The muscles in his shoulder tightened and he drew her back to him, but the moment he felt the lifelessness in her body, he let her go.

She splashed into the water back first and descended slowly, her hair floating above her head. Her feet hit the bottom and her legs folded. She remained there and he could only stare in shock. He tried to scream, but his throat closed up.

At first he was too frightened to do anything. Then he jumped into the water and swam until he could stand. As soon as he could, he rushed out of the lake. He squatted down in the bushes and looked back at the boat. It rocked gently. Everything was very quiet. His heart was pounding and he could think only of Jake's anger.

Keeping to the shadows and out of sight the best he could, he made his way back to the hotel and entered it through the side door. Although he ran through the hall quickly and got to the back stairway to the basement, many guests and staff saw him. He went right to his room and closed the door. He sat on the bed and tried to catch his breath. He was so scared he began to shiver and realized that his clothes were soaking wet. He took them off and threw them in a pile on the floor. Then he put on dry ones, but he didn't go out of the room.

It seemed like hours before he heard the screaming. He knew it was his mother, but the sound of her voice was the most terrifying thing he had ever heard. Jake came charging through his door, his grandfather right behind him. There were some other people there, too, staff people. Everyone was yelling at once. Jake was pounding him and demanding answers to questions. It took three men to hold him back. Nothing was more frightening than Jake's face, Jake's eyes.

"She . . . she . . . fell out," he said. There was

more screaming because his mother passed out in the hall. People were running everywhere.

The people left him, but he remained in his room. A long time afterward his grandfather came in. He looked tired and very old.

"Do you understand that Miriam is dead?" he asked.

"She . . . was . . . she was standing on the sea . . . seat and stamping her foot," he said. His grandfather just shook his head.

"Your mother is very bad," he said. "She's in the hospital. Stay away from your father. You realize what I am saying, Eric? This is the most terrible thing ever."

He cried. He even cried for a while after his grandfather left him. Then he got hungry and went upstairs to get something out of the kitchen. He was afraid of Jake so he went right back to his room. He thought about Miriam bouncing on the bottom of the lake and he thought about all the screaming. He didn't feel that sorry though. He even felt glad. Maybe now his mother would spend a lot of time on his hair, he thought.

But she didn't. She never came back from the hospital. He asked about her often, but his grandfather never wanted to talk about it. He would never ask Jake anything. He had to stay away from him all the time.

And he never went back to the lake. Until now. Until this new girl had come. He had to see what she and the boy were going to do out there. Even though he was still afraid, he slipped out of the hotel and scurried into the bushes to follow them. He clutched at the twigs and saplings before him, squeezing them so forcefully, they bent and broke within his fingers. As he drew closer and their voices became louder, his excitement grew. When he caught sight of the water, he stopped to catch his breath. He pushed Miriam from his mind and went on.

The lake was not clearly visible until they were practically in it. Suddenly it was there before them, so very isolated and quiet. Marty had taken a long, thick stick and used it as a machete, clearing a way for them.

It wasn't a very big lake, but it was long and wide enough to be interesting. They came to what had obviously been an entry point for swimmers. In the old days, before the hotel had a pool, the lake was probably the only bathing facility. The small sandy area, which was used as the lake's beach, had very little grass and weeds over it. About forty yards out a small raft, made of slats attached to oil drums, bobbed gently in the clear but brownish-colored water. They heard small splashes and saw the glimmer of fish scales.

"This is pretty," Judy said. Marty nodded and continued to survey it all. The forest and overgrown bushes came right down to the water's edge as far around the lake as they could see. "Look," Judy said. She pointed to two deer off to the right. They stopped drinking and looked up at Marty and Judy. "They're as still as statues."

Almost on cue, they heard the caw of a crow as it swooped down and landed on the raft. It paced about nervously at the edge, jerking its head from side to side as though it expected to be challenged for the spot at any moment. Its beak opened and closed with its steps and its wings lifted and fell gently.

They heard a lot of movement within the forest and bushes to their left, but they couldn't see anything. The trees were tall and thick here. Shadows over the water made it cool and attractive for bugs and all sorts of wildlife. It was possible that the lake had been changed or extended by man, but now, after years of no use, it looked like a natural, undiscovered place. It made Marty feel like an explorer.

"C'mon," he said, walking toward the water's edge. Their approach scattered the waterbugs and small fish. He cupped the water in his hands and smelled it. Despite the muddied bottom, the lake was fresh and clean. He suspected that it was fed by some mountain streams that could provide excellent drinking water too. From the corner of his eye he caught the quick movement of a black snake as it slithered for cover under some rocks. Judy didn't see it and he didn't point it out.

"I was hoping there would be boats," she said.

He stood up and looked about. The heavy grass and weeds had hidden the small dock from immediate view. Two overturned rowboats were beside it. From the amount of vegetation growing around them, it was obvious that they hadn't been used for years.

"There," he said, pointing. He cleared a way to the dock and tapped the bottoms of the boats with his stick.

"Where are the oars?"

He turned full circle and saw nothing. Then he knelt down and, grasping the first boat's end, turned it over in one move. Two large frogs, now exposed, jumped for the water.

"The seats look okay," he said.

"We don't have oars."

He turned over the other boat, revealing more frogs, a small garter snake, and a set of oars. Judy gasped at the sight of the little brown striped snake, but when he bent over to lift the oars, the snake disappeared quickly into the tall grass nearby.

"Well," he said, "ready for sea duty?"

"I don't know."

"Ah, c'mon." He pushed the sharp end of the boat into the water and got behind it to push the rest of it in. Then he took off his sneakers and socks and threw them into the boat. He rolled up his pants to his knees and moved the boat farther out, waiting to see if it would take in any water. After a while he was confident that it was still good. He brought it close to shore again. "Take off your sneakers and socks and get in," he said. She thought for a moment and then did it quickly.

He squatted in the bushes and reached forward ever so slowly to part the branches of leaves before him. He had a clear view of the old dock. He held his breath when the boy turned the boats over and discovered the oars. Seeing the boats and the lake reminded him of all the hours he had spent alone on the lake, rowing in silence.

He saw the deer run from the lake when the boy turned over the first rowboat. He saw the crow on the raft and he looked up and saw the birds circling and diving from treetop to treetop. He had almost forgotten how much he liked it here.

He wished he could take the girl out on the lake

and show her how fast he could move the boat. She would clap and laugh. He knew she would.

He glared out at the boy, watching his every movement. *If only he wasn't here,* he thought. *If only she was alone.* Like a predator, he studied the boy. An unfamiliar rage was building within him, causing him to growl so loud that he thought they might have heard it.

He'd have to be quiet. He'd have to watch and be quiet.

10

While Marty and Judy manipulated the boat and got themselves securely into it, the crow watched them and strutted nervously when the boat moved out. The deer were gone and the woods had become silent. Judy sat at the far end. Marty hopped into the boat after giving it a strong shove and then took the oars and placed them into their slots. He sat facing her and turned the boat around to head toward the raft. The crow waited until they were halfway there and then flew off into the forest, disappearing within the leaves and branches.

For a while the only sound was the rhythmic dipping of the oars. Judy turned on her side so she could dip her fingers into the water as they moved. Marty concentrated on making his strokes strong and even, with a minimum of splash. He saw that the boat did have a very tiny leak just under Judy's seat, but it wasn't anything to be concerned about. He pressed down a little harder on the right oar to steer the boat alongside the raft.

"Land ho," he said and let go of the oar so he could catch hold of one of the oil drums and stop the boat. As soon as he did so, he crawled onto the raft.

"Be careful. Maybe it can't hold you."

"Sure it can. It's in good shape, just like most everything else around this hotel. These boards aren't even rotten." He sprawled out on the dock and lay back with his hands behind his head so he could look up at the sky. "This is the life. Man, it's hot." He sat up and took off his shirt and then threw it into the boat.

"You think people could still swim here?"

"Sure. There's no pollution."

She sensed that he was going to suggest it soon. The idea made her heart beat faster and she looked away, over the lake and around at the forest.

"This is like a . . . like a secret paradise or something," she said. "I mean it's so quiet and so . . ."

"Untouched?"

"Yeah."

He looked at her sitting back in the boat, appreciating the lake. The look of pleasure on her face attracted him to her. There was something enticing about her innocent enjoyment. It made him feel carefree and safe.

"I think I'll try it."

"What?"

"Swimming," he said. He stood up and unbuckled his jeans. She looked away when his hands went to his underwear. He hesitated, then decided to leave them on. Without a second thought, he dove into the water. It was a lot colder than he'd expected. He reached the bottom fast. The mud was slimy and cool, but when he opened his eyes, it was all still very clear. He shot up just behind the boat and splashed her. Judy screamed and splashed back.

"How is it?"

"Refreshing and clean, just as I said."

She watched him swim and considered it. It looked so inviting, but when she thought about taking off the uniform, she became reticent. He seemed to sense her modesty and deliberately swam in the opposite direction. She unbuttoned the uniform quickly and slipped it off, watching him all the while. Then, before he headed back, she lowered herself over the boat and slid into the water.

"It's freezing!" she squealed. She stayed near the boat, practically hidden by it. He smiled when he saw her in the water.

"Oh, it's not that bad. It's because the air is so warm. You'll get used to it. I bet some guests used this lake even when they had the pool."

"Think so?" She swam a little and then took hold of the edge of the raft. Marty went around it and pulled himself up onto it to lie in the sun. Judy stayed in the water a while, swimming, floating, splashing him occasionally. When she struggled to get up, he had to reach down and take her hands to pull her. He was surprised and happy with his own strength. She practically flew out of the water to stand dripping beside him.

Her breasts rose and fell with her heavier breathing. The wet bra had slipped some, showing the depth of her cleavage, the roundness of her bosom. She wrung out her hair and laughed self-consciously. Marty forced himself to look away and sprawled out on the raft again.

"You're right. It's better when you're in a while."

162

She sat down beside him. "My hair's going to be a mess." When he looked at her again, he saw the very large black and blue mark on her right thigh. She saw what he was looking at; it wiped the smile off her face. She embraced her knees and brought her legs up against herself, resting her chin on them.

"When do you think we should go back?"

"To the hotel?"

"No. You know, home."

"Oh. Another day maybe," he said. Then he thought for a moment and added, "What if we never went back?"

"What'dya mean, never?"

"Never means never. We'd stay here for as long as we could and then go someplace else."

"Really? I don't know. What would my mother say?"

"She wouldn't say anything if she didn't see you to say it, would she?"

"I don't know." She looked very worried.

"Relax. We have to go back," he said. "I was just dreaming."

She lay back beside him and for a while they both simply stared up at the sky. Both began thinking the same thing, however: What would it be like to go on indefinitely with each other? She liked him, liked being with him. Despite the terrible thing that had happened, it was fun hiding out here with him.

"You could be happy never going back?" she asked. "Never seeing your friends?"

"Friends? What friends?"

"Buzzy, Tony . . ."

"We just hang out together. There's a difference between that and real friends."

"Did you ever have a friend?"

He thought for a few moments and said, "No."
"Me neither."

"Nobody close enough to me," Marty said, thinking on, "who I could trust enough to tell my deepest feelings without being afraid he'd laugh or be disinterested."

"I know what you mean," she said.

"Friends," he said. "I've told you more over the past twenty-four hours than I have some of my so-called friends."

"You have?" He looked embarrassed that he had said it. "Boy," she said, feeling she should change the topic, "I dried fast in this sun." She pinched her panties for him.

"Yeah." He touched them quickly. She had turned on her side toward him, revealing more of the inside of her breasts. Small blue veins were highlighted by the pressure. He looked away, but the image stayed with him, especially when he closed his eyes.

He felt a warmth rushing over his body and quickly turned to his left side to pretend interest in the raft's wood. He saw that the two deer had returned to the lake. They began drinking again, eyeing the raft cautiously. "Hey, Bambi," he said. They didn't move, but they stared now.

"I don't think they're afraid of us," Judy said.

"They're stupid if they're not. People can't be trusted."

"We can. You wouldn't hurt them. You told me how you hated to go hunting with Frank."

"No, I wouldn't hurt them." He lay back again and brought his knees up.

"I would've hated to be little and be with Frank,"

she said. He grunted. "You never talk about your mother. How come?"

"I don't know. Yeah, I know. When I think about her, I get mad. She never wanted me around that much either. I don't think she even wanted to have me in the first place. I was one of those accidents."

"Oh," she said. When he opened his eyes and looked up, he saw her staring down at him, but he sensed that she was thinking about something else. "Do you think that because . . . because of what Frank did to me I could have an accident?"

He thought for a moment and tried to recall the details of the scene. So much of it was vague now.

"Well, I don't think . . . I mean, don't you know . . . he didn't have an orgasm in you before I hit him, did he?" She just shrugged. "Ah, you would know that," he said, although he wasn't that sure about women and what they felt during sex. "Right?" She traced the lines of a rafter with her finger.

"I can't remember," she said.

"Don't worry about it. It didn't happen."

"I hope not. I'd hate to have a baby by Frank." He laughed at the way she said it. "Oh, I don't mean anything bad about you, I mean . . ."

"I know."

"I don't even think of you as Frank's real son."

"Really?"

"Really. You're so different. You care about people's feelings and you're so smart."

"Don't start that smart business again." He got up quickly. "I'm gonna take another dip," he said. He felt he had to get away from her for a few moments, not because he didn't want to be with her, but because of what the sound of her voice, the closeness of her body, and the sight of her partially revealed breasts were doing to him. He hit the water eagerly, welcoming the cold over his body. Judy moved to the side of the raft and dangled her feet over the edge. He swam back and forth, floated, dog-paddled, pretended to be a whale and then a shark. Her laughter echoed over the water and died in the pocket of trees.

At one point he went under and came around behind her. He snuck over and grabbed her ankles. She screamed with delight and he tugged a little harder until she slipped into the water herself. She grabbed hold of one side of the raft and he grabbed hold of the opposite side.

Facing each other, they first pretended to be waterspouts and sprayed each other and then kicked at each other. When they slid their bodies on a shelf of water, their feet met, sole to sole. He pushed her and she went back, still holding on to the raft. She did the same to him. They played like that for a while until he realized that their antics had forced Judy's bra down, revealing her breasts to the nipples.

"You're comin' apart," he said.

"Huh?" She looked down, saw what was happening, and laughed as she fixed herself. She wanted to resume the game, but he climbed back onto the raft.

"Let's get dressed and row to the end of the lake," he said.

"We're too wet to get dressed." She climbed directly into the boat. "We'll row anyway and the sun'll dry us."

She was right. He put his pants into the boat, but when he sat down to row, he sat with his back to her.

He was embarrassed by the prominence of his erection. He pushed away from the raft and headed across the lake. They weren't more than twenty or thirty yards beyond it before the crow returned. It looked at them as if to say, "And stay off." Marty moved on with harder, smoother strokes.

At the far end of the lake there was a turn hidden from view because of the heavy overgrowth along the shores. The branches of two large maple trees extended out over the water, their ends dipping so far that their leaves were inches from touching the surface. He headed close to the shore so they would pass under the branches, moving through a kind of natural tunnel.

When they came out, they were at the turn. He worked the right side only and they headed into the inlet. He looked back periodically and saw Judy lying against the boat's end, her arms dangling over the sides, her legs out and spread apart. Her eyes were closed and she was just enjoying the sun. He mumbled something about the turn and she opened her eyes. A few moments later, she screamed.

"What?" He stopped rowing and looked in the direction she was pointing. In a little clearing at the far shore, three stray dogs were tearing apart a deer's stomach. Sometimes their grips were so strong that they lifted the carcass off the ground in a kind of tug-of-war, growling and shaking their heads to tear the flesh. When a strip of it ripped clear, the dog who was successful gobbled what it could as quickly as it could.

The dangling deer's head shook from side to side as the dogs tugged. Its eyes wide open, it looked as though it were still trying to deny what was happening. Part of its tongue was just visible through the partially opened mouth. It looked like it had been a medium-sized doe. Marty started to row away.

"Wild dogs are always a problem up here."

"How could there be wild dogs?" exclaimed Judy.

"So many people, tourists especially, take on a pet and then give up on it. They return to the city and leave the animal to fend for itself."

"Oh, it's so terrible."

"What they do is gang up to run deer down. It's only natural instinct. They'd starve otherwise. Maybe they were lying around here in the bush, waiting to surprise it when it came to drink."

"Ugh," she said, covering her face with her hands.

"Things kill things," he said nonchalantly. Then he drove an oar in roughly to send a splash of water in their direction. The dogs paid no heed. "They would probably attack us if we got too close," he said.

"Let's go."

He headed back, this time going around the natural tunnel. He worked very hard and fast for a while and then let the boat drift toward the right direction as he put the oars up and slipped his pants on. Judy put her waitress uniform back on. Neither of them spoke. It was as if the sight of the deer slaughter had broken a spell and brought the world crashing back over them.

"It's still nice here," he said after a while.

"Oh yes."

"I wouldn't mind coming back."

"Me neither."

When the bottom of the boat touched land, he stepped out and shoved the front onto the shore. He helped Judy out and they pulled the boat up farther.

They sat on the ends to put their sneakers and socks back on.

"Think those dogs have rabies?" she asked.

"No. They're strays. They usually don't bother people if you don't go near them while they're eating."

"I hate them," she added. "I don't care if they're starving."

"Let's forget it. Come on, we'll see what the old man's up to."

He found the stick he had used as a machete and they started back down the path. She looked behind her once as they made the turn that took the lake out of view. It looked peaceful and still, frozen in time like a sepia photograph in an old family album.

They were so close when they passed by him that he almost reached out to touch the girl. His fingers moved through the bush, only inches from her skirt.

He hadn't taken his eyes off them for a second when they played around the raft, and when they got back into the boat and started toward the other side of the lake, he slithered through the tall grass and wove his way in and out of the trees to track along the lake as the boy rowed. Sometimes he got too close to the shore and stepped into puddles of water and thick, oozing mud, sinking nearly to his knees, but he didn't care; he didn't even notice. Always watching them, he just pulled his legs out and moved along as quietly as he could.

He heard the dogs before they saw them. He had seen dogs like these many times. They never bothered him and he never gave them much thought. But when the girl screamed, he looked at them with a new interest. If she didn't like them, then he wouldn't like them. He saw her bury her face in her hands to stop looking at what the dogs were doing. He had to laugh at the boy's attempt to scare the dogs away by splashing at them. This boy couldn't do anything for the girl. All he could do was row away.

He watched them go back toward the raft. Then he turned to the dogs. He spotted a thick dry hickory branch on the ground and grasped it like a club. Crouching low and moving on a floor of air, he came up behind the ravaging animals. They neither heard nor saw him. He straightened up, brought the stick back with both hands, and then delivered a stinging blow into the side of the closest dog. It was a cross between a police dog and something quite smaller, for it was only a third of the size of the average police dog.

The animal yelped and released its hold on the deer's carcass. The two other animals, both only slightly bigger, were encouraged by their partner's retreat from the food. They tugged faster and harder, pulling the deer's body farther away from Eric. He stepped forward and delivered another blow to the wounded animal. This time he hit the dog just behind the head. Its cry was cut short. It turned and fell over on its side.

Too bad the girl hadn't seen this, he thought. She would like him better than that stupid boy.

He didn't care much about the boy now. Watching the girl at the lake had gotten him even more excited about her. He wondered if it would be so bad if she saw him. He felt his face and looked at his reflection in the window. Maybe he should try to cut some of his beard. He even had long hair growing out of his neck. The boy had no beard.

What he should do is ask her. If she said he should shave, he would try, no matter how many times he cut himself. He clapped his hands with excitement. She should see him. She should. His mind was made up about it. He would go right downstairs to his basement bedroom and find Jake's old suit. He would get dressed up and wait for his chance to show himself.

11

"There's the old man," Marty said. Pop Levine was waving at them from the back of the hotel. "He wants us for something."

"He's probably mad we went to the lake."

"Why should he be? Let's see what he wants."

"I just took my wife a glass of tea," old man Levine said as they approached. He looked at them when he spoke, but to Marty it seemed as though he were talking through them. He wondered if he had forgotten who they were supposed to be.

"How is she?" he asked.

"How is she? She talks, gives orders," he said, swinging his hands about wildly. "According to her this place should be ready to be open in a couple of days."

"Doesn't she ever come out?"

The old man studied them as though he had just

realized they were there. It gave them both the willies.

"Come out? Sure she comes out. She was just on the porch for an hour."

"On the porch?"

"She got tired. She gets tired easily," he whispered. "It's not like the old days." He nodded after his own words. "Oy, what a tumult there was. You couldn't keep her down. She was everywhere." He paused, looked out toward the pool, and then raised his hands. "Ah," he said, dropping them. He turned to go back inside, but stopped as though he had just remembered something. "Oh," he said, "she says the casino floor must be washed. We mustn't forget."

"We won't. I'll get right to it."

"Good, good. If you need me for anything, I'll be in my office."

"Right," Marty said. "Crazy as a loon," he added when the old man entered the hotel.

"There couldn't really be a wife, could there?"

"No."

"Still," she said, looking up, "it didn't look like him watching us from the window."

"Why wouldn't she come out to talk to us and throw us off the grounds? No, there's no wife."

"Maybe she's as senile as he is."

Marty thought for a moment and then shook his head. "I doubt it, but if it'll make you feel better, I'll look around the place later."

"You're not really going to wash the casino floor, are you?"

"No. As a matter of fact, I'm tired. Let's switch to being guests again. To the game room," he said. "I challenge you to Ping-Pong."

"Ping-Pong?" She followed him through the back entrance.

He paused at the basement doorway for a moment. "You wanna go down and say hello to the old lady?"

"Marty!"

He laughed and they went on into the kitchen and out to the main dining room and lobby. He remembered seeing Ping-Pong paddles behind the main desk. He found them and three balls in an old cigar box.

There was a small game room just off the dining room. It had half a dozen card tables and one Ping-Pong table. He had made a mental note of it before. "C'mon," he said, coming out from behind the main desk. "I'll see what kind of paddler you are."

They both stopped when they heard the door open behind them. It was the door to the main office. Old man Levine looked out.

"Don't bounce the ball in the lobby," he said. Then he closed the door.

They looked at each other and then broke out laughing. Marty indicated they should be very quiet and practically tiptoe out of the lobby. He put his arm around her and led her to the game room. He closed the door softly and then straightened up.

"What do you think he's doing in there?"

"Taking reservations, what else? Look, as long as he's happy, what do we care. Let's go. Here's your paddle."

"It still gives me the chills."

"What, the paddle?" he kidded.

"You know what I mean."

He took it easy with her, deliberately holding back

so she could succeed. He let the games stay close and let her win a few. She sensed what he was doing, but she didn't say anything. *He doesn't want to hurt me,* she thought, *not even in the slightest way.*

Finally they both agreed they had had enough. The working and the swimming and the sun had tired them out. He found some chaise lounges by the entrance to the side patio and set them up out there. It was safe because no one could see them from the road. They sat facing the casino, hidden by the main building.

The sun was at the other side of the building by now so they were in a nice area of shade. Marty's face, neck, and shoulders felt a little crisp from the burn he had gotten working in the pool and swimming at the lake. Judy's face had a lot of color in it too.

"Right now we both look like satisfied guests," he said. She smiled and nodded, closing her eyes.

Although he was tired, Marty felt relaxed, even contented. As he looked out across the fields at the tall, richly green-leafed maple, birch, and oak trees that made up the surrounding forest, it occurred to him that this area of the world, this place where he had spent all his life, was really a beautiful spot.

"Some of the guys should see me now," he said. Judy opened her eyes slowly; it looked like it took a great effort to do so. "I don't know if they'd think I was crazy or if they'd be jealous."

She closed her eyes again. He could hear bees droning in the tall grass. The shadows extending over the lawn revealed circles of tiny flies moving in a madness he thought was brought on by the heat. He was glad the day was cooling down. The birds seemed to be glad too. They became more active.

He watched them flying to their nests in the eaves of the casino and the main building.

He turned to Judy. A slight breeze lifted the small strands of hair from her forehead. They danced and fell, danced and fell. She looked so peaceful.

Finally he closed his eyes. He didn't remember when he drifted off, but he woke with a start, his whole body jerking upward. There was a familiar sound of a car or truck, much too loud to just be passing. Whoever it was had turned up the driveway and was approaching the hotel. He was sure of it.

His pulse quickened. He glanced at Judy, but she was still fast asleep. Her lips were puffed out and she had turned on her side to face the building. He went to the corner and peered out at the front lawn of the hotel. Someone in a late-model dark blue Ford pickup was coming up the driveway. He didn't recognize the truck or the man inside. It wasn't one of Frank's friends; he was sure of that. It couldn't be anyone looking for them.

Still, it was frightening and depressing to see anyone turn up this driveway. It was as if their private shield of protection, their imaginary fortress, had been violated. Whoever was in that truck must be the person who takes care of the old man. He's the link with reality, the man who brings him fresh food. What was the name the old man used? Jake? Yeah, Jake. Who was Jake? What would he do if the old man told him about them? This looked like it was probably the end of their stay here.

He waited until the truck went around the other side of the building and then turned back to Judy, but she still slept. She didn't have to know what was happening.

That was it, he thought. He would go and spy on

the old man and this guy Jake and see what was said and what was done. Then he'd know what to do. He tiptoed past Judy and slipped silently through the side entrance. He waited a moment to be satisfied that she didn't realize he was gone, and then he continued on toward the back of the hotel.

When Frank opened his eyes, he was shocked at how low the sun was in the sky. The living room was gloomy in subdued late-afternoon light. He had slept the day away. He sat up slowly on the couch, happy that he felt some renewed strength. He scrubbed his loose and unevenly cut hair with the palms of his hands and then listened hard. Was anyone in the house? Had they come back? Before he could begin to search, the front door opened and Elaine came in. She confronted him seated on the edge of the couch.

"Ain't they back?"

"The Plymouth out there?"

"Didn't see it."

"Then they ain't."

"Christ," she said and started up the stairs.

"Yeah, Christ." He stood up. His upper back muscles were stiff and sore, so he stretched and pumped his arms in and out. Despite his soreness he was feeling better and he was even hungry.

"Hey," he said, calling up the stairway, "let's go for a pizza."

"Pizza? You're up to it?"

"All I need is a drink or two."

"The doctor said you shouldn't."

"Fuck the doctor."

She was quiet for a moment and then said, "Where the hell are those kids?"

"They can't be far," he said. "Can't be far," he

177

muttered. "And they got to come back soon. When they do, I'll be here."

He insisted on driving. She didn't argue with him because she sensed the aggression in him.

"I'm surprised at Judy," she said, "not even leavin' a note or callin'. What are you goin' to do when you find 'em, Frank?"

"I ain't got nothin' against Judy," he said quickly.

She was quiet until he pulled into the Village Inn. "What do you think, they're here?" she said. She knew he wouldn't want to go there for any other reason. The Village Inn was a popular hangout for younger people.

"Let's go," he said abruptly and stepped out of the car. She sat there for a moment, realizing how determined he was to get back at his son. For the first time the whole situation began to frighten her.

He didn't wait for her to get out of the car. He walked in and stood in the doorway looking down the bar. Everyone turned his way. He studied their faces, disappointed at first because he didn't recognize a single one. Then Buzzy Lipkowski came out of the men's room that was located just on the other side of the bar. He saw Frank looking his way, but he didn't acknowledge him. He went back to his spot at the bar. Frank smiled. *That bastard knows somethin',* he thought.

Elaine came in beside him, but he didn't move. He just glared ahead. The young crowd went back to their conversations and laughter. She touched his arm.

"Let's get a table then."

"Yeah," he said, but he didn't move toward the tables. He walked down the bar and edged himself in between Buzzy and one of his friends. A short, chubby boy with a perennially jolly face, Buzzy was certainly no match for Frank's hateful glare and insane eyes.

"Seen my boy around?"

"Marty?" Buzzy laughed his nervous laugh. "Not for a while. Almost a week or so."

"I mean yesterday," Frank said, spitting his words between his teeth.

"No, I ain't seen him," Buzzy said, his face losing the forced smile.

"He took the Plymouth."

"Plymouth?" Buzzy looked to his companions, all of whom looked down at their drinks.

"Shit, all he could do is go on some back roads with that car, Frank." He looked at his own glass of beer to avoid Frank's burning eyes.

"If you saw him and lied to me . . ."

"I ain't lying. Why should I lie? What's the problem?"

Frank just stared at him a moment and then turned away. Elaine had already taken a seat at a table and held a menu in her hands. He didn't sit down.

"Come on," he said.

"What?"

"I said come on. I ain't eatin' in any playpen."

"Well, what the hell . . . Frank," she said, but he was already at the door. She looked up at the waitress, shrugged, and got up to follow him out. He was in the car before she left the restaurant. "Frank," she said, getting in.

"Shut up," he said. "Just shut up."

He backed up quickly and sped down the road.

* * *

Marty slipped through the dining room doors and crossed to the kitchen entrance. He opened the door slightly and peered inside. Pop Levine sat at the table nibbling on some bread and cheese like some small animal, holding the food tightly between his forefingers and thumbs.

Suddenly the back door was flung open and the man Marty assumed was Jake entered with a carton filled with perishable foods. He set it near the refrigerator and moved quickly to unload it, paying little attention to the old man.

Pop Levine didn't seem to notice him either. It was as though the guy walked in and out all day long. Pop continued to stare forward at nothing and eat. Jake glanced at him a few times as he finished emptying the carton.

Jake was a stout man, broad-shouldered and a little stooped. He had a bull neck and kept his gray hair cut very short, almost in a military style. When Marty caught sight of his face, he saw that he had large features, a wide forehead, and a sharp, protruding jaw. There was definitely an air of hardness about him, but also a sense of fatigue in the way his shoulders turned in and his back slouched at the base of his neck.

When he finished emptying the carton, he crushed it in his hands and shoved it in the garbage bin by the sink. Marty narrowed the opening in the door when Jake turned to the old man. Although there were no physical resemblances between Jake and Frank, Marty sensed something similar. He experienced the same kind of fear when he looked at him. It was as though Frank and this man, Jake, were members of the same tribe. It was in the haunting glare of their eyes, the roughness in their mannerisms. The very air around them was charged with a violent electricity. He recognized a common note in the sound of their voices.

"So, Pop, how ya doin' this week?"

"How should I be doin'? I'm doin'."

"Good."

"We'll have the pool scraped down and ready to be painted in another day."

"Is that right?"

"And I'm going to have the grass cut."

"Sure. That's a good idea."

"The staff's beginning to arrive," the old man said with more enthusiasm in his voice.

"Is that so? Well," Jake said, looking around the kitchen. Marty moved away from the crack in the door. "I'll just have to get myself organized."

"What about the linen?"

"Oh, I think we're in good shape with the linen. Did any of the chambermaids arrive or was it just dining room staff?"

"Just dining room."

"Good, good. Listen, Pop, try to understand me for a moment, will ya. I have to go somewhere so I won't be back for at least three days. Do you know what that means?"

"We're goin' to be busy, Jake. I can tell by the way the reservations are startin' to come in."

"I know. I know. Look, I left you extra milk and eggs. I know how the food disappears around here," he said, directing his voice toward the ceiling. Marty began to wonder if he weren't as crazy as the old man.

"Mrs. Levine wants you should talk to the baker," Pop said as though he didn't hear a thing Jake had told him. They're just not on the same channel, Marty thought. "She thinks he's putting too much salt in the breakfast rolls. We've had too many complaints, and from old-timers who should know."

"Right. Okay," Jake said. For a moment Marty thought of *Our Town*, a play that had brought him to tears when they read it in his class years ago. The old man was like Emily Webb's mother, locked in the past, unable to hear words from the present. Thinking about it brought tears to his eyes again. He really liked this old man. He was the grandfather he never had, the past he never knew. Whom could he ever return to? He had no heritage.

He heard something behind him and turned around quickly. It was Judy. She saw his teary eyes. He wiped them quickly.

"What is it?"

"Shh." He gestured for her to walk more softly. Then he turned back to the kitchen. Jake had started for the back door. He paused to look around as if he thought something was different. Then he continued out. Marty closed the door quietly, took Judy by the arm, and led her through the dining room.

"Somebody came to the hotel, a man called Jake. He brought the old man food."

"Marty, let's get out of here quickly!" Judy whispered vehemently.

"No. He's leaving. I heard the whole conversation. He's not coming back for a few days, at least three. We've got it made here."

"I don't like it now."

"Why not?"

They stopped in the lobby. She embraced herself and looked around. Then she sat down in one of the easy chairs.

"I've got the chills," she said.

"That's from your sunburn."

"When did you leave me?"

"As soon as I heard the truck coming up the driveway. I figured I'd spy to see what was what. You were still asleep, so I didn't want to wake you."

"I woke up because I thought someone was standing right near me, Marty. I know I felt it."

"Maybe you woke up right after I left."

"I thought so. I heard footsteps behind me. I thought you had gone into the hotel again."

"I did."

"But the sounds came from the card room where we played Ping-Pong, not the dining room."

"You just got confused, probably still groggy from sleep."

"I went in there."

"So?" She didn't say anything. "There wasn't anyone there, right?"

"I don't know."

"What'dya mean, you don't know? That's stupid. Either you saw someone or you didn't, and I know you didn't. The old man was already in the kitchen."

"I felt someone."

"What? A ghost walked by you?" He smiled.

"It's not funny." Judy looked worried.

"All right, all right," he said. He went to the card room and looked inside. After a moment she came up beside him. "So? I'm looking in here and there's no one around, not a sign. And I don't feel anyone either," he added.

She nodded. "I guess I imagined it."

"You must've had a dream. You fell asleep so fast out there. The sun can do that to you, you know."

"My shoulders sting."

"Mine too. I bet there's something for sunburns behind the main desk. We'll look."

"Marty." She touched his shoulder as he turned.

"What?"

"That thing on the wall there."

"Where?" She pointed. "What about it? It's a grate, an opening for air or exhaust. So?"

"Was it like that? Away from the wall?"

He considered it for a moment. "I don't know. What's the difference? It was probably always loose. This place hasn't been maintained for quite a long time now. Things are bound to fall apart here and there. Come on."

He walked back to the lobby to the main desk. Judy hesitated in the card room doorway for a moment and then followed. Even though everything he said seemed right, it didn't seem satisfactory. There was something . . . she had the same feeling she'd had the first moment they had walked into this place. What was more important, she suspected he did too, but he was ignoring it. Why? How could he?

As she approached him he indicated that they should be quiet again. They heard the truck as it came around from the back and started down the driveway. Marty peered out one of the front windows and watched it turn onto the road and head away.

"He's gone," Marty smiled. His smile looked almost evil—as though he'd been locked inside a candy store. He rubbed his hands and took a deep breath.

"I don't like this, Marty. Not anymore."

"Why not?"

"I don't know." She looked around. "I don't know. There's something. I can't . . ."

184

"Listen to me," he said, his voice sounding more desperate than ever. "It would be stupid to leave now, now that we know it's going to be safe for a few days."

"Safe?"

"Sure. I mean, what else could you ask for?" His expression changed. He looked more angry than anything else. "Why can't you see that?"

"I see it."

"In another day or so things should have settled one way or another back home. Then we'll know better what we should do." His tone turned more reasonable. "You know I'm right. Don't you? Don't you?" he insisted.

"I know," she said softly.

"It's going to be okay, Judy," he said. He touched her chin and forced her to face him. He was smiling now, but she thought there was something different about it. Maybe it was his enthusiasm for the place. Whatever. There was something in his expression that created a nagging fear in her mind. A fear she couldn't express, at least not well enough for him to understand.

"Look," he said. "We'll keep doing things to keep our minds off what happened, all right?" She nodded. "Good, good. All right, let me look for something to ease sunburn. There must be something for it here. This place has everything!"

"It doesn't have everything."

"Sure it does," he insisted. He started for the main desk. "After I find something, we'll go see what's for supper. Maybe you can cook something for me and the old man."

"Oh, Marty, you know I'm not that good a cook."

"At the Mountain House you can do anything

well. You'll see. It's magical. You'll make believe you're the hotel's new cook. We'll tell that to the old man," he added and laughed.

She watched him for a few moments. She wanted to tell him that that would be wrong, that they couldn't keep doing these things, that this wasn't a magical place. It was just an old deserted hotel with a senile old man in it and dust and dirt and dampness. What's more, she felt there was something else, something that might be dangerous. *Oh, I can't describe it exactly,* she would say, *but, Marty, I know you feel it too.*

She approached him, planning to begin such a speech, when he popped his head up from behind the counter, his eyes lit up, his smile wide.

"I knew it," he said, holding up a medicinal-looking white tube in his fingers. He read the small print: "'For painful discomfort due to sunburn.' What did I just say? This place has everything!"

She stood there, unable to start a sentence.

12

He was watching them sleep when he first heard Jake's truck. He knew its sound so well that he could tell it was Jake long before he could see the truck on the road. See, it was Jake's day, he thought. This was not something he knew from an understanding of time or a knowledge of the days of the week. It was something he knew from instinct, something that had been built into the rhythms of his life. As soon as he woke up on the morning of Jake's day, it came to him: Jake would be here. Jake's coming. Be careful.

When the truck approached the driveway, he squatted even lower behind the bushes. Now he was sorry he had come outside to spy on them from the untrimmed hedges that grew near the patio. This bravery, however, was his way of building up to the most courageous act of all: his showing himself to the girl. He was so eager to do that, he had forgotten Jake would be coming.

He was happy when the boy left the girl alone and went into the hotel, but he expected him to reappear shortly. When he didn't, his heart began to beat madly. The girl was still asleep and the boy was gone. This was his chance!

It took all his courage to stand straight up and step out from behind the hedge. He went forward, moving slowly, hesitantly, ready to lunge back into the bushes if he had to. Close up, the girl was even prettier. He knelt down to look directly into her face. When her eyelids flickered, he got frightened and stood behind her. Then he reached out to touch her hair.

The girl moaned and he lost his courage. He decided to just stand there until she opened her eyes. When she did, he would tell her his name. He would say, "Hello, I'm . . . Eric." It had been a long time since he heard anyone say his name. Even his grandfather rarely said it. Sometimes he thought he might have forgotten it. But the girl wouldn't forget it.

But then he realized he couldn't do it. Maybe it was because of all the warnings Jake had given him and the fact that Jake was here right at that moment. He couldn't forget that. If Jake caught him here like this . . .

It would be bad. Jake might hit him in front of the girl. He wouldn't like that. The boy would see it too and he would laugh like the other boys used to. He couldn't forget that. No, he wouldn't let that happen.

He thought he heard something in the hotel, so he

slipped back inside just as the boy had done. He panicked, thinking the boy might confront him any moment. Maybe Jake would be with him!

The sound of his own feet chased him faster. He ran into the card room, and when he heard her coming into the hotel from the patio, he practically lunged for the grate and pulled it too hard. Instead of just bending it out and sliding it away like he always did, he pulled a few screws out of the wall and it dropped to the side to dangle.

He couldn't waste time about it now. He just pulled himself up and manipulated his feet in, turning his body from side to side to slip through. He was able to grip the lip of the insert and hold his entire body weight with his fingers. He had barely done so when the girl appeared in the doorway of the card room.

He was on his back looking behind himself through the grate opening. The girl looked upside down. Because of the darkness of the shaft, she couldn't see him looking out at her. He waited, holding his breath and not moving a muscle. It seemed to him that she looked directly at him and then turned and left the card room. He waited a moment longer and then started to work his way down the shaft in the direction of the kitchen.

He arrived just at the tail end of Jake's conversation with his grandfather. As soon as Jake left, Eric worked his way back through the shafts, listening for the sound of the girl and the boy. For a while he heard nothing. Then he understood that they were walking back to the lobby.

By the time they arrived at the card room, he was almost to the opening again. He heard the girl talk about someone being there. He saw her point to the grate, so he pulled back, angry and frustrated. Why did she have to tell the boy? He clenched his teeth and his left eye began to twitch. The boy, he thought, and then like Jake would say, he muttered, "Damn him."

To get Judy's mind off her imaginings, Marty decided to make a big deal out of the preparations for dinner. He found some aprons in a closet and put one on himself and one on her. He even found a chef's cap. That made her laugh. They searched the stockroom to see what sort of special meal they might create. Judy thought she could do something with the noodles, the cheese, and the tomato sauce. Marty announced that he would attempt a cake.

The work began. Their laughter and joviality increased when Judy discovered half a bottle of kosher wine. They poured it and made toast after toast. Marty toasted the eggs, Judy toasted the noodles; Marty toasted the milk, Judy toasted his chef's cap. By the time everything was in the stoves, they were feeling very light and silly. While they sat and waited, the old man returned.

"We hope you're hungry, Pop, because we got a great meal comin'," he said.

"Eat, eat," he said, shuffling his way back to the table. "Tomorrow's a big day."

"I know, I know. We've got to paint the pool and cut the lawns and vacuum the lobby, and—" Marty started to laugh.

"Marty!" Judy looked at Pop to be sure he didn't realize he was being teased.

"It's check-in too," the old man said. He sat down

and clasped his hands. His long bony thumbs met in cathedral fashion.

"No, no," Marty said. "We have a few more days yet."

"You can't imagine what check-in used to be around here," Pop said. "Especially in the old days when the trains were going."

The smile left Marty's face as he thought about the railroad. "My friends and I used to play along the old track bed in Woodridge. The cinders are packed down enough to ride bikes over them."

"Yeah, we made our pickups in Woodridge," the old man said. "I used to make four or five trips a day in those days. I'd stand on the station platform when the trains came in, you know, and then sing out, 'Mountain House, Levine's Mountain House.'" He put his hands to his mouth and called "Levine's Mountain House." Judy smiled. "All the other pickup jockeys from the other places did the same. We called it the 'Resort Chorus.'" He smiled and nodded at the memory.

"Must have been somethin'," Marty said.

"We were in *Summer Homes!*"

"Summer Homes?"

"That was a brochure the O. and W. Railroad put out. It listed the tourist houses and small hotels. The railroad wanted to build the tourist industry so it would have a market for travelers." He stopped and just stared. Marty looked at Judy and saw the compassion in her face. He wanted to reach out and put his arm around her shoulders and hold her to him. He even felt like offering some sort of protection to the old man.

Somewhere in his dream world, where all illusions

were soft and good, he saw the three of them forever suspended in time, away from all turmoil and trouble. Nothing could hurt them and they could play and live in the resort and listen to the old man tell his stories.

"Those must've been good days," Judy finally said.

The old man looked at her sadly and nodded.

"What happened to Mrs. Levine?" Marty asked softly.

The old man looked at him and shook his head gently.

"Marty," Judy said. She touched his arm.

He realized that he shouldn't have asked the question. It demanded that the old man face reality. The mood was broken and Marty didn't want to lose it. It was part of what attracted him to this place, part of what kept him here. In the magic of the fantasies they could live in the hotel, live in a world that was much gentler than their own. As long as they were here, they were a family; they had something.

There's a kinship that comes from the same illusions, Marty thought. Even now, by sharing the old man's memories, they were borrowing from his past so they could feel what it was like to know love and affection. *It's not so terrible a thing to do,* he thought, *not so terrible.*

"Hey," he said suddenly, "that stuff smells good. Huh, Pop?"

"I've got to go check the guest list," he said, standing. "The maitre d' will be coming to work out the dining room arrangements."

"Don't you want to eat first?"

The old man kept moving as though he hadn't heard. They watched him leave the kitchen.

"Better check that stuff," Marty said. "I don't know if we have the temperatures right." He went to the stoves and looked in.

"I still don't understand why they just leave him here. It's like torture for him."

"It would be worse torture to take him away. C'mon," he said, bringing the wine bottle to the table. "Let's finish this."

She watched him pour the wine. They sat back and sipped it and looked at each other thoughtfully. When the food was cooked, they ate with delight, taking great pleasure in the fact that they had created the feast. Judy made coffee and they had Marty's cake. Although it had no frosting, it wasn't bad. They sat congratulating each other, buoyed by their ability to survive and survive well.

The shadows in the hotel swelled and stretched against the retreating afternoon sun. The diminished light cast a more melancholy glow over things. It made everything dreamlike and gave them the feeling they should whisper and walk softly. Judy cleared the table and Marty helped her wash and dry the dishes and silverware. All the while they moved softly, gracefully. It was as though they were afraid to shatter the moment.

When they were finished, they turned to each other as though drawn by the same melody. Their eyes met with such intensity that it created tingling sensations along each of their spines. Judy felt the tips of her breasts press firmly against the inside of her bra. A warmth settled in Marty's loins. Their bodies moved closer, magnetized by the moment.

But before they kissed, the old man came back through the door.

He waved a long sheet of yellow paper above his head as he shuffled by. They turned to him with surprise and he shook his head as though he had just had a terrible argument with someone and remained steadfast in his position.

"I've got to ask Mrs. Levine," he said. "The Mortmans' daughter, I think she's already nineteen. We've got to get a single at her table."

"Right," Marty called, but the old man was already well past them and out the rear entrance, heading for the basement. Judy and Marty looked at each other and then laughed. Their intimate moment was gone, but it had left its effect. It was the same as if they had completed their kiss. There was something new between them, a different sort of closeness.

"Come on," Marty said, a little frightened by the intensity of his feelings. "Let's go out front. It's getting dark in here."

They went out to the lobby. Marty looked out the front door at the impending twilight. Judy picked up a brochure at the main desk and sat on the couch to read it.

"I bet it was fun working here when it was busy," she said.

"I'd rather work here than in some of the bigger places. That wasn't such a bad job," he said, pointing at the counter.

"What?"

"Receptionist."

She contemplated the counter and then walked around behind it. He smiled at the way she stood there with her hands on the counter as though she were waiting for business. She fiddled with the keys in the room boxes, making them all hang evenly, and then she straightened up the papers on the counter. He opened and closed the front door and then pretended to be carrying a heavy suitcase.

"Mr. Martin O'Neil," he said.

"What?"

"Martin O'Neil. I have a reservation for the weekend."

"Oh." She reached under the counter and came up with a registration card and pen. Without smiling, he began to fill it out.

"I need a bellhop," he said.

"What?"

"A bellhop, a bellhop."

"Oh." She looked around.

"No, no. You hit the bell and say 'Front.' Just like in the movies." She did it. "Better check your chart and tell him the room."

"Room . . . room three-oh-six." She took the key out of the box and put it on the counter.

"Three-oh-six? Does it look out over the pool? I want to look out over the pool."

"Three-oh-six looks out over the pool."

"How are you fixed for single women this weekend?" he asked, smiling licentiously.

"We have our share."

"Share?" He laughed. "That's a good way to put it."

"Well, what am I supposed to say?"

"Just wink. Anyway, I hope they're as pretty as you, lady," he added and pretended to walk off. When he looked back at her, she was filing away the registration card. He reached out and hit the bell and she jumped. "Hey, I saw a flashlight under the counter, right?"

"A flashlight? Yes," she said, showing it. "It works too," she said, flicking it on.

"We'll take it."

"Where to?"

"The casino."

"What?"

"The casino. C'mon," he repeated. He headed for the front door. "Will you hurry up?"

"Martin, what are you doing now?" she asked, coming around slowly. He took the flashlight as soon as she was close enough. Then he stepped out and looked toward the casino.

"We might as well have some fun tonight. I wonder what sort of stuff's left there."

"I don't think we should."

"Who'd care? The old man's in his own world and that guy Jake left." He started down the steps. She hesitated and then followed.

The casino looked like it could have once been an old barn. There was not much style to it. It had a sort of modified A-frame roof, and there were no windows on the sides. The only windows they could see were high up in the front. They looked like they opened to an attic. There were half a dozen concrete steps in the front that led up to a cement landing with a railing of pipe running around it. There were two wide, wooden front doors. A considerable amount of paint had peeled off them, revealing the bare wood beneath.

The tip of the sun was just below the horizon now, and although there was enough light to see well outside, Marty was sure it would be pretty dark in there, even with the big doors left wide open. He studied how the wires ran to the building and wondered how electricity was cut off from various parts of the hotel. He imagined that Jake took care of all that by shutting the circuit breakers. If he could find the casino's master switch, he might be able to turn on the lights in the place.

"How do you like that, they're locked," he said, trying the front doors.

"Where are you going now?"

"Around back to see if there's any other way into the place."

"We shouldn't be doing this," she said, following. "We're only going to get ourselves into more trouble."

He didn't respond. He'd spotted a landing going down to basement doors in the back. There were two pipe railings on the sides of that. These steps, however, were chipped and cracked very badly. Some of the concrete gave way as he started down.

"Careful."

He saw that the doors were locked with a latch and padlock. The lock was still good, but the latch was badly rusted. He tugged on the lock a few times so that the screws holding the latch would pull out. It took very little effort for him to do so. All the while Judy complained. When he ripped the latch off, she gasped.

"Relax," he said. "Nobody cares." He threw the latch and lock to the side. "My friends and I were always good at breaking into places. I don't know how many times we broke into the school to play basketball on weekends when I was younger."

He pushed open the doors. The hinges squeaked and complained. Then he turned the flashlight on and directed the beam inside. There seemed to be a lot of dust.

"You're not going in there?"

"Sure. What's to be afraid of?"

He located a switch just to the inside of the doorway and flicked it. Nothing happened. As he suspected, the electricity had been turned off.

The floor of the basement looked like poured cement. He had expected a plain dirt floor. He ran the light to the left and saw that there was still a great deal of stuff in storage. He couldn't tell what much of it was, but when he brought the flashlight beam down the wall and back toward the door, he spotted what looked to be a large fuse box.

"There it is," he said aloud, but really to himself. He turned around. Judy had come down a few steps. "You wait here until I see if I can turn on the electricity in the place, okay?"

"Why don't we just forget about it, Marty?"

"Relax, relax. You should see what's in here." He went forward and entered the basement. There was no doubt that a rat, or what had to be one of the biggest field mice around, scurried inches from his right foot. He moved back quickly, but he didn't make a sound. That was all Judy had to see, he thought, and she'd run for cover.

She waited in the doorway while he continued to make his way. There were cartons of what seemed to be old clothes. One opened carton revealed a collection of magazines; another was filled with shoes, both women's and men's. All the way in the corner was a rack of clothes. He couldn't tell what kind of clothes they were.

He opened the outlet box and ran the light along the inside of the small metal door. There was a sheet of numbers with scribbling in pencil beside them. The pencil writing had long since lost enough darkness to be legible, but he quickly understood that the top switch was the master. He gazed back at the doorway for a moment and then threw the switch. The basement light went on.

"All right," he said. "We're in business. Holy shit," he added, looking around. "Judy, come in here and look at all this stuff."

She stepped through the door and they both gazed upon what was the storage room for the theater. On the right wall were stacks of stage scenery flats. In front of one of the stacks was a make-believe wishing well built out of cardboard and Styrofoam. There was a lot of crepe paper and some paper lanterns strung over the flats. With the light on, he could see that the cartons he had walked through were filled with stage props and costume material. All of the clothing on the rack was costume stuff as well. He recognized the outfits for the mock-marriage Pop Levine had described to them.

He found a box of makeup, some wires and microphones, a magic wand, a fake bullwhip . . . there were all sorts of things. Judy began to sift through the junk too. When he came across some masks, he put them on and made noises.

They started out slowly and timidly and then became wild and silly, grabbing different garments, trying on shoes, playing with props. Eventually he put on the mock-marriage groom's coat and tails and she put on the veil and gown over her own clothes.

"Wait," he said when she started to take it off, "let's go upstairs and see what this place was like." He indicated the wooden stairway at the other end. "I'm sure we can get in that way."

At this point Judy was game for anything. Still dressed in their costumes, they went to the back and climbed the wooden stairway, being careful not to smash their heads on the thick floor beams that hung a few inches lower than the stairway ceiling.

As Marty expected, the doorway to the casino was unlocked from the basement side, but when he opened it, they looked into pitch darkness. He flipped on the flashlight and ran the beam across the wooden floor, up and down the walls, until he saw the light switches by the front doors. There was a row of switches, each for a row of lights in the casino. One switch lit up the front steps. He turned that one off again, but turned everything else on. They stood looking at the large playroom.

"Well," he said, heading for the small stage. He walked up the stage steps and disappeared in the corner for a moment.

"Marty?"

"Ta da," he sang out and the curtain began to travel across the stage to close at the center. A moment later he stuck his head out of the opening. She laughed again. Then he stepped forward and gazed about the room.

The walls of the casino were still decorated with faded loops of crepe paper. The stage was framed in tinsel. Some of the tinsel had fallen off, leaving bald spots. There were some folding chairs against the right wall and two piles of them in the far left corner of the casino.

On the stage behind the closed curtain, he had seen more scenery flats, microphone stands, some stage furniture, a lectern, lighting wires left in rolled circles, bulbs and fixtures, cans of paint, and some brushes. The blue backdrop that covered the rear wall had large tears in it.

Once again he had the feeling that the hotel had just come to a complete halt one day. Things had stopped abruptly. It was almost as if they had had some sort of air-raid drill, left the place, and never returned.

Now, gazing out over the brightly lit casino with Judy dressed in a bridal gown and veil and looking up at him, himself dressed in the tuxedo and standing on the stage, he felt as though they had slipped completely out of the real world and, like Pop Levine, had traded sanity for illusion and happiness.

13

He saw them walk to the casino and he watched the boy try the doors. He followed close behind. He saw the lights go on and he heard them laughing. Lying on his stomach, he looked through the opened basement doors and saw them walk to the stairway and go up and into the casino.

Carefully he slid down the cement stairs and shot through the basement doors. He pressed himself against the sides of the basement and listened hard. The sound of his own quickened breathing was so loud that he thought he'd be unable to hear them if they came down the stairs again. He tried pounding his chest to slow down his heartbeat. Then he went to the stairway.

Little by little he made his way up, lifting and dropping his feet as though they weighed tons, climbing as though a rope had been tied to his waist and ten men were pulling him back. When he got to the top, he heard them laughing again. Why were they laughing so much? He peered around the corner.

The curtain on the stage was closed. He shot forward to the back entrance of the stage and moved in, falling to his stomach immediately. The boy was saying something funny because the girl was laughing and clapping her hands. He stood up and tried to remember the stage as he had known it. He almost knocked over a mike stand but caught it quickly as it tipped.

With his eyes more accustomed to the darkness now, he made his way to the ropes that dangled from the ceiling. For a moment he wondered if they could hold him like they used to. *I'm bigger now,* he thought.

His indecision was short-lived. He was too excited about going up to the fake ceiling and looking down on the boy and the girl. He leaped up and caught hold of the rope. Then he began his smooth, muscular ascent, hand over hand, pulling himself up through the darkness with an ease that made it seem that he was half his weight. He was excited by the memories it brought back.

The feel of the rope, the darkness, the scent of the curtains and stage scenery, returned to him like old friends. He was eager to pull himself up on the lighting bar and swing forward to the ledge above the casino floor. There was just the slightest groan of metal as he did so.

It was a lot dirtier and dustier than he remembered, but he was still able to find his footing on the frame of the false ceiling. He straddled the beams and inched his way out over the casino floor, working his way slowly toward one of the familiar openings.

They looked silly dressed in those costumes. He nearly laughed right away. The boy went behind the curtains and then reappeared with a microphone in his hand. The girl clapped her hands and took a folding chair from the side of the casino. She put it right out in the middle and sat on it. *What game is this?* he wondered.

"Welcome," the boy said, "to Levine's Mountain House, where a good time is easy to come by if you come by easy." He laughed after he spoke and then leaned forward. "I heard that line at a hotel once."

"Bravo, bravo," the girl said. She looked very happy.

"We have all sorts of entertainment for you tonight. No, ma'am, there is no bingo tonight. It's Saturday night. We're going to give you a show."

The girl clapped again and the boy took a big bow. That wasn't so good, Eric thought. He wished he had brought up one of the curtain weights with him. Then he could have crawled over the boy and dropped it. That would shut him up. He fantasized doing it and then imagined himself swinging down to the stage and taking the microphone. He would sing and the girl would clap for him, just like she was doing for that dumb boy. He could do that. "I could," he muttered. "I could."

"What's that?" Marty pointed to a large phonograph at stage left. Judy came to the stage as he marched across to inspect it. It was built into a tall cabinet. "This is an antique," Marty said. "It only plays seventy-eights." Sure enough, there was a carton filled with old records just behind it. He knelt down and looked at a few.

"What sort of music is that?"

"Al Jolson? Ever hear of Al Jolson? The Andrews Sisters. Here's a Frank Sinatra. A lot of Jewish music. I can't read the writing," he said, taking them out faster. "Ha, square dance music: 'Duck for the Oyster,' 'The Virginia Reel.' Oh, wow, look at this one, 'Row, Row, Row Your Boat.' Can you imagine listening to a recording of that?"

He tried the machine and discovered it worked. They listened to one of the recordings of Jewish music. While it played, he investigated the sound system. He saw that there were two small speakers high up on the walls just to the right and left of the stage. He played with the amplifier and got a loud hum and then, after adjusting the tone, eliminated it. He found a microphone wire and attached it to the mike he had, attaching them both to the amplifier. It worked and his voice reverberated through the casino.

He found a recording of Tony Bennett singing "I Left My Heart in San Francisco." He had heard that before and liked it so he played it. It was a bit scratchy but all right. He hopped off the stage and held out his arms and said, "Madam, may I have this dance or is your card full?"

"My card?"

"Sure," he said, taking her hand and putting his arm around her waist. "Didn't you ever watch those old movies where the man had to sign his name on the woman's dance card to get to dance with her? A popular woman always had her card filled fast. Your card would be filled fast," he said, moving her to the music. Gradually they moved closer.

With the veil on and the wedding gown over her clothes, Judy looked very grownup to him. She fit snugly in his arms and moved gracefully to the music. Her chin rested on his shoulder and he could smell the delicate fragrance of her hair and skin. There was something deliciously fresh about her, something that made him remember past summer days when he would fall in love over and over with different city girls.

At first he looked clownish and silly dressed in that tuxedo, but as they danced and he held her tightly to him, Judy's view softened. He was humming to the music and his lips occasionally grazed her hair. She felt her face flush and her body tingle in anticipation.

"'Where little cable cars . . .'" He sang along with Tony Bennett. When she lifted her head, their cheeks touched. He let go of her right hand and put both his arms around her as they swayed to Tony Bennett's final phrase. The record ended, but the old phonograph had no automatic arm return. The needle simply got caught in the smooth area and scratched softly over and over. For a while they even danced to that. Then she said, "The record's over."

He laughed to cover his embarrassment and ran back to the stage. She stood there looking up at him, the fingers of her right hand twirling strands of her hair. He took the record off and picked up the microphone.

"Ladies and gentlemen," he said, "the time has come. You have all waited for this moment." Judy smiled widely, not sure of what he was doing. "Direct from Las Vegas nightclubs to Levine's Mountain House, we are proud to present the one, the only, Judy Collins." He clapped wildly and gestured for her to come up on the stage.

"No."

"You can't let all these people down."

She looked around as if there were really people there, which made him laugh. Then she shook her head again. He clapped harder and louder.

"I can't sing anything."

"Sure you can."

"Anyway, not without music."

"I've got it," he said, raising his hand in stop-traffic fashion. He went back to the pile of records and found "Row, Row, Row Your Boat." "I'm sure you know this one," he said and put it on.

"Oh, Marty."

"Come on. You'll sing along with the record."

"I don't want to."

"What's the big deal? Hey, this is opening night at Levine's Mountain House. You've got to." He jumped off the stage and took her hand. She moaned, but she could only follow him up the stairs to the microphone. He stood her right in front of it. "Get ready," he said. "I'll start it again."

"This is stupid."

"Folks," he said, looking out at the imaginary audience, "do you think this is stupid? You see, they're anxiously awaiting your debut." He went to the phonograph and started the record again. She didn't do anything, so he stopped it and started it one more time. "Just join in."

Judy saw that he wasn't going to stop until she did so. She reluctantly began to sing along. He gradually lowered the phonograph volume until her voice was considerably louder. He didn't think she sounded bad at all. She stopped when she realized what he was doing. Immediately he jumped up and stood beside her, clapping.

"What'dya say, folks? Isn't she fantastic? Just as we promised."

"Marty, you're crazy."

"Crazy? Listen to that applause. Don't you hear it?" She smiled. "What are you going to do for an encore?"

"Encore?"

"They want another. You've got to give them another." She looked out again as though there really were an audience in the casino. "You have a nice voice. Really."

"Do I?" He nodded emphatically. "Do you have anything more modern in the box?" she asked.

"No. Sing something without music. Go ahead. I really want to hear you."

"What should I sing? I don't know what to sing."

"What song do you know?" She thought for a moment.

" 'You Light Up My Life.' "

"Great." He jumped off the stage and stood looking up at her, his arms folded. She didn't do anything, so he clapped. Then she moved closer to the microphone again. He could see from her expression that this was not an unfamiliar fantasy for her.

" 'So many nights, I sit by my window . . .' "

He was really amazed. She did sound good. When she saw the pleasure and surprise on his face, it encouraged her even more and she sang louder. He was hypnotized by the way she got into it, losing herself in the meaning of the words, holding the neck of the microphone as a professional singer would do. When she finished, he didn't clap. He just stood there looking up at her.

"That was fantastic," he said.

"Really?"

"Really. This has convinced me," he said, slapping his hands together.

"What? Marty?" She laughed.

He ran back up on the stage and got down on one knee before her. "Miss Collins," he said, taking her hand, "will you do me the honor of marrying me?" She laughed again and shook her head, but he didn't let go of her hand. "Well?"

"Of course."

Judy's eyes widened as Marty stood up, put his arms around her, and brought his lips to hers. He kissed her softly but firmly. He was surprised by the intensity of the passion he felt. He didn't want to back away; he didn't want to stop. He wanted to kiss her forehead, her eyes, her cheeks. He wanted to hold her closely and tightly and tell her how afraid he had been all his life and how much he had wanted someone like her. What he felt wasn't just a tremendous sexual desire; he felt a longing to be wanted and to want.

When he stepped back, she stood there confused but obviously affected. It wasn't just a casual kiss or a part of make-believe. When their lips touched, she felt herself draw into him. Her surprise was quickly pushed aside by her own need to be held affectionately. She couldn't explain why, at the moment, but her eyes began to tear. She wanted him to come back to her and hold her tightly. She wanted him to stroke her hair and make her feel secure. She had an instinctive need to welcome sex again, to want it cleanly and purely as she knew it could be with him.

Their confrontation left them both speechless for a few moments. Their eyes moved quickly over each other's faces, searching for similar responses. They held their breath; it was as though time had paused long enough for them to settle back into their bodies. Because the kiss had been so passionate, something had changed between them. Right now it was a subtle change, but nevertheless one they both sensed. The discovery they had made about themselves turned them into strangers for a moment. It was hard to speak, and when their eyes locked, it was hard to look directly at each other.

"It's party time!" Marty announced to break the embarrassing moment. He jumped onto the stage and located one of the Jewish dance records. As soon as he got it started, he skipped and clapped his hands to the happy music. Judy relaxed. She spun around and danced in the center of the casino floor. He spotted some fake flowers made of plastic in the corner of the stage and threw them out at her.

They both laughed and danced until the record ended, moving frantically and wildly. It was as though they were trying to drive the sexual energy out of themselves before it was too late. Afterward he sat on the stage to catch his breath and she sat on the casino floor. For a while they just stared at each other and let the excitement wind down. Then he got up and shut off the phonograph. She stood up and pulled the wedding gown over her head. Then she folded it and placed the veil on top.

"I left the lights on downstairs," he said. "I'll take that and go down to put them out." He took the wedding costume from her arms. Every time they looked at each other now, their gaze seemed to linger. "If we can open the front doors from the inside, you can go out this way," he said. He tried the lock and found he could open them.

For a moment they both looked over the casino. It

was as though they were the last ones to leave a great party and they wanted to cement the room, the decorations, the night's events, into their memories. He switched off the lights a row at a time.

"Be careful," she said. "I'll wait in the doorway."

"Okay. Where'd I leave the flashlight?"

"It should be right on the stage in front."

"Yeah." He touched her arm and then moved through the darkness. She waited until he found the light and turned the beam her way. "Be right out," he said and went off to the basement.

Still in the doorway, she turned and looked out at the now darkened hotel grounds. Although there was no moon, the sky was electric with stars. That, plus the warm night air, made her feel melancholy. Suddenly she heard something behind her, something in the casino. She looked into the darkness.

"Marty?" There was no response, but she heard the noise again. "Marty, is that you?" Nothing. The sound stopped. She waited, listening hard. "Marty, you're not being funny if you're doing that." No response. Judy took a step forward and listened even harder. She was sure she heard something; it was the sound of someone singing in a loud whisper. "Ninety-five bottles of milk on the wall, ninety-five bottles of milk . . ."

She peered into the darkness, trying to determine the direction from which the sounds came, but they seemed to have come from above her. It didn't make sense. She looked up. Marty wouldn't keep this up, she thought. Then she realized it couldn't be him. He would never frighten her deliberately.

It started again, a lot lower, but . . . it was almost a whisper. She wanted to turn and run out the door, but her feet were frozen. She couldn't turn.

She closed her eyes. It was still there.

"Ninety-four bottles of milk on the wall . . ."

She brought her hands to her ears. "STOP IT," she screamed. "STOP IT, STOP IT."

There was complete silence and then the sound of something behind her. She spun around, terrified.

"Hey, hey. Judy." He was in the doorway, silhouetted. She couldn't see his face so she backed away. "What is it?" He turned on the flashlight and she saw that it was Marty. "What the hell's going on?"

"Marty, oh, Marty." She ran to him.

He was surprised by her embrace and ran the flashlight's beam over the casino's floor and walls. "What happened?"

"Were you singing something?"

"When?"

"Just now."

"I . . ." For a moment he wasn't sure if he had been singing something as he walked around the building. All the music had been in his head.

"You were?" She stepped back in anger.

"What are you talking about?" He laughed. "Maybe you heard the ghosts of Saturday night shows or something."

"You're not funny, Marty."

"Look, sometimes when you play music a while, it lingers in your mind."

"We didn't play a song like the one I heard: ninety bottles of milk on the wall, something like that."

"We played 'Row, Row, Row Your Boat.' That's like that," he said, but she didn't seem convinced. He looked into the darkness again. Her fear was beginning to get to him. He was anxious to leave the darkness of the casino. "Come on, what else could it be?" He turned the beam toward the outside and pulled the doors of the casino closed.

"Maybe you left the phonograph on."

"No, I didn't."

"It was sung almost like a . . . like a little kid would sing it," she said. She embraced herself as the chill ran through her body.

"A little kid, huh? Listen," he said, taking her hand. "Hey, you're cold. Let's get away from the casino. You'll feel better," he added, still holding her hand. They walked as quickly as they could. "It's a beautiful night anyway," he said. "Let's sit out on the big porch for a while. No one can see us from the road if we turn off the flashlight, especially behind those weeping willow trees."

They found two porch chairs in relatively good shape and pulled them close together just to the right of the steps. He sat with his feet up on the railing. The night was alive with the sound of insects.

"I don't think I've ever been aware of how much racket there is on a summer country night," he said. "No wonder some city people complain they can't fall asleep up here."

They heard an owl off to the left and then they heard the snorting of deer that were just a few feet in front of them on the lawn.

"What's that?" Judy asked, reaching for his arm.

"On warm nights like this, deer make that sound. Most people think they don't make any sound."

"Sounds like a giant cat."

"I know." He had taken her hand when she reached for his arm. She didn't let go and slowly, almost unconsciously, he pulled her closer and closer to him until their shoulders touched and he could put his arm around her. She lowered her head to his shoulder and they sat like that without speaking for a while.

His eyes had grown accustomed to the darkness now and he thought he could make out the forms of the deer as they grazed and sauntered by. Out of the corner of his right eye, though, he caught sight of something that looked much larger and moved in a strange way. He knew that eyes could play tricks on you in the dark, but it looked a lot like a big man crouched and running.

It sent a cold chill through him and his heart began to beat faster. It pumped so hard that he was afraid Judy would sense it, but after what had just happened in the casino, he couldn't help it. He was both afraid and ashamed of his fear. Then Judy raised her head from his shoulder at the sound of an approaching car. It seemed to slow down when it came to the Mountain House driveway, but then it continued on.

"For a minute I thought . . ."

"Naw," he said, trying to sound convincing, "no one would be out looking for us at night."

"Will we go back tomorrow?"

"Maybe, maybe."

"Even though I got scared back there," she said, "it was fun in the casino."

"Yeah. Hey, you have a nice voice. I mean it."

"Thanks."

"You shouldn't put yourself down so much."

"You neither," she said. "You are smart, smarter than a lot of people."

He brushed some hair back off her forehead and she rested her head against his shoulder again. The night air had gotten considerably cooler and sent chills through them. He felt her shudder and held her closer and tighter. Both of them felt tired, but it was a comfortable fatigue.

"Maybe we should go inside to our room," he said.

"Yes," she whispered.

He turned on the flashlight and drew the beam in an arc across the front lawn, deliberately aiming in the direction where he had seen that large form moving quickly. There was nothing there.

"What is it?"

"I thought we'd see some deer." He stood up. She did so, too, and kept her arm through his. He turned the light off. "We have to be careful about it. If someone drove by and saw it, they might report vandals or something."

"It's so dark in there now."

"I'll flash it on and off so we don't bump into anything."

"I'll stay right by you," she said and pressed her breast against his arm. He thought he felt her quickened heartbeat as they started in, but he wasn't sure. It could have been his own.

14

When the boy had left her alone and gone down to the basement of the casino, he'd thought his chance had come. But it hadn't, and he was angry. He'd almost gotten caught by the boy.

He didn't come to realize the two of them were on the front porch until he was nearly there himself. He heard a chair squeak and he stopped. After a moment he rushed to one of the hedges where he squatted and waited. He saw the boy flick on his flashlight and then he heard them get up and go into the hotel. He followed.

They were going to their room, he thought. Maybe they would do that candlelight thing again. He slipped into the hotel and moved quickly behind a tall chair. He waited there for a few moments and then made his way across the lobby, weaving behind small couches, chairs, and tables.

When he reached the entranceway to the corridor, he stopped to listen. They were talking very low. There was no light, but he knew which room was theirs. He took deep breaths as though drawn to them by their scent and slid along the hallway wall, moving by inches toward their doorway. Their voices got louder in slight degrees. He could almost make out words. He pressed the palms of his hands tightly to the walls to feel the vibration of their voices. Everything excited him now: the darkness, the mystery, the thrill of discovery. He could barely contain himself from making small noises. Soon he would be at their doorway and when he was there . . .

"I feel a lot more afraid tonight than last night," Judy said.

"Still thinking about the kid singing in the casino?"

"Well, it's hard to forget it."

"It doesn't make sense," he said, but she could sense the anxiety in his voice. They sat on their beds and faced each other, though they could barely see in the darkness. He reached forward and took her hand. There was a small but determined tug and she got up to sit beside him. Her leg just touched his. Neither moved; they just remained quiet, staring into the night.

"It's cooler than I thought it would be," she said, so softly he almost didn't hear her. He moved over in the bed and pulled the blanket toward them. She lay back and let him tuck the cover in around them both.

They were so close now. When she turned toward

217

him, he felt her breath on his cheek. His heart thumped so hard with excitement that he thought she could hear it for sure. There were all sorts of voices in his mind at that moment, all telling him in one way or another that he should forget she was a girl and remember she was supposed to be his stepsister, but he wouldn't listen.

Instead he heard the sound of her breathing, smelled the scent of her hair, and remembered the feel of her lips against his. His face moved closer, almost as if it had a will of its own. He moved his lips gently over the edge of her nose and . . . they kissed again.

"Judy . . ."

"I can't help it," she said, unable to relax her body. "I'm afraid."

"I know."

"I'm afraid but I want to . . . I want you to . . . to touch me. I want to make believe I've never been touched and you're the first."

"You don't have to make believe. No one's touched you. It wasn't touching, loving. It was hurting. Don't think of it as anything but that."

"Is that the way you think of it when you think of it?"

"Yes," he said, but it wasn't completely true. There was a part of him that placed him in Frank's position. He saw himself vulgar and animal and he was terribly afraid that he would make love to her in that way. He had to overcome it, as much for himself as for her.

"I was afraid you wouldn't like me . . . never like me because of it."

"That's silly."

"I felt, feel, almost polluted because of it, like I could take a bath for the rest of my life and never wash it away."

"It's washed away. It was washed away at the lake."

"You think so?"

"I know so. You've returned to innocence and tonight's your first night."

"Marty . . ."

He rested his head against his propped-up left hand and with his right hand he stroked her hair and caressed her face. She kissed his fingers as they traveled down to her neck and followed the line of it to the opened top button of the waitress uniform. She closed her eyes as he unfastened the next button and the next until he had opened them all to the small of her stomach. She didn't speak, but when he went to part the garment, she lifted herself on her elbows so he could slide the uniform over her shoulders and down her arms.

He left it at her waist and kissed her naked shoulder, moving down slowly until his lips found the tops of her breasts, just above her bra. When his hand traveled behind her, she turned cooperatively so he could find the bra clip. It seemed to jump apart at his touch. He moved the now softened garment ever so gently and slowly down her breasts until his fingers found her taut nipples.

She moaned softly and he brought his lips to them, holding them tightly and touching them with the tip of his tongue. She turned her hips in an effort to press her body harder against his.

All their hesitation left them. His erection had grown so hard that it began to pulsate with an ache against the tightness of his pants. In unison they pulled back from each other, she to slip the uniform completely off, he to open and lower his pants.

They touched each other with the tentativeness of first love. To eliminate any comparisons with Frank, Marty felt it was important that he be in complete control of himself and that he touch her gently, caringly. But it was hard; it was hard to keep the rush of blood from driving him into a frenzy.

When their lips met again, their mouths were wet and demanding. Her aggressiveness frightened him because it chipped away at his discipline. He couldn't keep control; he wouldn't keep control. He wanted so to surrender to his screaming sexual voices. He longed to be defeated.

They pressed their tongues against each other's. For a moment Marty thought there was still time to stop, but he ignored that final warning. She was whispering his name over and over again, driving him mad with the sound of it. He could feel himself sinking. It was going beyond his control. He was nearly there.

"Judy." He sounded like he was pleading, but it was more like begging her to be his. At least that was the way she heard it.

"It's all right," she said. "I'm not afraid anymore. Not with you."

The fragile grasp he had on himself broke. He settled between her legs and pushed on. She came to him with a tiny cry. He was afraid to make another move, but it was as if a giant hand pushed and turned him until he entered her gently. She moaned and turned. The old bedsprings groaned. She clasped his head between her hands and scrubbed his hair as they moved rhythmically toward the demand they made on each other. Her moans grew louder and louder until they both climaxed in a nearly perfect act of love.

The moment it was over, his initial reaction was shock, shock at how quickly his body had gotten away from him. His first thought was that he was no better than Frank because he took advantage of her. He took advantage of her fear and her loneliness.

But she was still with him, kissing his face, embracing him. She wasn't spent by the lovemaking; she was invigorated. Her energy calmed him. It *was* different; it had to be different. All men and women didn't behave like Frank and his women behaved. People could be gentle with one another.

They both turned onto their backs and looked into the darkness. Then he found her hand and held it tightly in hers.

"I used to dream we would do this," she said and immediately regretted her confession.

"You did?"

"I was even jealous of that *Playboy* picture in your room." He laughed. "Don't laugh. Did you ever think of me . . . I mean, as you would a girlfriend?"

"Not right away. You were kind of funny-looking when you first came to the house."

"I was not," she said indignantly.

"Yeah, you were. But you changed soon afterward too."

"I did?"

"Damn right you did. One day I woke up and you had your hair fixed nicely and you wore . . ."

"What? What did I wear?" She propped herself up on her left elbow. "Tell me, Martin O'Neil."

"You wore that tight black pullover with the V-neck and I thought . . . this is no junior high kid."

"Why didn't you ever tell me?"

"I couldn't. Well," he said quickly, "I was getting around to it."

"You were getting around to it? I probably would've been old and gray by the time you did. I thought you were sexy in those tight old jeans and that sweatshirt with the sleeves ripped off."

"What do you mean, you thought I was? I am."

"Don't get conceited, Martin O'Neil."

"What's this Martin stuff?" He reached up and felt for her nose. When he found it, he squeezed it gently. She lowered her head to his chest and he stroked her hair. "You know," he said, "I wish we could stay here forever. I want it to stay like this for as long as it can. I want to forget there's another world out there, forget there was ever a Frank or an Elaine, forget it all and just live here with the old man and his old world. It was better. People cared about each other."

"People can care about each other now too. We care about each other, don't we?"

"Yes, but I'm just afraid of what will happen to us when we leave here."

She lifted her head away from him.

"You mean, you'll change. You won't care about me like you do here?"

"No, that wouldn't change. It's just . . . easier for us here. We're safe, at least for a while, and we've got so much. There are many things we haven't done here yet, and we've got the lake and endless food . . ."

222

"You make it sound like a paradise."

"Well, in a way it is."

"But there are things that frighten me here."

"Me too, but those are things from our own imaginations, fears we've brought to the place."

"I wish I could be sure you were right."

"I'm right, I'm right."

She put her head down again and they were quiet for a long moment. Then she ran her finger along his stomach.

"I was afraid," she said, "of what I'd feel . . . that I wouldn't feel anything, you know what I mean?"

"Uh huh."

"But it wasn't that way. It was good. It makes us something special now, doesn't it, Marty?"

"Something special. I think we were always something special."

"Did you?"

"That's why the hotel has been kind to us. It recognizes that we're something special."

"You talk about it as if it's alive."

"In a way it is. I felt different from the moment I came into it. Didn't you?"

"I think I was too afraid to remember any feelings."

"You're not afraid now, are you?"

"No," she said. "Yes," she said.

"You'll see, after a while you won't be. I know it."

She was quiet. It seemed so important to him. She couldn't understand why, but it only increased her fear. It was as though he could no longer think clearly, sensibly, about the place and what they were doing.

She looked into the darkness to see if she could

feel anything like he described, but all she felt was anxiety. The walls didn't breathe and the windows didn't see, but there was a presence in this place, something alive. Why wasn't he more afraid of it?

He leaned forward and kissed her hair. She pulled back and they kissed again. Then they laid their heads against their pillows. With their silence, the darkness closed in tightly.

"Good night," Marty said. He fell asleep first. It came in easy, undulating waves of fatigue. She fell asleep, too, but woke soon afterward. Even in sleep she had sensed something, something very near. She could have sworn something had touched her. It was so dark now, she could barely see her hand before her.

When she turned toward Marty, she could hear the rhythm of his quiet breathing. She knew he was in deep sleep, but she was afraid and she was growing more and more afraid every moment. But of what? Where? She nudged him gently. He didn't awake.

"Marty?" she said in a loud whisper. "Marty?" she nudged him more urgently.

"Huh? What?"

"I think something touched me; it woke me. I felt it."

"What? An insect?"

"No. It felt like fingers."

"Must've been me in my sleep," he said.

"No," she insisted. "I would have realized it was you."

"C'mon. Next you'll be saying it was the old man."

"It wasn't the old man."

"I'm glad to hear that."

"Someone's there. I feel it. Don't you feel it?"

He didn't move a muscle. She moved closer to him, nestling herself against his chest. He let his hand drop to her shoulder. Studying the darkness, he listened hard. He heard nothing and saw nothing, but there was something. Instinctively his body tightened.

"You feel it, too, don't you? Don't you?" she insisted.

"No, no one's here. Relax. It's all right." He sat up and searched for the flashlight at the foot of the bed.

"What are you doing?"

"Shh."

His fingers touched it and he brought it up slowly. He was tense with expectation. He aimed the flashlight and then pushed the switch. The beam of light shot out and he thought he caught sight of a moving shadow, but he wasn't sure. It reminded him of the shadow he had seen in the darkness outside.

"Nothing," he said.

"Look in the hall."

"This is ridiculous," he said, but he didn't think it was. He found his underwear and pants and slipped them on. Then he went to the doorway and directed the beam up and down the corridor. There was nothing there, not even a rat or a field mouse. He directed the beam to the linen closet door because it looked a little ajar. He studied it and then decided it was nothing. "Not a guest in sight," he said.

"I felt it, Marty. I really did."

"Could you have dreamed it, Judy?" Marty asked hopefully.

"Maybe."

"Let's just go to sleep. Maybe we'll leave tomorrow, okay?"

"I'm sorry I panicked," she said as he got back under the blanket.

"Forget it."

"I really do feel safe with you," she said, drawing herself closer to him.

"Half the time I'm scared to death myself."

"Really? You don't show it."

"Big brave me," he said, curling his arm around her. She pressed her face against his chest. Outside the partly opened window, the crickets and peepers continued their nighttime symphony while the owl voiced another list of complaints. All during their lovemaking, he thought, the sounds of the night had been turned off. Now they came back seemingly louder than before.

After a while he heard her soft breathing. He was happy he could make her feel secure. He was lucky he was able to hide his own fears so well, for something had stirred him and left him feeling uneasy.

He kept his eyes opened and listened in the darkness for as long as he could until sleep overtook him again too. Maybe it was time for them to leave paradise.

He had done it! He had done it! It had taken him so long because he had moved inch by inch across that floor, continually stopping to listen to their breathing and be sure they were asleep. And then . . . he touched her!

First he found some strands of her hair at the sides

of her pillow. He ran the tips of his fingers over them and followed them up to her forehead. Then he pulled his hand away and brought it down ever so gently to touch her cheek. When she stirred, he lifted his hand away as though he had touched fire.

He didn't take a breath, but he knew her eyes had opened. He inched back slowly and when he heard her call to the boy, he moved faster and faster until he reached the door. He was at the entrance by the time the boy sat up, and he had just managed to turn the corner when the boy flicked on the flashlight.

He was afraid he had been seen, but he didn't wait to find out. Not wanting to make any noise in the hall, he kept his back to the wall and slid along until he reached the linen closet. He got into it and peered out through the crack in the door. He saw the boy shine the light down the hallway. When he put it on the door, Eric pulled back. Right then and there he made up his mind.

"Won't let him tell Jake," he whispered. "If the boy comes to the door, I'll pull him in and keep him from going out."

. He wasn't sure how he'd do that, but afterward, he planned to go to the girl and make friends. "Then she won't wanna tell Jake. Tomorrow I'll take her on the lake and show her how to row a boat."

That idea sounded so good, he was almost hoping the boy would come to the linen closet. He could put his hand around his neck and squeeze it hard like he did to the cat when the cat scratched him. He remembered how its tongue fell to the side of its mouth. It was a bad stray cat. His grandfather hated it and threw rocks at it whenever he saw it. Sometimes he did too.

After the boy turned off his flashlight, Eric remained in the linen closet for a while. He sat there remembering what he had just heard and seen. He had heard them moving on the bed and knew they were kissing again. He moved into the doorway and stared so hard into the darkness that he could see them holding each other. He had seen scenes like this before.

The girl is showing him her "hidden places," he thought. He listened hard to every movement. Once in a while he caught a glimmer of naked skin. The tingling sensations that traveled up his legs and settled in the small of his crotch filled him with a delight he had almost forgotten existed.

He had touched himself many times before, but never when he was so close to other people who were touching. That made it better. He rose to his knees and opened his pants. As always, the hardness both shocked and delighted him. He nearly moaned as loud as the girl when his hot semen spurted over his hand. Afterward he waited and listened hard for their sounds of sleep. When it came, he began his slow movement farther into the room.

Now at the linen closet door, he listened hard again. He wasn't sure the boy was gone from the doorway. Maybe he had just turned the flashlight off and was still standing there. He waited a long, long time, peering out of the crack into the darkness of the hallway. Finally he decided it would be safe. He inched the door open and went to his knees. He waited a moment and then scurried down the hallway.

He moved quickly into the dining room, weaving

around the tables, barely touching a chair even though the room was in total darkness. No rodent, no bat, no creature of the fields, could move better in the darkness.

In the basement he stopped at his grandfather's bedroom door. The light was still on. Curious, he nudged the door open slightly and peered inside. His grandfather was in his rocker beside the bed. One of Eric's grandmother's nightgowns was sprawled out again, the straps of it resting on the pillow.

His grandfather was talking softly, so softly that Eric could barely make out a word. He strained to hear him say, "Reservations are coming in ahead of last year." Once in a while his grandfather would stop rocking, stare at the nightgown, and lean over to stroke it gently. Then he would lean back and look up at the ceiling. After that he would begin talking softly again.

He closed his grandfather's door and went on to his own bedroom. All he had was a dresser with a mirror and a single frame bed with two blankets. The white pillowcase was gray with grime and dirt. The blankets were crusty. The sheet was ripped so badly that portions of the mattress stuck out.

Once he tried stuffing everything into the washing machine, but it didn't work. It never occurred to him that he could go to a linen closet and take a clean sheet. Many nights he slept in the attic anyway. His bed wasn't that important to him.

When he stepped into the bedroom and turned on the light, he was surprised at what he looked like. He had forgotten that he had come down before and put on the suit. What was once a halfway decent pair of pants and a jacket were now torn and smeared so badly that they looked like he had worn them for years and years. His shoes were scraped and coated with grime as well.

"Ugly," he said. Now he would have to find something else when he met the girl. Where would he look for something? Jake's room, he thought and sucked in his breath as though he had just been punched in the stomach. Jake's room? What if Jake found out? He doesn't go there anymore, he thought. "Jake won't know."

He was surprised at his own courage. The need to meet the girl and let her see him was great. He stripped down quickly. When he looked at his naked body in the mirror, he saw the streaks of grime and dirt on his chest and neck as well as his forearms and legs. His cheeks and forehead had patches of black and gray from the dust and grease he touched and then brought to his face.

He went to his closet and found an old hotel towel and began to wipe himself off. He realized the need for water and went out to the sink by the washing machine and dryers. After he cleaned up, he went back to his room and crawled into his bed. For a long time he just lay there in the fetal position with the old blanket pulled tightly to his face.

He listened to the different sounds of the hotel as the various loose parts moved in the breeze and the slight wind wound its way through cracks and under doors. He thought about the boy and the girl sleeping beside each other in one of the rooms above him. He remembered the feel of the girl's hair and the softness of her cheek. He dreamed of what it would be like to have her beside him, to feel her breath on his skin, to feel her "hidden places" pressed against him. It filled him with a longing the likes of which he had never known. He knew he had to have her for himself.

15

Elaine was up and gone by the time Frank opened his eyes in the morning, and the only reason he did open them was because of the banging and screaming coming from the front door. He groaned and sat up, looking down at himself and realizing he had fallen asleep with his clothes on. Passed out was more like it, he thought.

"O'Neil, you bastard!"

"Hold on," he shouted. The effort sent his head into a painful throb and he had to close his eyes and rub his temples repeatedly.

"O'NEIL!"

"Jesus," he said. He stood up and went to the bedroom door. "Who the fuck's there?"

"Why the hell ain't the car ready?"

"Shit," Frank said, realizing it was Sam Cohen. He had promised the fifty-five-year-old plumber he would have his car finished the day before yesterday.

He tried to think of a good excuse as he made his way down the stairs, but it was too hard to think after being awoken so abruptly. The pain in his head was worse today than yesterday. Maybe that hospital doctor had been right; maybe he should have stayed there a day or two.

"What the hell, were you on a drunk or somethin'?" Cohen said. The short, bull-necked man was so wide and barrellike that he looked as though he would have to turn to come in the front door. He had wide wrists and very thick forearms, his arm and back muscles hardened and thickened from years of struggling with wrenches and pipes. His father had been a plumber and he had worked with him from the day he could hold a wrench.

"Naw, I just . . . I had an accident," Frank said, twisting himself to the right so Cohen could see his bandage.

"Sure, an accident. I told you I definitely needed that car by today."

"Yeah, well . . ."

"Well, shit," Cohen said. He turned away and went out and over to his car. The fender had been smashed and a torn section of metal was bent in so far that it prevented the wheel from turning properly. Frank saw Cohen's son sitting in their truck, glaring at him. Then he watched as the plumber reached in and grabbed hold of the torn fender. He pulled the metal out with such ease that even Frank was amazed.

"That ain't gonna . . ."

"It's gonna for the time being," Cohen said. He got into the car and started it up.

"I can have it for ya by the end of the day," Frank said. He was nearly pleading. It wasn't going to be that hard of a job and he had been counting on the money.

"I'll tell you somethin', O'Neil. It's not your fault," Cohen said, putting the car into gear. "It's my fault for being stupid enough to believe you could be somewhat reliable. Don't worry, I won't put you in that spot again." He backed the car up and his son started the truck and backed it out too.

Frank watched them both drive off. When they were obviously out of earshot, he screamed, "Fuck you, you dumb bastards!"

Again he was shocked by the surge of pain traveling from the back of his head to his forehead and temples. He gritted his teeth and tapped his knuckles against his forehead in frustration.

It's the kid's fault, he thought, *all of it. The loss of money too.* He turned and looked up the back country road and nodded. They hadn't come home and they hadn't gone to any of his friends. They couldn't put that car on the major highways. It was a good possibility they had camped out in one of the bungalows at that old deserted colony not more than two miles away. If they weren't there, he would move on down the road to the Levine place, he thought. He knew that Marty was aware of it.

He went into the shop and located a wrecking bar. With it he could break into anyplace, but more importantly, he could break open the kid's head. *He'll suffer at least the same pain I suffered,* Frank thought. He opened his car door and threw the bar into the front seat. Then he went back into the house to have some coffee.

He found he could hold down that and a sweet roll, which seemed to make him feel a lot better or at least strong enough to disregard the constant ache in his head. Then he started out again.

The fact that they hadn't returned after two nights surprised him. He was beginning to believe they could go off and not come back at all. When he gave it some thought, he realized that Marty was capable of it. He always suspected that his son was smarter than he was, and because of that he never fully trusted him. Whenever he obeyed him or agreed to something he suggested, Frank was wary of it. He always wondered if the kid didn't have some secret motives, some hidden reasons. He always had the feeling the kid was doing something to outsmart him.

Well, he wouldn't outsmart him this time, Frank thought. He knew which way they had to go and how they would have to travel. He could track them. In a way it was like hunting for prey, he thought. He gazed up at the house and thought about his gun. For a few moments he seriously considered it. Then he shook his head.

"Naw, I don't need it," he said aloud. He continued on to the car. When he opened the door, he stopped and looked out at the back road ahead of him. "Run, you little bastards," he said. "I'll find ya and when I do . . ."

He got in and slammed the door shut behind him. Then he started the car and headed down the road that ran past Levine's Mountain House.

Marty woke with a start, swinging his left arm up to ward off a blow. He had dreamed that Frank tracked them down, came into the hotel, and found them in the bed. He was staring down at them and

235

smiling. He carried the same coal shovel Marty had hit him with and he was about to use it on them when Marty awoke.

Realizing it was a dream, he wiped his forehead and sat up. Judy was still asleep beside him. She had pressed her head between their pillows and slept with the blanket clutched between her hands. In sleep she was doll-like. He brushed some hair from her cheek and her eyelids fluttered.

"Hi. Is it late?"

"I don't think so. It's another nice day," he said, indicating the view. He got up and went to the window facing the pool while she began to dress. Their lovemaking seemed like a dream now. Had it really happened? When he stepped just a little to the right, he caught Judy's reflection in the glass. She still maintained a sense of modesty, dressing with her back to him. After she put on her blouse, he turned around.

"The old man's already up," he said. "He's out at the pool inspecting the work."

"Really?"

He nodded. She looked so cute now, so deliciously cute. He wanted to put his arms around her and kiss her more than ever. She seemed to sense it because her face looked flushed. When they confronted each other now, there was a longing. The night before had only been a taste. They sought to consume each other.

"I wish we had a watch," he said. He realized he was speaking lower, softer. There was a new tone in both their voices.

"I know. It might be the middle of the afternoon already."

"No, it's not much more than eight, nine o'clock," Marty said, considering the sun's position. "Did you sleep well after . . . when you finally did fall asleep?"

She smiled and stretched her arms out and over her head. "Yes," she said. "I feel . . . stronger, better. I'm eager to do something."

He laughed at her bright enthusiasm. Then his gaze went to her two yet unbuttoned top blouse buttons. She fingered them slowly, almost coquettishly.

"Hungry?"

"Yes, that's why I thought it was much later."

"Good," he said, slapping his hands together. "Let's go down to the kitchen and see what we can whip up." She saw that his excitement was revived, and once again she was impressed by the way the hotel stimulated him.

He put on his shoes and socks quickly and slipped his T-shirt over his head. Judy checked herself in the bathroom mirror. He waited while she brushed her hair. Then they walked down the corridor.

"Breakfast is on me," he said when they got down there. "You wash up and I'll get the coffee started."

He found the old man's pot of coffee still going and at least half was left. He located some of the fresh bread Jake had brought the day before and remembered where he had seen small containers of jelly.

"I worked as a short-order cook for a few weeks two summers ago," he called back as Judy came in and saw him whipping up some omelets. "In fact," he said, leaning toward her as though he were about to deliver some great secret, "there are some things I can cook better than your mother can. I just didn't want to say anything and make her feel bad."

"Marty," she said, sitting at the long table, "are we going to go home today?"

"Huh?" He worked on as though she had said nothing important.

"I said, are we going back today?"

"Oh. Yeah, yeah, we're going back. But first," he said, sliding the eggs onto plates, "I want to do a few things."

"What few things?"

"Ta da," he sang, bringing the dishes over. He went back to the coffee.

"Looks great.'

"Tastes even better." He poured the coffee.

"Marty, what few things?"

The toaster popped and he went for the bread. She waited for his answer. He knew he would have to express himself, express the feelings that had been growing within him ever since he first sat in the kitchen and listened to the old man.

After the old man's first talk, he had ransacked his brain for memories of family. He had never known any of his grandparents, although he had heard cousins and uncles talk of Frank's father. What he had been able to gather from these recollections was the picture of a man who devoted one hundred percent of his energies to the battle for survival. He worked two, sometimes three jobs to earn the income he needed to maintain his family. He wasn't close to his sons and he grew old way before his time. When he had his stroke and became incapacitated, they deposited him in the county infirmary and left him there to battle death for three more years alone. No one went to visit. He was already dead as far as the rest of them were concerned.

Whenever Marty came across old pictures or something that had belonged to his grandfather, he would think about him, but it wasn't until he met Pop Levine that he felt this sadness at never having known his grandfather. Now he wondered what he would have done if he had been old enough to know his grandfather well. Would he have gone up to the infirmary often? Would he have felt sorry for him, or would he have written him off the way the rest of the family had?

He tried to disregard it when Judy said they were taking advantage of old man Levine, but he understood that they were, and all of his fantasizing and rationalizing wouldn't diminish that fact. The old man was pathetic. Marty felt guilty now. Before he left here, he wanted to do something to make it up. But what?

It came to him while he was looking out of the window this morning, watching the old man inspecting the work around the pool. He wondered if Judy would understand why he wanted to prolong their stay.

"We've got jelly, too, as you see," he said, sitting across from her. "So eat."

"What few things, Marty?"

"I've been thinking. Here we've enjoyed this place, taken advantage of the senile old man, had fun . . ."

"So?"

"We should do something more for him before we go." He took forkfuls of omelet.

"What do you mean?" Judy asked. She began to eat her eggs. "It's good. Marty, what things?"

"Well, to start with, I think we ought to give the old man a feeling this place is really going to open up."

"How?"

"I saw where they kept their tractor and mowers in a shed out back. I'm going to see if I can get the tractor going and cut down the tall grass. At least in the back. I thought we might make up some rooms in our corridor. There was enough linen in the closet. Okay?"

"Are you sure that is the only reason you want to do these things—to make the old man feel good?"

"Sure. What else?"

"I don't know," she said. He sat there smiling at her, waiting. She thought she could say it now, that after last night they were so much closer. Still, it was hard. It was as if the hotel were stopping her. "You're different when you talk about the hotel. It's hard to put it into words, but you're like . . . like under a spell."

"You're not serious."

"I can't help it."

"Believe me, it's not true," he said, but the smile left his face. Maybe it was true. Was he really thinking about the old man or was he using it as an excuse? "It's just an old deserted place." He laughed. "Finish eating. It's too good to waste."

"Quit smirking," she said. "This is good, but you don't have to be such a bigshot about it." He laughed just as the old man entered from the rear.

"Hey, Pop, how's it going?"

"Good, good. The pool's almost ready," he said, raising his right forefinger.

"We'll run the water tomorrow."

"Yes," he said, nodding, "yes, that's true."

"You going to the lobby for calls?"

He looked at Marty as though the idea had simply slipped his mind. He nodded again, but his eyes looked glassy. Judy thought he appeared a little more tired and worn than yesterday.

"Do you feel all right, Pop?" she asked.

"What? Oh, yes, yes. It's my wife. She's not well."

"I'm sorry."

"I promised I'd do some of the things she normally does. It's the only way I could get her to rest."

"Of course."

"We'll help," Marty said quickly. "I'm going to help the chambermaid."

"Marty!"

"We're going to finish the rooms on the first floor this morning," he said enthusiastically. Judy could see the energy and determination in his face. It was kind of frightening that Marty believed his work would make a difference and would be significant. Did he think they could bring the hotel back and live here together?

"That's good, good," Pop said, brightening up a bit and looking around the kitchen.

"Don't worry. We'll clean up the mess we made in here too. None of the chefs will be upset."

"Oy, how they can carry on," the old man said, pressing his right hand against his face and swaying a little from side to side. "I'd better get to work myself. Gotta be a good example for the staff," he added and shuffled toward the dining room and out to the lobby. They watched him until he left the kitchen.

"He doesn't look too good today," Judy said. "He's all confused. He's not even mistaking me for his daughter anymore. I don't think he remembers we were here yesterday, or thinks we're the same people who were."

"Probably not," Marty said, scooping down the last of his omelet. "It doesn't matter. It's what we remember that matters. Let's do some of those rooms. It'll cheer him up. You saw how his face lit up when we mentioned the work we were going to do." He got up to put the dishes in the sink.

"Are you sure we should do this, Marty?"

"Positive. Besides, you wanted to work in a hotel."

"Not as a chambermaid."

"You've got to do it all if you want to appreciate what it's all about," he said and kissed her on the cheek. She was flustered by his excitement and his show of affection.

"Don't tell me you worked as a chambermaid, too, Martin O'Neil."

"I didn't say I did, but I was sort of a custodian once."

They walked through the dining room to the lobby. He kept his arm around her.

"I don't know when to believe you anymore. You're making things up as you go along, I think."

"Me?" He laughed and kissed her again. Then he went to the linen closet and began to hand out sheets and pillowcases. "You take the even rooms; I'll take the odd."

"I can't believe we're doing this," she said, but he didn't seem to hear her. He was off to a room. She shrugged and went at it. They worked for over an hour, even putting towels and washcloths in the bathrooms. He found a box of soap and put some in each room. When Judy looked in on him, he was wiping down furniture.

Afterward, he pretended to be supervisor of services and began a room-by-room inspection. They were running back and forth through the hotel, to the stockroom for cleaning liquids and sprays and to the kitchen for water and soap. The old man came out and watched them for a while, but he didn't say anything. Their activity appeared to reinforce his own and he went back to work on his guest list.

Finally Marty went to his office door and knocked. He opened it slightly, looked in and said, "Mr. Levine. Pop. We've completed the first floor and would like you to take a look, if you have the time."

Pop considered the request and then nodded his head slowly. Marty stood at mock attention and waited as the old man stood up and walked out.

"No one likes to check into a dirty room," Marty said as they walked across the lobby. Judy was waiting in the first-floor entranceway, a rag tied across her forehead to hold her hair back and a mop in her right hand, held like a standard. A pail of dirty water was at her feet. The old man stopped when he saw her. "My girls have been working pretty hard," Marty said.

"Good, good."

They went on to the first opened door and Pop Levine peered in. Marty walked into the room and ran his right palm over the dresser top. Then he showed it to him.

"Polished," he said.

"Very good. You've done a fine job," Levine said proudly.

They went on down the corridor, looking in at room after room. Judy stood by the linen closet, sorting out towels and hand towels. The old man nodded at her and she nodded back.

"Some of the windows still need some washing," Marty said as they headed back toward the lobby, "but we'll get to it before the first guest arrives."

"I wonder about the mattresses," Pop Levine said. Marty could tell that it was something he had said many times before.

"I'm replacing two, the one in room one-oh-eight and the one in room one-eleven."

"Good, good. Mrs. Levine hates it when they complain about the mattresses."

"There'll be no complaints this season," Marty said and looked back at Judy. "I feel I can guarantee that." She subdued a giggle, but he smiled with pride. The old man returned his smile and went back to his office, walking straighter and with dignity. Judy flopped onto one of the softer small couches. She fanned herself with a dustpan.

"That was really work."

"Now you know what it's like to be a chambermaid."

"I told you, I don't want to be a chambermaid."

"Well," Marty said, slapping his hands together, "on to the dining room."

"What are we going to do there?" she asked, sitting up quickly.

"We're going to complete the setting of the tables and get it ready for our first hotel meal, what else?"

"Marty?" He was already through the dining room doors. She pulled herself up reluctantly, looked at the old man's office, and went on to join him.

Some of the tables had goblets on them and some dishes. None, except for the table they had set when the old man asked them to, had much else. Marty came back from the dining room supply closet carrying a pile of tablecloths and napkins. He set them down on the corner table. Then he went around taking all the chairs off the tables and placing them neatly around each. Judy watched him work.

"Here's how you do it," he said and proceeded to show her how to set up a table. He covered a table quickly, sliding the cloth back and forth until the ends looked equidistant from the floor. He folded the napkins into triangles and placed them to the right of where each setting would be. Then he went to the nearest server and brought out the silverware, organizing the soup spoon, dessert fork, coffee spoon, salad and main dish fork and knife.

"This looks like more work than the rooms!"

"You just do the tablecloths and napkins and I'll put out the silverware and dishes," he said. He went off carrying a deep busboy tray. By the time he returned, she had already done three tables. He put his tray of dishes on the serving table and set out the dishware on the finished tables. He went back for more. They were a good team, because she remained a table or two ahead of him. While he caught up at the end, she went around and wiped out the goblets. When it was completed, they stepped back and contemplated the results.

"It looks good, really good," she said.

"Yeah," he said, "but I wish we had some centerpieces for each table: bowls with flowers in them. That would make it more authentic."

"I don't think he's going to notice that."

"We'll soon see," Marty said. He went back to the lobby and found the old man behind the check-in counter. "Pop," he said, "if you have a minute, can you look in at the dining room? It's just about ready for the first meal."

The old man stared at him a moment, blinking quickly. His jaw worked up and down slightly, as though he were chewing some remaining food. Then he came around the counter, almost too fast because with his slight bend and his arms swinging, he looked as though he would fall face forward. Marty went right to the dining-room doors and slid them wide open. Pop stopped in the entrance and looked in.

For a moment he said nothing and Marty was afraid the old man had no concept of what had been done. Then he saw the tears in his eyes. His face lit up, the aged, tired look disappearing. His eyes widened; he stood up straighter, losing his stoop. He was rejuvenated. Even Judy was impressed with him and was suddenly filled with satisfaction.

"It's beautiful," Pop said. "Another opening at Levine's Mountain House." He closed and opened his eyes as though to be sure it was all still there. Then he slapped his hands together. "I've got to get back to my work," he said and left quickly.

"See what I mean?" Marty said. "See the pleasure in his face?"

"I just hope we won't cause him any greater sadness when we leave."

"Naw. He won't even remember we were here. In the meantime," he said, holding his arms out wide, "he has all this to dream with. Now, for the final thing."

"Which is?"

"The grass in the back."

"I'll be right with you," she said. "I just want to clean up a little. I feel as though I just dusted half of America."

"See you in a while," he said and kissed her quickly on the lips. Then he went out back. There was a shed just to the right of the help's quarters. It was a small A-frame that looked as though it had been built out of leftover wood. Grass and weeds had grown right up to the doors, which opened out like barndoors. The hinges on both sides were badly rusted and the doors wouldn't open easily.

To his left was a small, ten-horse International tractor. All of the tires were still good, even though the cushioned seat was worn down to its metal base. Behind the tractor was a set of rotary mowers. The tractor would tow them and they would cut down the grass and weeds.

On the left wall were shelves of tools, parts of other machines, and rolls of wire. There was a small cabinet to the right and on its shelves were cans of paint, brushes and rollers, empty containers, paint thinner and turpentine, old gloves and mixing sticks. He saw a case of motor oil on the floor, a grease gun, and an old jack.

"Not really in bad shape," he muttered as he checked the tractor engine. He checked the oil, saw that it needed half a quart, and put some in.

This model had a hand start, but there wasn't any pullrope on it. He checked around the shed for something suitable and found a piece of rope tied to a mixing stick. He wound the rope around the hand start and gave it a tug. The engine barely sputtered.

Gas, he thought, and spotted a gas can in the rear of the shed. It had more than what he needed. He shook it and then poured the gas in until the tank was filled. Then he tried to start the engine again.

Finally the engine sputtered and ran. He let it idle while he hooked up the rotary mowers. Then he put it in first and slowly edged the tractor and mowers out of the shed.

He began to cut the back lawns of Levine's Mountain House. It was probably the first time it had been done for years.

On his second turn he saw the old man standing by the back door, shading his eyes with his right hand and looking out at him. He waved to him and Pop waved back. It seemed to Marty that the old man waved with renewed vigor. *This is a good thing we're doing,* Marty thought, but then he thought about Judy's comment at the table.

He looked up at the hotel building that loomed wide above him. The windows had turned into so many eyes. Could it be? Could a place possess him? He drove on, ignoring the sense of foreboding that had begun to come over him.

When Eric heard the sound of the engine, he rushed to one of the windows that looked out on the back of the hotel. For a moment he didn't understand what was happening, and then he saw the boy on the tractor. His mouth opened with amazement and his eyes widened with envy. Why was the boy doing this? He had always wanted to do it, but no one would ever let him. It wasn't fair; the boy was getting to do everything. He had seen them preparing the rooms and setting up the dining room, and now he was cutting the lawn! Look how the tractor worked!

No wonder that girl liked him so much, Eric thought. Jake let him do everything. He stood by the window staring out, watching him cut deep lines in the tall, wild grass. It looked so easy and seemed to be so much fun.

It made him angrier and angrier to watch. He pressed his face to the window so he could look down at a sharper angle and see where the girl was standing. He was sure she was looking out at the boy and admiring him for how well he handled the tractor and mowers. But he couldn't see her anywhere. She wasn't with Pop by the back door. She must be inside somewhere, he thought.

Maybe now, with the boy and Pop out there, he could see her and let her see him. Maybe now he could have her for himself.

He went to the stairs and made his way down slowly, keeping close to the wall. He didn't know where she was, but he wanted to surprise her. He wanted to see her first. When he got to the lobby, he listened for sounds. He turned his head in little jerks, tuning his ears to the slightest noise. He pressed his fingertips against the nearest wall to pick up vibrations.

Where is she? She's alone somewhere. He closed his eyes and waited. Then he heard it—almost imperceptible at first, and then louder, louder. Water was running through pipes. Their joints shook and rattled.

He followed the flow mentally. Water was running in the women's bathroom off the kitchen doorway. She was there. He clapped his hands with satisfaction. Still hovering against the hotel walls, he scurried swiftly to the dining room.

He was thinking so hard about the girl that he almost didn't notice the dining room. He was halfway through it when he saw. It was all ready! It had been a long time since he had seen it like this. He paused and looked around. People were coming. People were coming. That's why the boy was cutting the grass. People.

Then he thought, *If people come, Jake'll come too*. He would never get near the girl and she would never see him. *Have to move fast*, he thought. When he came to the door marked WOMEN, he stopped. His heartbeat was quick and hard now. He put his hand into his shirt to feel the thump, thump, thump.

He licked his lips, then moved forward to turn the knob of the restroom door. He paused to listen every few seconds to be sure no one was coming. The doorknob's click was very slight, but he heard it. The sound increased his excitement. She was just a few feet away now . . . just a few feet. He moved the door inch by inch and then stepped inside. He stood there for a few moments listening to the running water. He recognized the sound of a towel being dipped and rinsed out. He took a deep breath and continued on. When he peered around the corner and looked in, he saw that the girl had her naked back to him. The sight of it stunned him. For a few moments he was unable to move or utter a sound.

Judy stood by the sink and mirror. There had been so much dirt and grime in all those rooms. The sleeves and the bodice of her uniform were streaked with the gray-black dirt. The dampness of her own perspiration, along with the musty odor of the hotel, made her long for a shower or bath. With that not possible at the moment, she decided to scrub down her upper body as best she could.

She unbuttoned the uniform and peeled it off to her waist. Then she undid her bra, slipped it off, and draped it over the adjacent sink. She wet and soaped down a clean dishtowel she had found and proceeded to scrub her arms, shoulders, and breasts.

As she washed herself, sensual memories of their lovemaking the night before returned. The dream had become a reality. Marty had loved her, had wanted her. He had seen her as beautiful and desirable. She felt grown up and more self-confident than ever before. And Marty was right—what Frank had done to her had nothing to do with their kind of love. Real love came from trust.

And she trusted him because he was so strong and so caring. He had feelings and dreams, compassion and tenderness. It seemed as though they could do anything as long as they were together. At this moment she was happier than she had ever been. She believed in herself and it felt good.

As she lifted her breasts and washed down her chest and shoulders, she found herself appreciating her shapely figure: the lines of her neck, the softness of her shoulders, the fullness of her bosom. She had good color in her face from the sun. It brought out the color of her eyes. She was very pleased with her image in the mirror.

When she recalled the sexual pleasure of the night before, her nipples became firm and her neck and chest reddened. She mouthed Marty's name and imagined him coming up behind her, embracing her, kissing her neck and lifting her breasts. She closed her eyes and moaned, appreciating the vision.

When she opened her eyes again, her heart nearly stopped. Reflected in the mirror was the most distorted and wild-looking creature she had ever seen. Her body went numb. She couldn't even lift her hands to cover her breasts. She closed her eyes, hoping he would be gone, but he was still there when she opened them, only a few feet behind her. A creature made of hair whose mournful eyes gazed at her.

She opened her mouth to scream, but her vocal cords seemed paralyzed. He took a step toward her, his long right arm outstretched, the long, dirt-corroded fingers wiggling like long thick worms. She turned and stepped back but everything began to spin. She reached out wildly for the edge of the sink, still struggling to scream.

She felt herself sinking in an endless descent. There was nothing solid around her. She tried to push back the darkness that was closing in, but it rushed over her, sending her reeling into unconsciousness.

He looked behind himself to be sure no one had heard her fall. It was silent. Carefully, hesitantly, he approached her. For a few moments he simply squatted and stared at the back of her head. Then, gingerly, he reached out and took her right arm. His touch was so gentle he nearly lost his grip. He was finally holding her hand.

Her eyes didn't open and she made no sound. He gazed down at her half-naked body and admired her breasts. The undersides of them were so white. He had never looked at a naked girl this closely before.

. He moved his hand out slowly, jerkily, watching her face to see if her eyes would open. They didn't, so he touched her. He had a strange feeling. It was as though parts of him had minds of their own. His lips wanted to touch her breasts and her face. His cheeks wanted to press against her cheeks. But he was afraid to do anymore here.

He looked about quickly and saw her bra dangling off the sink. He took it and stuffed it into his pocket. Then he knelt down again, slid his arms under her, and scooped her up off the floor as easily as someone lifting a sheet of paper.

Her head turned in to his chest and the scent of her hair reached him. He brought his face closer to it and pressed his lips to the strands. He held her tightly to him. She was the greatest prize of his life and he felt so happy he almost cried.

When he got to the door, he listened. Satisfied that there was still no one around, he rushed out with her in his arms. He didn't look back. He would never look back. If they saw him and yelled, he would keep on running. Nobody would take her from him now.

He moved through the dining room to the lobby. Once there, he turned to the stairway and took it two steps at a time, practically leaping up to the top floor. He knew there was only one place to take her, one place where he could see her and talk to her without being afraid.

He had never brought anyone there. She would see things no one had seen. He might tell her stories too. She would have fun and she wouldn't want to be with the boy anymore.

A great smile formed on his face as he released the lever to unfold the stairway and ascend into the attic of the hotel. She was his; she was really his!

16

For a while Marty lost himself in the work—in the hypnotic sound of the engine, the scent of freshly cut grass, the rhythm of the mowers and the circular design he was creating as he went around and around. The circumference of the circle got smaller and smaller. Pop Levine had become inspired by the sight of real work and had gone to get a hammer and some nails. While Marty cut the grass, the old man repaired the frame around the back door of the hotel. Marty smiled to himself when he saw that.

Toward the end of the circle he felt hot and sweaty and thought about going out to the lake. It was then it occurred to him that the whole time he was working, Judy hadn't come out to watch. What could she be doing? He guessed that she might be cleaning up the kitchen.

He drove the tractor back to the shed, shut off the engines, and detached the mower. He looked back at what he had accomplished. The long strands of cut grass would soon turn to hay in this terrific sunlight, he thought. For it to look neat back here, he'd have to rake it all up. He was sure Judy wouldn't want to stay over an extra night just so he could do that, and he wasn't anxious to do any more work in this hot sun. *One more dip at the lake,* he thought, *and then we'll head out.* The prospect of returning home drove fear into him, but he realized that there wasn't much more he could do to postpone it.

"It's been nice," he muttered to himself and headed for the hotel. "But now I have to face Frank."

"Terrible the way Jake lets things go," the old man said as Marty approached. "I got to be everywhere, after everyone."

"Ain't it the truth," Marty said. He wiped his face with his shirt and looked around. "Did you see the"— he paused for a moment trying to remember whether Judy was a chambermaid last or a waitress —"the waitress?"

"I ain't seen nobody. When there's work to do, everyone disappears," Pop said and continued to nail up the loose moldings. Marty watched him for a moment and then went into the hotel.

"Hey," he said, entering the kitchen, positive she'd be there. He was going to kiddingly chastise her for not coming out to help with the cutting of the lawn, but he was confronted only with the silence and emptiness of the big room. "Must be in the lobby," he muttered and headed out through the dining room.

When he discovered that she wasn't there either,

he looked around, puzzled. He would have never expected her to go wandering off by herself. She was just too timid. It was possible that she might have gone back to their room to lie down. She could have been tired from all the work. He ran up the corridor, convinced that was where she was. When he got there and found the room empty, he experienced his first sense of panic. She would never leave the hotel without him.

He ran back to the lobby. Disappointed again, he put his hands to his mouth and yelled for her. He waited but heard only the reverberations of his own voice as the sound wound its way around the empty hotel, echoing with a hollowness that left him even more frustrated.

"What the hell . . ."

He went into the dining room and shouted for her. He pounded the doors of the kitchen and stood shouting her name. Nothing. He listened. Everything was so quiet, but he could hear the sound of running water. Realizing what it was, he breathed relief and went back out to the restrooms. Yes, the sink was running, but still she should have heard him.

He opened the door slightly and peered in. "Judy?" Just the smooth sound of water running into water came back to him. "Judy," he said a little louder. He entered the bathroom and came upon a rapidly flooding floor. The faucet in the sink was running full blast and the filled basin was overflowing. There was a soaked towel at the foot of it.

"What the hell . . ." He turned off the faucet and looked around. He was suddenly scared. He went back through the kitchen quickly and out the rear door.

Pop Levine was out at the pool again, staring down at it with his hands on his hips. Judy was nowhere in sight. All he could think of now was that she was walking about. He put his hands to his mouth and yelled at the top of his voice: "JUDY! JUDY! JUDY!"

There was no response. He rushed across the newly cut lawn, kicking the long blades of wild grass out of his way as he crossed the field. He turned around frantically as he moved, shouting again. Pop looked his way but didn't move.

"Have you seen the girl?" Marty said.

"The girl?"

"The girl, the waitress, the chambermaid, whatever the hell she is. Have you seen her?"

The old man just looked at him.

"Christ," Marty said with impatience. He shouted her name a few more times. The old man went to a nearby bench and sat down. He ran his right hand over his forehead, cheeks, and jaw. Then he dropped his arms to his lap and stared out blankly. Marty ran up to him.

"Listen," he said, "there was a girl with me. Don't you remember the girl who was with me?"

"The girl?"

"Oh, Jesus. Pop, you called her . . . you called her . . . Sylvia, that's it. Where's Sylvia?"

"Sylvia," he said. He nodded slowly. "Poor Sylvia."

"Yeah, Sylvia. Why poor Sylvia, Pop? What happened to Sylvia?"

Marty's imagination was running wild now. He pictured Frank arriving and discovering Judy. Something terrible must've taken place, and he couldn't have heard it because he was riding the tractor. That's why Judy didn't come out to watch him. It had to be. He cursed himself for his foolish fantasy.

"Sylvia," the old man repeated. Marty sat down next to him. He got hold of his frustration and excitement, realizing that he couldn't pressure the old man.

"Something bad happened to Sylvia?"

"Little Miriam."

"Little Miriam? Was that her name?"

The old man turned to him, his eyes filled with deep sadness, and nodded.

"I shoulda known, too, I shoulda known."

"Known what, Pop?"

"That the idiot would hurt her. But it was busy. We were all so busy."

"Sure. We're busy, I know. What did the idiot do to her, Pop?"

"Jake hates him; Jake won't look at him," the old man said in a loud whisper. "He doesn't even want to know he's alive."

"Who's alive?"

"But he's alive," the old man said, ignoring him and looking back at the hotel. "He's in there . . . somewhere. Where he goes, I can't tell you; and what he does"— the old man shrugged—"only God knows."

"Who knows? What? Pop," Marty cried, losing his patience now. He grabbed the old man's wrist. "What did the idiot do to her?"

"He took her to the lake."

"The lake?" Marty turned toward the path. "The lake."

"Everybody told her, all the time—don't go to the

lake with Eric. Never by yourself and never with Eric," he said, waving his forefinger at an imaginary little girl.

"Eric? Who's Eric?" Marty asked. The old man just stared. "Pop, who is this Eric?" Marty nudged him.

"My grandson." Pop nodded and smirked. "Such a grandson my worst enemy wouldn't wish on me."

"What did your grandson do?"

"He let her go in the boat. Oy, oy, oy," he chanted and folded his upper arms over his stomach as he rocked his upper body back and forth.

"Pop, what happened to little Miriam? What happened exactly?"

"She drowned. She drowned!" he said and tears began to form.

"She drowned?" Marty could barely hold down his panic. Was the old man talking about Judy? A little girl drowned and someone named Eric lived in the hotel. Now? he wondered. "Eric," he said, shaking the old man's arm. "Is Eric in that hotel now? Is he here?"

"He's here, he's here. Who knows where? Jake don't give a damn. Jake hopes he dies. Poor Miriam," he said, silently continuing to rock back and forth.

Jake, Sylvia, Miriam, Marty thought. "And Jake's your son-in-law," he said out loud. "Sylvia's your daughter. Miriam was your granddaughter. And Eric was an idiot and caused her death? How old is he? My God," he said, standing. "What is he? He's in there? Why haven't we seen him? What's wrong with him? Why is he an idiot?" He looked at the old man, but the old man stared out as though he hadn't heard a word. "This Eric caused the death of Miriam and that's why Jake hates him. And he lives in the hotel," Marty concluded.

"Yit-ga-dal ve-yit-kadash," the old man chanted.

Marty vaguely remembered that was the Jewish prayer for the dead. He looked back at the hotel.

"Judy," he whispered. "Oh my God, Judy," he said and ran back toward the building, leaving the old man rocking and chanting his tragic memory.

A spinning, multicolored circle brought Judy to consciousness. She tried to cry out, but she couldn't find her voice. When her eyes began to focus, she was looking up at ceiling beams in an attic. She had no idea where she was. She felt the mattress beneath her and then his hand stroke her hair. The memory came flooding back.

He was on his knees just a little behind her, and she screamed, this time getting the piercing sound out. She tried to turn, but his grip on her hair was too tight. She could barely lift her head from the mattress. She was still half naked, the bodice of her uniform folded at the waist.

When she flared out to break free, he took hold of her left wrist and brought her arm back to the mattress. Then he released his grip on her hair and caught her other wrist to do the same. His strength was too great. He had her pinned back, and although she could lift her head some, she could do little more. Exhausted from the effort and nearly hoarse from screaming, she fell back completely. His grip on her wrist relaxed, but he didn't let go. She closed her eyes and sobbed. After a moment he did let go, but she sensed that he was still hovering right above her, his face very close to hers. She kept her eyes closed because she didn't want to look at him.

Afraid to move, she remained that way. She could feel his breath on her forehead. It was as though he were inspecting every inch of her. She felt him move on the mattress. His weight shifted and he positioned himself on her left. He began to stroke her hair again.

Her body heaved spasmodically as she gasped. She fought to keep herself from panicking. To do so, she had to keep her eyes closed, but every time he stroked her, she cringed and winced, waiting for something more painful to happen. His hand left her hair, but before she could take any hope from that, she felt his fingers on her breasts. She sobbed louder, and when his forefingers and thumbs caught her nipples between them, she screamed again and pushed herself up with her elbows. He retreated as she turned to sit back against the wall. She embraced herself protectively and opened her eyes.

He was like a creature from a science fiction movie. His long dirty hair was draped around his head and reached below his shoulders. He seemed to be made of hair. There was no bottom to his beard. It grew over his neck and out to meet with the draped hair emerging from the collar of his shirt.

The eyes that peered out at her looked as though they were the eyes of a child trapped within the gross form. Although he was big, his shoulders were turned and stooped so his true height was not immediately discernible. His arms dangled long and apelike, with large hairy hands at the end.

The creature wore sneakers without socks. His ankles and shins were scraped and scabby. Wherever skin was visible, there were blotches of red. He was a monster of shadows and mildew, covered with spider webs and dust, the very pores of his skin grimy and crusted with the filth of basements.

So close up, the sight of him was even more terrifying. He was perspiring profusely, and the drops of sweat that ran along his forehead created streaks in the dust and grime. His beard glistened and there was saliva on his lips and in the corners of his mouth.

The dank, musty odor was very strong here. Judy felt as though her skin were covered with crawling insects and tiny creatures. While she surveyed the room, she continued to sob and hold herself. He didn't move, but he stared at her intensely.

She struggled to speak, but her throat kept closing. She closed her eyes and concentrated with all her being. "Who are you?" Her difficulty seemed to please him.

Actually he was happy to answer the question. He had been wanting to for so long. He smiled and went forward, catching himself on his hands. He seemed more comfortable on all fours. The move sent her pressing harder against the wall and screaming again.

"I'm . . . I'm . . . Er . . ." He couldn't say it. What a time for his voice to fail him! Just because he hardly ever used it. He slammed his hand onto the mat, sending up a cloud of dust, and clenched his fists in frustration. She thought he was going to strike her. She wailed, raising her arms above her head, and turned in to the wall. She pressed her face against it and cried hysterically. He was getting annoyed.

"Stuh . . . stuh . . . stop," he commanded sharply. She quieted her sobbing and peeked out over her arms. He was sitting back on his legs, the smile no longer on his face. She tried harder to control herself. "Here," he said. Judy shook her head. When he reached forward, she cringed in terror. He caught hold of the bodice of the uniform and pulled her away from the wall.

She groaned and started to scream again, but his hand was over her mouth. The scent of his skin and the taste of it made her stomach churn. She gagged, her eyes widening. He had her against his lap, her legs folded to the side. She stopped screaming and he lifted his hand from her face. She swallowed hard to keep from heaving.

Satisfied that she would be quiet, he began to stroke her breasts again. She closed her eyes and tried to pretend it wasn't happening. Then he stopped and sat her up. She opened her eyes and waited. He pointed to himself and spoke again.

"I'm . . . Errr . . . ic." He had to close his eyes to say that much, but he quickly opened them as soon as his name was out.

He started to stand and she gasped at the sight of his huge bulk hovering above her. "Marty," she moaned desperately. "MARTY!" she shouted. "MARTY!"

"NO." He reached down and scooped her up under the arms, lifting her with ease and holding her before him. When she looked into his face, she fainted again.

The panic that Marty had begun to feel outside gripped him completely as he once again confronted an empty kitchen. The echo of his own footsteps terrified him. Why hadn't he listened to his own sixth sense? Judy had been right. Someone had always been watching them, following them. He recalled what she had said about hearing someone in the casino after he had turned off the lights. What kind of a person was it? Who would do such a thing?

Last night in the darkness of their room, when he felt another's presence . . . when Judy said something touched her . . . he had been there too. To watch them that way and never speak or try to attract their attention . . . what was he?

Could the person Pop called "the idiot" be something supernatural, a creature of the dark? What could he do against such a thing? It might be too late for Judy already.

He began to scream her name at the top of his voice as he ran through the hotel rooms. Every time he opened a closed door, he braced himself for something terrible. He looked in the main office at the lobby; he went to the card room. He stared at the broken grate on the wall and remembered Judy's suspicion that someone had just been in there. He walked in slowly and approached the grate. For a moment he just stood before it. Then he peered into the darkness of the chute. This is crazy, he thought, and yet . . .

"JUDY!" he screamed into it. The sound carried throughout the lower floor, echoing through the walls. The metallic corridors caught his cry and sent it vibrating into a distortion that became a scream. He couldn't be sure if it was Judy or a dying echo. He backed away, staring in horror at the opening. He envisioned her body stuffed in a chute. It was a terrible image.

He ran back up to the first-floor corridor, opening every door along the way, shouting her name and pounding the walls. He knew his panic was keeping him from thinking clearly, so he forced himself to stop and catch his breath. *Why doesn't she hear me? The casino,* he thought. *She must be at the casino.*

He practically tore the front doors off their hinges as he lunged into the big room. He stood gazing about, the memory of their good time bringing him to tears. Why hadn't he listened to her and left this place when they had the chance?

I'm responsible for all of it, right from the start, he told himself. The thought drove him into a greater frenzy. He ran back to the hotel and pounded the steps as he climbed to the second floor. Once there, he caught his breath and started down the corridor, opening doors, calling her name, listening. There was nothing, nothing but the sound of his own quickened, heavy breathing.

He wondered if he should go on to another floor or down to the basement. The basement would be most logical, he thought. They had never been to the basement. If someone else was really living here all the time they were here, he most probably would be down there. He started to go back down when he suddenly remembered Judy telling him she had seen someone looking out at them from a third-story window.

He looked up the stairway. Marty was suddenly certain he was up there; and whatever he had done to Judy or was doing to her, he was doing it up there.

When Judy awoke this time, she was on the mattress, but there was a cushion of some sort under her head and a sheet over her. She groaned and turned. He was sitting in a corner, his knees drawn up against him, his arms embracing them. He rocked very gently as he stared at her.

Suddenly he stopped, stood up, and approached her again. She saw no sense in resisting as he reached down to take her hand and stand her up. She tried to hold on to the sheet as he pulled her across the room to where there were chests and cartons.

"Sit . . . dow . . . down," he commanded. She did so quickly.

He opened one of the chests and took out a photograph album. He held it out toward her and she took it slowly. As soon as she did, he pulled the sheet away from her body, rolled it into a ball, and flung it across the attic. She leaned away from him, holding her left arm up. But he didn't come at her.

"Pictures," he said and sprawled out by her side. He propped his face on his hands to stare at her as she opened the album cover hesitantly. Her fingers trembled and the pages shook. She was afraid she would rip one and he would go berserk.

"Pictures," he said again, this time with more authority, and she looked down at the first page of them, still watching him out of the corner of her eye. He was intent on her every move, his eyes traveling from her face to her breasts to her hands and back to her breasts. When he moved his hand toward the book, she jumped. He pressed his finger onto a picture of a man standing on the first step of the front of the hotel.

"Grand . . . pa," he said. She looked.

"Grandpa?" she whispered. She was breathing so hard that it was difficult for her to speak. But when she studied the picture, she recognized the face. "Pop?" she said. The realization came to her. "Pop Levine is your grandfather?"

"Pop."

Judy felt her first wave of relief. Anything to do with Pop had to be all right. Even him, even this creature . . . there had to be some explanation. An idea came to her.

"He'll be mad you brought me here. You've got to let me go back."

"Mo . . . mo . . . more pictures," he said gruffly. He poked her in the ribs and it stung. She was frightened more by the shock of it than the pain. She sensed that this monster, whatever he was, had no understanding of his own capacity to inflict pain or do harm. That made him even more dangerous. She closed and opened her eyes, trying desperately not to panic. She had seen how wild he could get. At least for the moment, she could keep him calm, keep him from hurting her.

She turned the pages. As she moved on through the album, the pictures became clearer, the setting more developed, the clothing people wore more modern. He stopped her on a page again and he pressed his finger against the figure of a pretty woman standing by the pool. She was in a one-piece bathing suit.

"Mo . . . moth . . ."

"Your mother?" she said. He nodded. "She's pretty. What's her name?"

"Syl . . . Sylvia."

"Oh, yes." She could barely make her fingers work but she forced herself to stay calm. She bit her lower lip and closed her eyes. Almost immediately she felt his fingers on the nipple of her breast. She backed off.

"Nice," he said, as if in justification.

"No, not nice," she responded. It took all her courage to do so, but she sensed something about him from the way he looked at the pictures. She shook her head. "You can't do that unless I want you to do it." He took on the look of a little boy who had been chastised and she became more confident. She pulled the uniform up again and shoved her arms into the sleeves.

"No," he said, but not belligerently.

"If you don't let me, I won't look at any more pictures."

He looked down at the other albums in the chest and then at her determined face.

"Pic . . . pictures," he said. She buttoned her uniform closed and turned another page in the album on her lap. As she looked at the pictures, she watched him, watched the way the smile formed and remained on his face. When a little girl began to appear, he seemed especially happy.

"Who is she? She's a pretty little girl."

"Mmm . . ."

She looked at him and he looked up at her. She saw the fear in his face.

"Is she a . . . a relative?"

He didn't respond. He just stared at her. She became very afraid again and looked down at the photographs, deliberately turning the pages a lot more quickly. He just continued to watch her. She looked about the room as best she could without making it too obvious. Where was the door? If she saw the door, maybe she could make a dash for it.

Then she came to a picture of a little boy. She could tell from the size of his head and the length of his arms that this boy was him when he was small. He was standing by swings and looked very sad and frightened.

"This is you," she said, pointing. His gaze went to

the picture and he nodded. The smile returned to his face.

"Er . . . ric," he said, and he pointed to himself.

"Is this where you live now?" He shook his head. "How come Marty and I didn't see you before?"

"Ja . . . Jake said no."

"Jake?" He nodded. "Jake said you shouldn't let us see you?" He nodded harder. She thought for a moment. Jake. "Well then," she said, "when Jake finds out you took me here and wouldn't let me leave, he's going to be mad then, isn't he?"

The smile left his face again, but he took on a more resolute expression. His eyes became small and his lips tightened. He was going to be big and strong. Jake could tell him not to do a lot of things and he could take many things away from him, but he wasn't going to take the girl away.

"No," he said. "Ja . . . Jake won't find out."

"He will. My friend will tell him, won't he? You'd better let me out of here. I won't tell them what you did. I'll say I got lost in the hotel, okay?" He just stared at her. "That way you won't get into any trouble. You don't want to get into trouble, do you? So let me out now." She started to move in hopes that would get him to agree, but he put his hand out immediately.

"No. Pic . . . pictures," he said.

"I'll look at your pictures. We'll take them out with us. My friend Marty wants to see them too."

"No," he said. "No," he repeated sharply. He seized the album and held it to himself.

"All right. So we won't show them to Marty, but I want to look at them someplace else, okay?" He looked at her, but he didn't respond. She started to

270

stand up again because he looked confused. "How do you get out of here?"

She saw a collapsed and folded ladder on the far end of the attic floor, but before she could walk to it, he was up, his huge body looming beside her. She smiled and took a step back. The heel of her right foot hit the base of a smooth mahogany chest. It had gold trim and a sheen to it, obviously from hours and hours of polishing and care.

"Mmmm . . . Mi . . . Miriam's," he said, pointing.

"Miriam?"

He took her wrist and knelt down, forcing her to kneel beside him. Then he lifted the lid. Inside were half a dozen beautifully kept dolls that looked as new as the day they had been bought. There was some dolls' clothing and a small hand mirror with a long handle, combs and toy bracelets too. He handled it all gingerly and brought a doll out for her to touch. It was the kind that could be fed with a toy baby's bottle.

"Very nice," she said.

"Miriam's," he said. He brought out another doll and another. She looked at each one and smiled. This encouraged him to take out each and every item in the chest.

"Where is Miriam?" Judy asked. He stopped taking things out.

"She fe . . . fell in the la . . . lake."

"Fell in the lake? You mean she—"

So close to her, he was unable to resist touching her hair again. She caught his hand in hers because his strokes were getting too rough. He resented the interference.

"I'm very thirsty," she said, "and you have nothing to drink here."

"Drink?"

"Yes, milk, soda, juice, something."

"Milk? I . . . I can ge . . . get milk." He smiled with confidence. "You wa . . . wa . . ."

"Yes," she said. She thought that if she could get him out of here, she could get away. She saw that he was beginning to think about it. "I'll wait here and look at the pictures," she said and went back to the carton of albums. "Hurry up."

"You wa . . . wait."

"I'll wait." She took a picture album out and pretended great interest in it. He studied her for a moment. She looked sincere.

How wonderful, he thought, she wanted to be here and she was interested in his things. And he had so much more to show her! He backed away slowly, watching her. She didn't turn away from the pictures. When he reached the drop ladder, she looked at him and smiled.

So pretty, he thought; prettier than Miriam, he concluded defiantly. He would get her the milk and come back here and they would look at all the pictures and he would show her things until it got too dark and then . . . the candles, he thought, remembering her first night here with the boy. He would get candles too and they would sit around them and talk. She would sleep here. Tomorrow he would take her out on the boat the way the boy did and they would swim around the raft. He would show her how he chased the dogs away from the deer, how he had killed one of the dogs. That would make her happy and proud of him. She would like him more than that boy.

He would chase the boy away. That's what he might do, just like Jake chased people away when the hotel was opened. If he didn't like the way a waiter worked, he told him to leave. Well, he could do the same thing.

He pushed the drop ladder out and took one more look at her before descending. She was still looking at the pictures intently. It was all right; everything was going to be all right. He went down quickly, eager to get the milk and come back as fast as he could. When he stepped off the ladder, he lifted it and heaved it back up to the ceiling with such force that it slammed into place. He considered it for a moment and then went to the door that opened to the top floor of the hotel.

For a few moments he thought it might not be necessary. After all, she did want to be with him. But then he thought how terrible he would feel if he lost her, now that he had her. So he took the skeleton key from his pocket and inserted it into the door lock. It clicked closed. He tried the handle and then, satisfied, he hurried on to the kitchen. She was his for as long as he wanted her!

Marty gripped the bannister and started up the stairs to the third floor slowly, listening as intently as he could while he walked. The silence had become threatening, frustrating. The hotel he had come to trust had now turned against him. Every corner, every shadow, was ominous. There was no longer anything magical and good about the place. It was a trap. Perhaps it had always been a trap. What was it Judy accused him of? Falling under its spell? Now he believed it was so.

When he reached the third floor, he paused.

Hearing nothing, he started down the corridor, turning doorknobs, peering into rooms, bracing himself for trouble. With every door he opened, he held his breath and clenched his fists. His heart, pounding so fast as it was, quickened each time he tried a knob or approached an entrance. A terrible cold sweat had broken out along the back of his neck. Every once in a while, an icy shudder traveled over his back and made him pull his shoulders up. Why were there no sounds? Why couldn't she at least yell for him?

He was disappointed when he reached the last door on the third floor and found nothing. He looked up at the next flight of stairs, feeling like a person who was playing Russian roulette. The chances were fifty-fifty that she'd be on the next level and with her would be . . . would be what?

He moved swiftly but quietly up to the next level and once again began the nerve-racking exploration of each guest room. Every time he confronted an empty one, he listened hard in hopes that he would hear something that would prepare him for the next.

At the end of the corridor he began to feel it was useless and leaned against the wall to catch his breath. As he confronted the dimly lit vacant corridor, a heavy depression set in. He pounded his fist into his hand. His chest ached from his effort to hold back tears.

God, how stupid I was, he thought. *How could I not realize someone else was here? All that food Jake brought—the old man could never have eaten it all. I should have known; I should have thought about it. I didn't want to think about it. I wanted it to be perfect. I deliberately ignored things.* He pressed his fists against his temples.

"Calm yourself, O'Neil," he said. How bad could this guy be, he thought. So they called him an idiot, so what? How many of his friends were called idiots and how many times had he been called that? It's nothing, nothing. He laughed at his attempt to diminish the seriousness of the situation.

Why did he stalk us like that? Why didn't he ever show himself? He must be crazy. He's not an idiot; he's a lunatic. That's why the old man said Jake didn't want to know him or see him. They've kept a crazy relative hidden away here because they're ashamed of him, and now he has Judy. Somewhere.

Realizing that he was carrying on this insane debate with himself, he stepped away from the wall and started for the stairway to the final floor of the hotel. He was just to the corner of the corridor when the sounds of heavy feet pounding the steps above him froze him in place. The whole building seemed to shake. He pressed his body to the wall, swallowed hard, and clenched his fists, bracing himself for whatever would come.

17

When he didn't see any sign of the old Plymouth at the bungalow colony, Frank almost continued on to the Mountain House. But then he thought, *The kid's too smart to leave the car anywhere obvious.* He'd search this place first. He backed up a little and turned into the bungalow colony's driveway, stopping at the first unit. Before getting out, he leaned over to take out a half-full pint of Old Harper. He took a long swig, wiped his mouth with the back of his hand, and then grasped the wrecking bar.

He opened the car door and stepped out. For a moment the stillness unnerved him. The dilapidated bungalows looked angry and sorrowful to him, each haunted by the sounds of its long-gone inhabitants. A half-torn screen door on the bungalow across from him squeaked and rapped against its jamb. He spun around, lifting his wrecking bar as he moved. He was embarrassed by his own fear and lowered the bar quickly. Then he put the top·back on the whiskey bottle, dropped the bottle on the front seat, and began his unit-by-unit search of the colony.

He had raided this place a few times before, each time coming away with a piece of kitchen equipment or furniture. He was able to sell most of it to people who were grateful to get a kitchen table and chairs for twenty dollars or a toaster for two. The owners of the colony had long since deserted it. All of the units needed painting; some had broken windows. Overgrown grass and weeds climbed the sides of the bungalows and into and over the small porches.

The small children's playground looked as though a herd of wild children had run through it, turning over swings and sliding ponds. Everything was rusted. There were weeds growing in the sandbox.

Frank opened the doors of the bungalows by shoving the wrecking bar against them. Most swung open onto empty rooms. Some had worn couches and chairs. He made a mental note of any good stuff he saw. After the search was over, he would come back and pick up what he could sell.

Although there were only twenty-four units in the colony, they were spread in a half circle over more than three acres of land. Normally that wouldn't have been too difficult for Frank to cover, even plodding through the tall grass, but with his head beating away, it seemed like it would take him an eternity to complete the search.

He realized they could still be in any one of the remaining bungalows, waiting for him to walk into one so they could rush out and away. He was careful to watch for a few minutes after he entered each unit. That added to the time.

A couple of times he stopped, thinking that he would give it up and continue on down the road, but he knew this place would make a good hideout, and it seemed logical to him that they would choose a place close by.

His anger mounted as he searched. He had thought they'd return home after a day or so, repentant and hopeful that the time that had passed had softened him some. That they hadn't returned was outright defiance.

Well, they're not here, he thought. *There's really no sign of them*. He knew now where they had to be. He had to get up to the old hotel, Levine's Mountain House, as quickly as he could.

Marty saw Eric charge down the next flight of stairs. He looked with horror at what seemed more like a creature than a human being. The mound of hair on his head and the wild beard that connected with it framed his face and emphasized his wild-looking eyes. As the weird-looking man pounded down the steps, he seemed to be muttering the word "milk" over and over, chanting it in rhythm with each step.

He disappeared below and Marty emerged slowly and waited, listening to the echo of the giant's footsteps. Then Marty considered the fifth floor, now more concerned about Judy than ever. She was up there with that! He ran up the flight as quickly as he could, and when he reached the corridor, he began to shout her name.

After Eric had slammed the folding stairs back into the attic floor, Judy decided to wait a few minutes to be sure he had really gone. She considered sticking her head out the window and shouting for Marty, but then she thought that might attract the wild man and bring him running back. She couldn't take that chance.

When she thought she had waited long enough, she went to the ladder and pushed it as hard as she could. It opened only partway because it had long since lost its spring action. Now it took brute strength to shove it down and shove it up. She leaned over and pushed as hard as she could. It moved a few inches more.

She began to panic, thinking that he would return and see that she had tried to escape. Who knows what he would do to her then, she wondered, if she were still trapped up here. She had to get down. She put her right foot on the top rung of the first section, hoping that if she placed her weight on the ladder, it would unfold sufficiently for her to walk down. It did move, but it was very unsteady.

"Oh God," she cried. She was sobbing now, although she wasn't really aware of it. She put her left foot on the rung and gradually lowered her full body weight to the ladder. Without warning, it unfolded nearly all the way. She almost lost her grip on the sides of the opening. Shaking with fear, but driven on by an even greater fear of what would be if she didn't go, she started her descent.

When she reached the bottom, she found the door was locked and burst into tears. She shook the handle and pulled and pulled, but the heavy old wooden door didn't budge. The small room she was in was tiny and bare. There was no place to hide when he came back. She was trapped with the ladder down. He would know she tried to escape and he would have her.

She crumpled at the door, crying hysterically now.

She couldn't think or move. Her legs felt so weak that she was sure she was unable to stand. She tried desperately to get hold of herself. There was only one more possibility. If she could push that ladder back up and then hide behind the door when he opened it, he might just go up and not see her standing here. She could rush out and get away before he discovered what she had done.

The plan renewed her strength. She rose to her feet and took hold of the folding ladder, lifting and pushing it with all her might. She half expected what followed. When she shoved the ladder, she didn't have the strength to drive it all the way up, so it stopped in midair just beyond her reach.

"No, no, no," she said, jumping to push it a little more. It barely moved. Now she was surely trapped. She couldn't go back up and she couldn't get out. The moment he entered the little room and saw the ladder like that, he would look around and discover her. She couldn't hide behind the door. It was hopeless.

"Marty," she moaned. Where was he? Why hadn't he come looking for her by now? "Marty," she said a little louder. It didn't matter if the wild man heard her now. "MARTY!" she shouted. She began to pound the door. "MARTY, MARTY, MARTY!"

He was just midway down the fifth floor corridor when he heard her and located the door in the old part of the hotel. When she heard him call back, she began to cry even harder, now out of happiness.

"Are you all right?" he asked, his face to the door.

"Yes, but the door's locked."

"Stand back," he said. He stood back and then

lunged at the door, smashing it with his shoulder. It barely moved off the jamb. He hit it again and again, but he wasn't making much progress. The door, being part of the old structure, was thicker and stronger than the doors in the more modern sections.

"Marty," she called anxiously.

"Hold on. I've got to find something to pry it open with," he said.

"Hurry. He went down for some milk."

"Milk?" Damn, he thought and looked up and down the corridor. There was nothing there, nothing he could use. He began to panic himself. He went into one of the guest rooms. There was only a stripped-down bed, an empty dresser with a mirror, a night table, and another small dresser. He opened a closet. There was nothing in it but some hangers. Hangers, he thought, and wondered if he could shove an end in and manipulate the door lock. What else could he do?

He ran to another room and another, but there was nothing different in any of them. The hanger idea was the only hope. He seized one quickly and bent it out. Then he went back to the door.

"I'm going to try to trigger the lock," he said. "There's nothing here I can use as a wedge."

"Hurry, Marty."

He shoved the hanger end in and probed. Skeleton key locks weren't that complicated, he told himself, but the faster he worked and the more she pleaded, the clumsier he was at it. The lock itself might be too old and rusty to be jabbed open, he thought. In any case, time was running out. Frustrated, he went back to slamming his shoulder into the door, bashing it and bashing it until his arm and shoulder ached. When he paused to catch his breath, he heard him returning.

The wild-looking man was pounding the steps with a fury. He could hear the bannister squeaking from the creature's grip as he pulled himself upward.

"Stand back," Marty whispered loudly, "he's coming."

"Oh God, no," she said. Marty retreated to the doorway of the room across the way and waited.

Eric had been so excited about Judy that he ran the entire way to the kitchen and back. When he went through the dining room, he slammed into a table and sent goblets crashing to the floor. On any other occasion that would have been enough to send him into hiding, but he disregarded it completely now. Nothing else mattered but getting her some milk and getting back to her. They were going to look at all the pictures and the toys and all the old things.

Pop was sitting in the kitchen when he got there; he was having a cup of tea. As soon as he saw Eric, he looked up and began to chastise him.

"Where have you been? You hide when there's real work to do. Don't you see what we're doin' here? Why aren't you out there? The grass has to be raked. I want the grass to be raked."

"Not now, Paa—Pop, nnnn . . . not now."

"Why not now? You're so busy?"

"We're lookin' a . . . a . . . at pic . . . tures."

"Pictures? Lookin' at pictures don't get work done."

"No," Eric said defiantly.

The old man's eyes widened. He watched him take a bottle of milk and glasses and run out of the

282

kitchen. Then he shook his head and nodded. "An idiot," he said, "an idiot."

Eric attacked the stairway with a vengeance. It was all that stood between him and Judy. He tripped a few times, trying to take too many steps at once. At the third floor he grabbed the old bannister so hard that he tore a section of it away. He let the wood go crashing below. When he reached the fifth floor, he jogged down the corridor with glee.

He forgot that he had locked the door and nearly tore off the handle trying to open it. He had to put down the milk and glasses to reach into his pocket for the key. He fumbled it into the lock, turned and clicked it open, and then put the key back into his pocket. He turned the handle and opened the door. As it swung open, he bent down to pick up the milk and glasses. At that moment Marty charged forward.

Marty knew it would be a matter of split-second timing. With someone that big, the only hope lay in hitting him when he was off balance. Judy was just behind the door. He had to shove him through the doorway sufficiently for her to get by. He crouched and ran forward, turning his aching shoulder in and hitting the giant like a football linebacker.

He caught Eric at the center of his buttocks and sent him flying forward. Surprised and awkward, he went crashing and sliding to the floor of the little room. The milk bottle flew out of his hands and the glasses smashed against the wall.

"QUICKLY!" Marty yelled and Judy was around the now-open door. Marty pulled it shut and they began to run down the corridor, taking no time to look back. He held her hand as they turned the corner and practically leaped down the stairs.

For a few moments Eric was too stunned and confused to react. He heard the boy yell "Quickly" but he didn't see the girl get out. Instead he sat up and gazed at the half-folded ladder. He saw the milk pouring out of the bottle and the glasses broken into bits. That angered him more than anything.

"Her milk," he said. He clenched his fists and stood up. The boy just didn't want them to have fun, he thought. He pulled the door completely open and stepped out in the corridor. They were gone, but he could hear them descending the stairs. It wasn't fair. He was sure the girl would have enjoyed herself if the boy would have left them alone.

He started for the stairs, walking slowly and deliberately at first. He was unsure about what he could now do, but he knew he had to do something. When he reached the corner, he broke into a run. He would catch them; he could catch them. Then he would tell the boy to leave them alone and he would bring her back upstairs. That's what he would do.

He flew over the steps in pursuit.

It had taken longer than Frank imagined it would to check out the old bungalow colony. The walking had tired him out and started up the pain in his head again. Back in the car he took half a dozen good belts of whiskey before he felt good enough to go on. The more pain he felt, the angrier he became. He started the engine, pulled out of the colony, and headed for Levine's Mountain House.

He arrived at the driveway and stopped the car and studied the buildings and grounds. There were no signs of anyone about, but Marty could have parked the Plymouth behind the main building. He started up the driveway slowly. Halfway up he caught sight of the car parked in the tall grass to the right. Despite his head pain he smiled to himself and looked at the hotel. They were in there somewhere.

He decided to pull his car alongside the Plymouth, check to be sure the key wasn't still in the Plymouth, and go looking for them. If they fled from him, they'd have to flee on foot. The key was still in the car. He took it and put it in his pocket. Then he grabbed hold of the wrecking bar and headed for the hotel. He would go in through the side entrance. If the door was locked, he'd just pry it open.

He wasn't surprised that the door was unlocked. He didn't give it a second thought; he just entered the hotel and started down the first-floor corridor toward the lobby, hugging the wall and listening as he went.

He thought of nothing else but confronting them. He wanted one good swing at Marty and then he would be at the girl. Damn her for teasing him and teasing him and causing all this, he thought. He listened hard for the slightest indication of where they could be. He was nearly to the lobby when he heard them coming down the stairs.

As Judy and Marty made their turn to the final flight of stairs, they were both looking up behind them. They didn't see Frank as he stepped forward and swung the wrecking bar into Marty's stomach. Judy screamed as Marty doubled up and fell forward, tripping on the last step and throwing his hands out to break his fall.

Frank grabbed Judy and pulled her to him, embracing her from behind. Her piercing screams reverberated throughout the hotel. The nightmare had surrounded them. They had descended into the hell where madmen awaited them.

"Thought you had me fooled, didn't ya?" Frank laughed hideously. "Thought if you stayed away long enough, it would all be forgotten. Well, none of it was forgotten, girl," he said savagely, keeping a tight grip around Judy. He laughed as Judy kicked out and tried desperately to pry his arms loose.

"Some son I have," he said, looking down at Marty. "Takin' her part against me." Marty was still face down, his hands on his stomach. Frank took a step forward and kicked him in the ribs. Then he spun Judy around.

"Let me go!" she screamed.

Frank laughed again and brought his face to hers, pressing his lips against her ear.

"Where are your teasin' ways now, little princess? Huh? Where?" He lifted her from the floor and swayed her from side to side. "Why don't you wag your ass now, huh?" He turned her around so they both faced Marty again. "Look at your hero there. Come behind me and smash me, huh." He kicked Marty in the buttocks. Judy reached back to claw his face. He caught her hand in the air and twisted her wrist so hard, he nearly snapped it. She cried out in pain until he laughed and released it. Then he embraced her tightly again and turned her away from Marty.

This time he seized her by clamping his hands over her breasts and lifted her so hard against him that her feet left the floor. With her arms pinned against herself, she was helpless.

On the floor behind them Marty crawled and gasped, trying to regain the breath that had been knocked out of him. His eyes bulged with the effort and his face turned red from the strain. He had to help Judy. Frank had torn open her waitress uniform and had her naked breasts in his hands. She continued to scream and kick, now from the pain he was causing.

Frank turned toward Marty, who was now on all fours, and before he could stand, drove his foot into Marty's rib cage, sending him over on his back.

"Bastard," he said. "I ain't finished with you yet. First I'm goin' to take the little princess here to the honeymoon suite." He started toward the first-floor corridor of rooms. Judy was hoarse from screaming. She continued to fight weakly, almost in shock.

When Eric heard Judy's first scream, he stopped on the stairway in confusion and listened. She probably wanted to come back and the boy wouldn't let her. He charged forward in anger. But the sight he saw when he reached the top of the last flight of steps stopped him and confused him again. There was the boy holding his stomach and moaning on the floor, and there was this man carrying the girl away. He could see that she was trying to get loose.

He reacted purely out of instinct. Frank neither heard nor saw him. Eric seized both of Frank's arms at the elbows and pulled them back so he would have to release his hold on Judy. The moment she broke free, she ran back to Marty, who had gotten to his knees again. They both watched Eric lift Frank off the ground. Frank bellowed from the pain that formed in his shoulders as his arms were twisted back. Eric let him go and Frank fell to the floor.

"N . . . n . . . no hurt her," Eric said. Frank gazed up at him in amazement. He cowered back, rubbing his shoulders.

"Who the fuck's your moron friend?" Frank said.

"Sons of bitches." He lunged for his wrecking bar and got it firmly in his grasp.

"Eric!" Judy called. "Watch out."

He looked at her questioningly, but before he could turn back to Frank, Frank swung at him and struck him in the left leg, right at the knee. The blow brought Eric to his knees. Judy screamed as Frank raised the iron tool with both hands to bring it down on Eric's head, but Eric reached up, catching the bar in his hands. Both men struggled to break the other's grasp on the wrecking bar, but Eric looked awkward and unsure of himself in a battle with what he considered to be an adult. Frank was able to take advantage of his hesitancy and break his grip on the wrecking bar. He stepped back and swung it at Eric again, this time catching him on the right upper arm. The blow stung and Eric went back. Frank pursued him, swinging the tool again and again. Eric seemed unable to defend himself.

"DON'T LET HIM DO THAT TO YOU!" Judy screamed. Both she and Marty were backing toward the door.

Eric sidestepped the next blow and Frank, lost in the momentum, went completely around. Eric went forward and hooked him under the chin with his right arm. Bewildered and frightened by the pain from the blows he had received, he violently pulled Frank toward him. Frank clawed at the giant forearm, but he was unable to break the grip.

"He's goin' to kill him," Marty said. Judy saw he was right and stepped forward to intercede, but before she could do anything, Eric lifted Frank off the ground and snapped his body to the left. There was a distinct, deadly cracking sound from the back of his neck. Frank went limp. Feeling no resistance,

Eric released his grip on him and Frank crumpled to the floor, the iron bar bouncing out of his hand.

For a few moments no one moved. Then Eric stepped back as both Judy and Marty approached.

"Oh my God," Judy said.

Marty knelt down and took Frank's wrist to feel for a pulse. Getting none, he opened Frank's shirt and put his ear to his chest.

"Is he . . ."

"Dead," Marty said, looking down at him unbelievingly. "It's like he rose from the grave."

"He would have killed us," Judy said.

Marty just nodded and continued to stare down at Frank.

"Dea . . . dea . . . dead," Eric said. They both turned to him as though they just remembered he was there.

"Marty!" Judy took his arm as Marty rose. They backed a few feet away.

"Stay calm."

"He could come after us now."

"Na . . . na . . . not my fault," Eric said, shaking his head at Frank's body. Marty thought for a moment.

"It is your fault. You killed him."

"Marty!"

"It's all right," he whispered. "I know what I'm doing."

"Jake be . . . be mad."

"Yes." Marty moved back to Frank's body. He saw the tag from the old Plymouth's car keys in Frank's pocket and found the keys to Frank's car too. "Jake be mad," he repeated. "We can't let him find out. We've got to hide the bad man's body. Do you know a good hiding place?"

"Marty, he's too dangerous."

"No, it's all right. I know who he is and what he is. He helped you before. He stopped Frank."

"Hide?" Eric said. He looked at Frank.

"Yes." Marty moved toward him. He wasn't sure whether it was dangerous or not, but he had to do it. "We need a good hiding place. Then Jake won't know and everything will be all right."

Eric looked to Judy. Marty moved his eyes and nodded toward him. He mouthed the words, "Say something."

"Yes, Eric," she said, "a hiding place. Do you know a good hiding place?"

He thought about the old foundation room in the basement. Then he nodded.

"Take him to it," Marty commanded in the strongest voice he could muster. Eric knelt down and, with only the slightest visible effort, lifted Frank's body and draped him over his shoulder. He started away, but stopped when they followed.

"Can we see the hiding place too?" Judy asked. He thought for a moment. He wasn't happy about the boy seeing it, but if this was what the girl wanted . . .

He continued to the basement, Frank's head bouncing rhythmically with his every footstep.

Judy took Marty's hand and they followed him into the depths of the hotel and the darkness of his own past.

18

Eric went through the children's dining room to a back door that opened to a stairway down into the older portion of the hotel's basement. The stairway probably hadn't been used very much, even during the hotel's heyday. The cobwebs from the ceiling to the walls were thick and heavy with dust. The steps of the stairway were very shaky. Each slat groaned and squeaked as they made their way down. The entire flight shook as though it could tear away from the wall and go crashing into the darkness below.

Marty held Judy back until Eric was nearly down. They could barely see anyway. When Eric reached the bottom step, he pulled a cord and a naked lightbulb in a ceiling fixture threw a sickly yellowish glow over the hard dirt floor and reinforced field-stone foundation walls. Marty saw a few rats scurry into the safety of shadows. There was the distinct sound of rodents squealing in fear. With reluctance, he and Judy started down the steps.

Eric didn't look back; he continued on into the darkness, stopped, and pulled another cord. A similar light fixture went on, extending the reach of the weak, yellowish glow. When Marty and Judy were halfway down the stairs, they were confronted by a pungent, dank odor. Things had died down here, Marty thought, and the putrescent scent of their decomposed bodies filled the air. This place was already a tomb of sorts.

Judy held his hand tightly. The dampness and the shadows sent a shudder through her body. She felt as though they were all descending into a living grave.

"Marty," she said, but he quieted her immediately. She wanted to tell him that maybe they shouldn't follow, that maybe Eric was leading them into some horrible danger.

"We have to see where he puts him," Marty whispered. "So that we can be sure."

"I'm afraid."

He stopped. "Do you want to go back up?"

"No. Not without you."

"Okay, then just stick close." She practically laughed at that. Even Eric couldn't pry their hands loose now.

Eric pulled another light cord and stopped. Just beyond the reach of this bulb's glow, Marty could see what looked to be the hotel's laundry. The foundation walls were Sheetrocked and there were half a dozen washing machines and dryers. Pipes ran along the ceiling. Even though the room had probably not been used for years, he caught the odor of detergent and Clorox.

Eric lowered Frank's body to the ground gently,

as though he didn't want to do any more damage. Then he went to the left and disappeared into the shadows. Marty moved forward, Judy right beside him. They heard the sound of stones being pulled out and dropped to the hard dirt floor. As they went closer they saw that the left wall jutted out and took on a box shape, the walls of that box parallel to the basement corridor. Eric was on his knees, carefully removing fieldstones to create an opening.

"What is this?" Marty asked. Eric stopped working and turned to him.

"My . . . my . . . hide . . . hide . . ."

"His hiding place," Judy said.

"Must've been some sort of storage room," Marty said, running his hand over the stones. "blocked up and forgotten when the hotel expanded and modernized."

"Is it good?" Judy asked.

"Perfect."

"Ja . . . Ja . . . Jake don't look here."

"I guess he wouldn't. You used to hide here?"

"Ye . . . yes. Don't tell . . ." he said pleadingly.

"You don't have to worry about that. This is our secret."

"Good." Eric pulled out more stones until he had an opening big enough for Frank's body. Then he got up and lifted the corpse under the arms, pulling it toward the opening. After a moment's hesitation Marty helped him. He lifted Frank's feet as Eric brought Frank's head and shoulders to the hole. Together they shoved the body in. The dark opening seemed to swallow the body, sucking in the legs and feet. As soon as it disappeared, Eric started to put the stones back. Marty admired the care he took in lining the stones up just right. Once the hole was closed, it was nearly impossible to tell that it had ever been there.

"Okay," Marty said, "back up." Judy moved quickly in front of him, heading toward the stairs. Eric remained a few feet behind them, pulling the cords and draping the old basement section in pitch darkness again. Neither Marty nor Judy looked back. They both felt a great sense of relief when they reached the stairs.

"Wait . . ." Eric called, but they couldn't help but rush up the steps. They welcomed the clearer, warmer air above. Without hesitation they moved through the children's dining room and out to the lobby. They heard him behind them.

"What are we going to do?" Judy asked.

"Just keep moving."

He led her to the first corridor. When they came to their room, he ran in and quickly gathered up whatever he could. Judy looked down the hall and saw Eric standing there, watching them.

"He's just staring at us," she whispered.

"It's all right. He doesn't understand. Let's move it."

"What about Pop Levine?" she asked as they continued down the corridor toward the side exit.

"There's no point in looking for him to say anything. He would just get more confused."

Eric was halfway down the hall when they reached the side entrance. He moved a little faster when they stepped out. She turned to look at him, but Marty pulled her along.

"We'll take Frank's car," he said, "and leave the Plymouth. Without plates, the junk heap will look like something someone abandoned."

Eric came out of the side exit and stood there watching them.

"Marty!"

"Don't look back," he said, but she couldn't help it. In the bright light he looked even more horrifying than before. "Get in quickly," he said. Eric came forward as they got into the car. Marty started it and backed up. Then he sped down the driveway to the road. As they turned left Judy looked back. It looked to her like Eric had lifted his hand to wave, but just held it in the air.

In a moment they were completely gone.

"I can't stop shaking," Judy said. "I can't." She started to cry and shiver. Marty stopped the car and put his arms around her, holding her tightly against himself. He didn't say anything for a moment, but she calmed down. He kissed her forehead and cheeks. Holding her and kissing her helped him to calm himself as well. His heart was still pumping like mad. He couldn't help but look through the rear window. They had been chased to the hotel, and now they had been chased from it.

"We'll be all right," he finally whispered. "It's over. It's over."

She shook her head and he rocked her gently in his arms. The maddening fight flashed before his eyes, and with his increasing calmness came the realization that Frank was gone forever and that the idiot had saved their lives.

"Who was he?" she said. "You said you knew all about him."

"Pop finally told me when I went looking for you." He proceeded to tell her all he had learned.

"How horrible. What will happen when Pop dies?"

"Jake'll have to stop ignoring him. We can't think about that now. We have our own problems. Now listen," Marty said, pulling back and sitting up straight, "today Elaine has the day shift. She won't be home from work yet. We'll leave the car in the driveway and say that Frank wasn't there when we got home."

"What about the Plymouth?"

"It broke down and we left it someplace. She won't care about that."

"Where did we go?"

"I want her to know the truth about Frank. We are going to tell her what he did to you."

"I don't know if I can," she said softly.

"You can. You have to. She has to know what he was. I mean, is. She can't know anything about . . . about this."

"But where will we say we were?"

"We went to a cousin of my mother's. She knows nothing about that side of my family. It'll work. Let me do as much of the talking as possible in the beginning."

"It's all happening so fast now. I can't think."

"I know. That's why I'll do the talking."

She looked at him and nodded. He was strong and she felt safe because of that. She touched his arm and he looked at her. Then he put his arm around her again and drew her beside him. He put the car in gear and they rode like that for as long as they could: both silent, both very much in need of the feel of the other.

The house looked different to them both. As soon as it appeared before them, they drew apart. It was as though they were moving from a dream back into reality. When Marty pulled into the yard and shut off the engine, they sat and stared at the building, waiting to be sure no one was home. The only movement about was the dance of an empty potato chip bag as the breeze carried it over the lawn. Nothing else had changed. The house looked more dilapidated than ever, the grounds cluttered with automobile parts.

"C'mon," Marty said, "let's get settled inside."

They took their stuff and went into the house. Marty found his bed in shambles, the mattress sliced, the pillow destroyed. He had to turn the mattress over and throw out the pillow. Judy regretted her room the moment she entered it. It seemed colder and lonelier than ever. Both created excuses to be near each other. The house had become alien to them, even threatening. Marty decided they should go downstairs and work on supper.

"We've got to appear as natural and as unperturbed as possible," he said.

When Elaine finally arrived, she found them both in the kitchen. Marty was mashing potatoes and Judy was setting the table. She had put down four places, as Marty suggested. Elaine thought it was Frank who was in the kitchen. She called from the doorway.

"Is that you, Frank?"

"No," Marty said. "It's us." She came in quickly.

"Where the hell have you two been? What the hell's goin' on?"

She looked as though she had been doing some drinking. Her hair was disheveled and her blouse was out of her skirt. Marty imagined that she had stopped at one of her hangouts on the way home from work. She leaned against the wall, her left hand on her hip. He moved forward.

"A cousin of my mother's," he said. "Is Frank with you?"

"I don't know where the hell he is. His car's out there; ain't he home?"

"No, and we're not sorry about that either."

"What the hell's goin' on? I was goin' to call the police if you two weren't back today. Why'd you go off without tellin' anybody?"

"Didn't Frank tell you anything?"

"Yeah," she said, looking from Marty to Judy, "he told me somethin'. What of it?"

Marty understood her look immediately.

"Well, he's a liar," he said quickly. "And I'll tell him to his face."

Judy started to cry. Marty thought that was a perfect touch, but he didn't say anything. He just stared at Elaine. Her expression softened and she folded her arms across her chest.

"Well . . . what's your side of it?"

"Better sit down," Marty said. *I'll play this up as dramatically as I can,* he thought.

"I don't need to sit. Talk."

Marty shrugged and took a seat himself. Judy sat down and looked at the floor.

"He sent me for some parts," he began. "When I came back, his car was here, but he wasn't in the shop. I didn't think nothing of it until I heard Judy's scream. I grabbed a shovel and ran around the building. Judy had gone to the backyard with a blanket to get some sun. Frank found her there in her bathing suit. By the time I got there . . ."

Judy began to cry again. Elaine looked from him

to her and then went to her. She put her hand on Judy's hair and stroked her gently.

"What did he do?" she asked, her voice nearly a whisper. Marty stood up, put his hands in his pockets, and turned his back on them. "Judy, honey." Elaine knelt down beside her. When Judy looked up, Elaine saw the remnants of the bruise on her cheek. "He didn't . . ." Judy nodded and began to sob again. "You poor thing," Elaine said. She caressed her shoulder. "He hurt you too. Do you have any pain anywhere now?" Judy shook her head. Elaine thought for a moment and stood up. She clenched her fists and pounded them softly against her thighs.

"I knew he was full of shit," she said. "When I found him bleedin' in bed . . ."

"I see he went wild in my room," Marty said, turning back to her.

"He's been huntin' both of you since you left, been lookin' everywhere, callin' people. Where did you go? You didn't tell the police?"

"No," Judy said, looking up and wiping her face with the backs of her hands. "I was afraid to."

"Probably wouldn't a done no good. So where have you been?"

"We went to a cousin of my mother's in Jersey. On the way back the car broke down and I left it on the highway. We hitched the rest of the way."

"You went on the highways with that Plymouth and no plates?"

Judy looked at him quickly.

"I stole some plates," he said. He made it sound as though he was sorry he had done it.

"I don't care about that."

"Well, now you know the truth," Marty said. "And when he comes home, we're ready to confront him with it, even if it means going to the cops." He said it with a lot of determination. Judy nodded and Elaine was impressed.

"When that bastard comes back, I'll throw him out myself," Elaine said. Then she thought about it for a moment and sat down. "We're goin' to have our troubles," she added. Marty agreed.

They decided to eat. Afterward, mostly out of nervousness, Elaine told one story after another about customers at the department store. She described a bad fight her friend Beverly Crawford had with her husband. "Put her in the hospital," she said, "with twenty stitches across her forehead." That got her thinking about Frank again and she decided she needed a drink. Marty got one for her, but before she started, she remembered a phone call he had gotten. "From Stanley Schwartz at the lumber company in Woodridge. They were looking for a new driver and delivery man. Someone recommended you."

"I don't want to work with Frank anymore. Might be a good idea. I'll call him tomorrow," he said and thought he would do it because they were going to need another income more than ever now.

Judy and he looked at each other during all the talk. Elaine didn't catch their side glances. It got very late and Elaine decided they shouldn't bother waiting around for Frank anymore.

"Yeah, I'm tired," Marty said.

"I spoke to the manager at the store," Elaine said as they all headed for their bedrooms, "and he said I should bring you around to do some shelf stocking and inventory work, Judy. Maybe you should come with me tomorrow. I don't want you around here by yourself anyway."

"Sounds good," Marty said before Judy could respond. She smiled at him.

It was a good hour after Marty had put his lights out and gone to bed that he heard her in the doorway. He sat up on his elbows.

"Judy?"

"I can't sleep," she said. "I'm afraid of nightmares."

"Me too."

"I wanna come in."

"What about Elaine?"

"She's asleep. I looked into her room first. She's snoring."

"Okay," he said, moving over in the bed. In a moment she was beside him. They lay quietly in the darkness and then he put his arm around her. "What's worrying you?" he asked. She didn't say anything for a few moments.

"What if he's not dead?"

"He was dead. This time I was sure of it."

"He was so ugly, so crazy, even for him. He was like another person."

"I know. I've been lying here trying to feel something about him, some sadness, some sorrow, but I feel nothing. He was a stranger; he was always a stranger."

"Oh, Marty," she said, turning her face into his shoulder. "I'm so afraid that I might say something or I might wake up screaming and Elaine will know."

"You won't. Try not to think about it."

"Marty, what happens when that man Jake returns and sees all the things we did in the hotel?"

"What happens? He'll think the old man and Eric did it. When the old man tells him about us, if he does, he'll just think it's part of his senility."

"You're so sure of everything."

"We've got to begin to put it behind us, if we ever can."

"As long as we're together . . ."

"We'll be together. Don't worry about that." He kissed her forehead and brushed away some strands of hair. "We'd better not take too much of a chance tonight. If Elaine should wake up . . . I mean, considering the story Frank told her . . ."

"You're right."

"In fact, let's try to be a little cool to each other, if you know what I mean."

"I do, but I don't like it."

He smiled and then brought his lips to hers. Their kiss was soft but reassuring.

"Go ahead," he said, "before I try to stop you."

"I'd like that."

"Please."

"All right, but what if I have a nightmare . . ."

"You'll start having them just so you can come in here." He kissed the tip of her nose. "Good night."

She slipped out of the bed, but he heard her turn in the doorway.

"Marty."

"What?"

"Do you think we'll ever go back there . . . to the hotel?"

"Why? What made you ask that?"

"I don't know. I just felt . . . like we've left something there."

"Go to sleep," he said. "You're just overtired."

"Night," she said again.

For a long time he just stared into the darkness, thinking about her question. He didn't want to say it, but he had felt it too. He didn't understand it, but he didn't want to think that much about it because it confused and terrified him.

Elaine woke him up in the morning to tell him that Frank hadn't come home all night.

"It doesn't surprise me," he told her. "He's done that many times before."

At breakfast she chatted on incessantly, happy to have them there to talk to again. Then she looked at Judy as though she just realized Judy had returned.

"You look different, honey," she said.

Judy shot a nervous glance at Marty, but he just blew on his hot coffee. "What'dya mean, different?"

"I don't know. You're wearin' your hair different. It looks good. You just look more . . . more grown up somehow. I don't know." She patted Judy's hand. "I know you had a bad time, but things'll be different now. You'll see."

After they left for the department store, Marty drove Frank's car to Woodridge and went to the lumber company. The job was still open and they wanted him to begin right then and there. He spent the day with another driver to learn the ropes, and by the time the day ended, he was exhausted but he felt good.

After he got into the car to go home, Merle Thomas, one of Frank's drinking buddies, pulled alongside. He slid over on the front seat and rolled down the window.

"How's the old man? Ain't seen him for a coupla days."

"Ain't seen him myself. He's been gone a few days. Took off on one of his drunks and he's still not back. You see him, remind him where he lives, will you."

Merle laughed. "Good old Frank. The dumb bastard," he said. Marty watched him drive off.

For a moment he thought about what he had told him. It was easier to think of Frank as being off on one of his drunks than to picture his corpse walled in under the deserted old hotel.

Elaine and Judy weren't back yet when he got home. He showered and dressed. His muscles ached as never before, but when he looked at himself in the mirror, he was proud of his build. He looked forward to doing the hard work, at least for the rest of the summer. As fall approached he would think more seriously about what he should do with his life.

He heard Judy and Elaine come in, talking and laughing loudly. When he appeared on the stairs, they both stopped and looked at him.

"All neat and clean," Elaine said. "How was your work?"

"Good. How'd you do, Judy?"

"All right."

"All right? They loved her there. The manager's thinkin' about movin' her right into a cashier's spot. She'll make good money this summer."

"Great."

"Don't tell me your father's not home yet."

"I haven't seen him."

"No one in town's seen him either," she said. "I asked a few people."

Judy's eyes met his, but neither of them changed expression.

"He's been off on a drunk before," he said. "Merle Thomas asked me about him and he thought it was funny."

Elaine considered that for a moment. "Probably. Good riddance to him, for all I care now. I'll make us some supper."

"I'll shower and come down to help," Judy said. After she went upstairs, Marty followed Elaine into the kitchen.

"You know, if Frank doesn't come home, we're going to have to think about the money situation, not that he added all that much to it on a regular basis."

"They're movin' me to the head cashier spot. I get a raise." She stopped working and looked at him. "You don't think he'll be back?"

"Could you stand it if he did?" She thought about it and nodded.

After supper Judy and Marty helped with the dishes. Afterward they all sat and watched some television. Marty complained about his sore shoulders and Elaine rubbed some liniment in.

"You're going to have arms and shoulders bigger than your father's soon," she said.

They all went to sleep early and followed the same pattern for the next few days. Elaine wondered if she should call the police but then decided against it. Marty was glad because he didn't want any kind of investigation. At the end of the week he and Elaine had a serious conversation about the future.

"We have to consider the possibility that he won't come back. At least not for a long time," she said.

"I don't have any problem with you, if that's what you mean. We can pool my check with the money you're bringing in to run this place. All we gotta do is pay the taxes on this place."

"It's too bad Judy didn't go to summer school. I don't like her being left back."

"Maybe she can double up or something. I'll help her more this year."

"I guess you two got to know each other a lot better when you ran off. I can see she has a lot more respect for you."

"We were pretty scared," he said. He wondered if she had sensed their new intimacy. She didn't say anything more about it.

She began to drink hard again. Finally one night she decided she was going to go out and have a good time. "What's the point in me sittin' around here sufferin' because of a son of a bitch like that. I hope he never comes back," she added and Judy and Marty felt a great sense of relief.

Marty went upstairs to his room before she left that night. When he heard the door slam and knew she was gone, he felt an excitement similar to the one he had experienced at the hotel. He knew Judy was downstairs waiting for him. He walked down the stairway slowly. She was standing in the living room entranceway looking up at him.

"Hi," he said.

"Hi."

"Missed you."

She laughed, but when he continued down, she ran to him and he held her in his arms. Their kiss was long and passionate and demanding. Gone was the innocent curiosity. The demands they made on each other were mature and determined. He took her hand and led her back upstairs to his room.

Although their lovemaking was more aggressive, it was slower and more careful. They handled each other with a tenderness born of the understanding of what loneliness really was. Afterward they lay beside each other, silent and thoughtful.

"It's not going to be good with your mother," he said. "She's really Frank's kind. She'll find someone else like him eventually."

"I know."

"She likes to drink and carry on. That's what brought them together in the first place." She nodded, rubbing her cheek against his chest. "Don't be afraid though. I'll always be around to take care of you."

"I'm not afraid." She was quiet for a long moment and then she said, "I wish someday we could go back to the lake. It was nice there."

"Yes, that was nice."

He was silent and she was silent, both deep in their own thoughts.

A strange feeling came over him again and ended his reverie. He sat up in bed and listened to the sounds of the night. Judy had fallen asleep but woke up when he moved.

"What's wrong?"

"Nothing," he said. "Go back to sleep." But he couldn't ignore it. He'd felt it on other nights, at the hotel. He got up and, appearing as nonchalant as he could, he went to the window.

"Marty?"

"It's all right," he said, but he peered down into the darkness intently. Something . . . something . . . it couldn't be.

19

After the car disappeared down the
road that day, Eric felt naked, vulnerable, and
confused. He had lost track of time. He was no
longer sure about Jake's days. The thought that he
could suddenly appear in his pickup truck was
enough to send him scurrying back into the hotel
walls.

He had gone to the room where they had slept.
The boy had taken nearly everything with him. Eric
found some orange peel on the windowsill and
peered out through the hole in the dust and grime
Marty had washed with it. He looked at the empty
pool and remembered how they had worked on it,
how they had played with the shuffleboard game,
and how the boy had held and kissed the girl. He had
seen it all and the memory of it made him unhappy.

He found some melted wax on the small table and
the butter knife they had used for their sandwiches.

He recalled their candlelight meal and wished he'd had the chance to do the same thing with the girl. He ran his hand over the pillow that had been her pillow and found some strands of her hair.

Very carefully and excitedly, as if he had discovered gold, he pinched the strands in his fingers and brought them to his nose to see if they still carried the aroma of her. Although he really smelled nothing, he folded them neatly and put them in his jacket pocket, along with the butter knife and the scrapings of candle wax he had taken from the table. Time passed by slowly.

One day he heard his grandfather in the main office and peered in. He was talking on the dead telephone. When he saw Eric, he stopped, put his hand over the mouthpiece, and gestured for him to come in.

"Go rake up the grass in the back," he said. Eric shook his head.

"No. I wa . . . wanted to cut . . . cut it."

"It's cut!"

"I . . . did . . . didn't do it. Tell the boy . . . to . . . to come back and do it . . . him . . . himself."

"Oy, such a dummkopf. Go, go, go play somewheres, I'm busy," Pop said and went back to speaking softly in the phone. Eric watched him for a few moments and then walked out. He was sorry he had to say no to his grandfather, but he was mad and that was that. He stalked through the lobby and into the dining room, stopping when he saw the table he had bumped into earlier. He was sorry he had smashed goblets, but he wasn't going to pick up the pieces. Not now, he thought.

He went into the kitchen and took out another bottle of milk. He poured it into a glass and drank it quickly; then he poured another and drank that just as fast. Milk was what the girl wanted. It had never tasted so good as it did now. He wanted more, but he was impatient with pouring it into a glass so he drank the rest from the bottle.

He went to the back door and looked out at the cut grass. The sight of it angered him, but he wasn't going to do anything about it. He thought about Jake coming and seeing the cut grass. Make the boy rake it, he thought. Maybe Jake would get the boy back to do it and the girl would come too. He smiled at that possibility.

But when he confronted the empty hotel, he became sad again and decided not to do anything else but go back up to the attic. He remembered how exciting it was to have the girl up there. He thought the room smelled different because she had been there.

He went to a small, nearly empty carton and shook the contents out. There were only some socks and some old shoes and slippers in it. Then he emptied his pocket, placing the butter knife, the pieces of candle wax, and the folded strands of the girl's hair in the bottom of the carton. He stared down at all of it for a few moments and then placed the carton in his favorite corner. He sat next to it, his legs pulled up against him, his arms around his knees, and he thought about the girl. Images of her face, her hair, her breasts, her eyes, flowed easily before him. It was as though he had his own private movie. She had been up here with him; he had touched her, and she had smiled at him.

The afternoon sun slipped below the ridge of mountains to the west. Its weakened rays backlit the rich green leaves of the surrounding forest until they became inky black and merged with the shadows to ring the hotel in darkness.

He went to the window and looked at the road until it became nearly impossible to distinguish it from the hotel's front lawn. Not a car approached; the world was draped in black silence. He felt as though the light within him had been turned off as well. It had been a long time since he'd suffered from such loneliness.

"She'll be back," he muttered. "She'll be back."

But she didn't come back the next day or the next, or even the one after that. Each day he spent hours by the windows waiting, watching. When he was bored with that, he wandered about the hotel to look at some of the things the boy and girl had done together.

He drank a lot of milk. Lately that was his favorite thing to drink. The creamy taste made him think of the girl again.

He often took some bread and cheese and went upstairs to the attic to eat it, even at night. Since Marty and Judy had left, he had taken to sleeping up there all the time. Lying on the mattress the girl had been on, he thought he could detect the scent of her hair. When he closed his eyes, he could see her vividly. He remembered her breasts and what it was like to touch them and to stroke her hair.

One time he heard a car approaching and he jumped up quickly to look out of the eyebrow window, but the automobile simply went by. It didn't even hesitate by the driveway. The sight of it encouraged him and he waited by the window for hours to see another one. Eventually he went back to the mattress, curled up under the same sheet he had placed over the girl, and fell asleep.

As the days passed, he didn't forget the girl; he thought more and more about her. One day he went out to the lake to stare at the water and the raft and the boat just to recall what it had been like when he'd spied on them. He threw some rocks in the water and left.

And there were new feelings, feelings that wouldn't leave him, feelings that drove him to think hard about the girl. He dreamed about her constantly and did whatever he could to revive the memories. Sometimes he spent his time simply walking through the places she had been in, touching the things she had touched. He even went out on the patio and lay out on the chaise lounge she had fallen asleep on that day.

But nothing was the same and nothing ever satisfied him. If anything, it made him more unhappy. He considered going into the casino and playing the music they had played, perhaps even wearing one of the costumes, but he decided against doing that at the last minute. When he finished the milk Jake had brought, he was terribly despondent and couldn't believe that he was actually hoping for Jake to arrive again so there would be more milk.

And then one day it came to him. The idea exploded in his mind. He had been staring out the attic window, looking down at the driveway, and remembering how the girl had run to the car. She had looked back once as the automobile pulled away and disappeared around the turn. The image of her face lingered as though it were frozen in the air out there.

He thought about how he had waved and how he had taken just a step or two forward. Suddenly it occurred to him: What if he had taken a few more steps and a few more? What if he had run after the car, followed it down the road? Maybe if he had done that, he would have seen where they had gone. Maybe he could still find out where they had gone. Perhaps they weren't that far away. He remembered the car. If he saw it again, he would know it.

His eyes widened with excitement. He clapped his hands together. He would do it. He would go down the driveway and follow the road until he found their car and then . . . then he would find the girl. He would call to her and she would remember him and maybe, just maybe, he could talk her into coming back to the hotel.

It was already late in the afternoon when he started out. Much of the low sunlight was blocked by the trees. He traveled as much as he could in the forest parallel to the road, sometimes stopping to hug a large maple or oak as he surveyed the road ahead of him. From the moment he left the hotel grounds, he periodically stopped to look back and see the roof of the main building. When it finally disappeared from sight, he was reluctant to go on. As long as the hotel loomed above him, he felt safe.

Was the girl so far away? How much farther could it be? He saw a car approaching and instinctively went to the floor of the forest on his hands and knees. The car was nothing like the car the girl had gone off in. This car was much smaller and a completely different color. He watched it pass and debated with himself as to whether or not he should go on.

It had already gotten much darker. He considered the possibility that he wouldn't find the girl and he wouldn't be able to find his way back. The thought terrified him and for a while he just stood there whimpering with indecision. Then, concentrating on his memory of the girl as hard as he could, he gathered his resolve and continued on, weaving and sliding in and out of the trees.

Eventually he reached a long, open field. Fortunately the grass was waist high and he was able to scurry across it, stooping as always. Satisfied that he was well hidden, he moved quickly to the forest at the other side and went on. Suddenly he came to a whole group of little houses on the other side of the street. He stopped, crouched down, and studied them.

There were no lights on in any of them and there were no signs of any people. He looked both ways by the road and then ran across, bending so low as he moved that his hands touched the pavement. He fell to his stomach in the grass and crawled closer to the entrance. Looking closely at the little houses now, he realized that the girl wasn't there; no one was there. It was as empty as the hotel. He felt it was safe enough to stand up again and continue on.

It was very dark now, but his eyes, used to years and years of perceiving forms in the dark, quickly grew accustomed to the deep shadows. He had no trouble going on; he moved slowly to be cautious and see as much as he could. He didn't want to pass up any houses. Once in a while he stopped to listen to the sounds of the night to see if he could hear any people. The crickets and peepers were noisier than ever. He wanted to scream out at them to be still for a few moments. Occasionally he would hear something in the forest across the road. Once an owl with a long wingspan swooped down a few feet before him and then went on to disappear in the black forest.

Now, when he stopped to listen, he did hear something. It sounded like . . . yes, it was . . . music. The sound was coming from the right, not very far off. He moved on, staying close to the bushes and trees, tunneling through shadows, draped in darkness. He had become a part of the night, almost indistinguishable from the swaying and nodding shadows of tree limbs and the different patterns created by the various configurations of leaves.

After a while he came to a turn. The music was louder now and very clear. He could make out the words. Slowly, hugging the bank of the road, he came around and then stopped immediately. The house was before him, lights on, someone visible in the upstairs window. Practically crawling, he began to approach it, and then his heart burst with joy. There, parked near the building, was the car the boy and girl had gone off in. He had done it. He had found her!

He was crawling closer when all of a sudden he heard laughter at the front door. He saw someone come out of the house. It looked like the girl. She went to the car and got in. A few moments later she started the engine and backed the car onto the road. He was going to walk toward it, but he decided too late. She headed in the opposite direction and was gone.

He sat on the ground, practically in tears. He was so close he could practically see her face and now she was gone again. He had come so far and now it was very dark. What was he to do? It must be her house, he thought. She would have to come back. He would wait and when she drove up again, he would run to the car to be sure she would see him and know he was here. It was a good idea.

He found a safe hideaway in a pocket of tall grass. From there he could see both the house and the road very well. He could even listen to the music. In time she would be back, he thought, and he would be here. He curled his body up and peered through the tall blades of grass and weeds. After a while he just closed his eyes and rested. Soon he fell asleep.

Hours afterward he awoke with a jolt. For a moment he forgot where he was. The music wasn't playing anymore and most of the lights in the house were turned off. He wiped his eyes and remembered. He was about to stand up when he saw something in the upstairs window. Although it was dark, he could clearly make out the silhouette of the boy. He was sure he recognized the shape of his head and shoulders.

Why was the boy just standing there, staring out? Did he see him here in the grass? He stared up at the boy and waited without moving a muscle. Then the car returned.

He heard it before he saw the beam of its headlights. The moment it turned up the road toward the house, he stood up and looked up at the boy again. He had moved away from the window. Eric imagined he was coming downstairs to tell the girl he was here in the grass. That had to be it! He had to make sure he reached her first.

The car tires squealed as Elaine floored the accelerator. She was quite drunk and excited and she was going too fast to stop right at the house. She knew it was there, but her perception was clouded and distorted. Instead of slowing down, she continued to accelerate. Merle Thomas was drinking a beer in the front seat. She had picked him up at the bar and was taking him home to bed.

She never really saw Eric run into the road. She was laughing hysterically, her head turned to Merle to tell him she had failed to see her own house. Suddenly they heard the thump and felt the car pause. Because of her slowed reflexes, Elaine hit the brakes a full second afterward and the car screeched to a halt.

"I hit somethin'," she said.

"Crazy . . ."

"I hit somethin'," she repeated.

"Huh? What?" Merle looked about stupidly and struggled to clear his thoughts. He had nearly finished a six-pack before they got there, throwing each empty bottle into the backseat. Elaine pressed her head against the steering wheel.

Upstairs Marty was sure he had seen Eric in the darkness below. When Elaine turned the car toward the house, the headlights had outlined him clearly against the shadows below. Marty had stepped away from the window as though he had seen a ghost.

"What is it?" Judy asked.

He barely had time to say the name before they heard the terrible thump and the screech of car brakes. Neither of them moved for a moment and then they both rushed out of the room, down the stairs, and out the front door. They stopped on the porch. Eric's immense body was sprawled face down on the road. He looked more gigantic than they remembered.

"Jesus Christ!" Merle shouted as he staggered out of the car. "Elaine, Jesus Christ!" He stood wavering over the body.

"What is it?"

"You hit some guy or somethin'! Jesus!"

Marty and Judy, holding hands now, approached slowly, silently. Elaine threw open the car door and struggled to pull herself out. She balanced herself against the car, then walked toward Merle.

"Oh God," she said. "Is he . . ."

"I don't know what the hell he is," Merle said. He knelt down slowly, cautiously, as though he were afraid Eric would rise up and attack him. He lifted Eric's left hand and studied it for a moment. "Hey," he called to Marty, "c'mere and help me." Marty looked at Judy. "C'mere, for Christ sakes. I can't move him myself. Look at the size of him." Marty stepped forward and helped Merle turn Eric on his back. The moment they did so, Merle stood up and whistled. "What the hell is it?"

"It's a man," Marty said. Judy came a few steps closer. Elaine put her hands to her ears to stop the ringing in her head.

"Is he . . . how is he?" she asked. Marty felt for a pulse and then put his ear to Eric's chest to see if he could sense a heartbeat. A line of blood had formed across his forehead so evenly that it looked as though it had been painted there. His mouth was open and his eyes looked like they were made of glass as they continued their death stare.

"Better call the cops," Merle said.

"Oh God," Elaine said. "I didn't see him. He came from outta nowhere. Oh God. . . ."

"Yeah, well, you're not exactly in any condition to have seen anything," Marty said. He looked at Judy, who had turned away. Elaine started to cry and beat on herself.

"It wasn't your fault. You couldn't a seen him anyway," Merle said. "Take it easy. Who the hell is he?" he asked Marty. Marty just shook his head. "So it's some kinda weirdo. Shit, you mighta saved someone's life hittin' him," Merle added.

"That doesn't make it right," Marty snapped, but neither Merle nor Elaine heard him. The two of them went back to the car. Elaine lowered her head against the side window.

"What are we going to do?" Judy whispered.

"Nothing. Don't say anything. If they find out who he is, they'll think he just wandered off from the hotel."

She looked back at him on the road, his arms twisted, his body contorted. Despite the grotesqueness, she couldn't help feeling a deep sense of sorrow.

"Oh, Marty," she said. He put his arm around her and led her back toward the house.

"I know," he said. "It's awful. He must have thought we were in the car."

They turned around when they heard Merle and Elaine shouting at each other. Each blamed the other now. They went at it for a few minutes and then Elaine looked at the body and became contrite. She broke into tears, her wailing almost as loud as her cursing had been. Merle became remorseful, too, but when he went to put his arm around her, she pushed him away.

"Well, fuck you," he said and started walking down the dark road. Judy ran to Elaine and put her arm around her mother's waist to lead her back to the house.

"I'll call the police," Marty said and went in ahead of them. Judy settled Elaine on the couch to wait. After he made the phone call, Marty got a blanket and brought it outside to cover Eric's body.

He remained with the body until the patrol car came. He felt a certain obligation to do so. After all, Eric had probably saved his life and Judy's as well. He had never meant them true harm. Nevertheless he was grateful when he finally heard the police siren in the distance. Now at least one nightmare was over.

Epilogue

The police never found out who Eric was. Marty realized it would be quite a while before Jake discovered that he wasn't in the hotel, and the old man would probably never know it. Neither Marty nor Judy told the police anything. They were afraid of what any kind of investigation would lead to and there didn't seem to be any reason to talk. Eric was dead, put out of the misery that came from no one really caring about him.

Elaine's license was suspended for two months and Marty had to drive her to work and pick her up whenever their shifts coincided. When they didn't, she had to take a taxi. But that was the least of her troubles.

Ironically, she was plagued with nightmares and remorse. Marty and Judy were surprised, even delighted, at the change that came over her. She didn't want to go out nights, and she rarely had anything to drink. She took to cleaning the house more, spending more time cooking, watching television, and reading magazines. She went to sleep early and got up early, even when she didn't have a day shift.

Although Marty worked hard at his job and enjoyed the physical labor, he didn't see any future in it. Toward the end of the summer he made a decision and announced it at the dinner table.

"I went to the high school during my lunch hour today and spoke to the guidance people. They're going to get me into a part-time program at the community college."

"Really?" Judy's eyes lit up with excitement. "You mean we'll both have homework at night now?"

"Yeah, I suppose so."

"That's very good, Marty," Elaine said. "That's very good. I hope you work hard and get yourself out of this rut."

"I'll give it a shot," he said. "I don't know what I want to do yet, but I'll see how it goes. I've been away from school for more than two years."

"I'll help you," Judy said and he laughed. Even Elaine smiled at that.

It was very warm that night, and after dinner was done and the dishes were washed, Marty went outside. For a while he just stood there on the porch looking into the darkness. There was still something bothering him and he knew he would never be satisfied until he had taken care of it. His nightmares were proof of it. He stepped off the porch and walked slowly toward the car just as Judy came outside.

"Marty?" she called.

"What?"

"What are you doing?"

"I was going for a ride," he said. She could barely see him in the shadows. "It's hot," he added.

"Why didn't you ask me to go along?" He didn't respond, but he didn't move either. "You're not just taking a ride."

"I won't be long," he said and started toward the car again.

She stepped off the porch and started to follow him. "I'll go with you."

"It's better if I go by myself."

"No it isn't, Marty. It's not something that happened only to you."

He thought for a moment. She stood beside him, her hand on his arm.

"Do you know what I want to do?"

"Yes," she said softly.

"Get in then." Without another word he started the car and backed onto the road. Neither of them looked at the other as he turned left and headed toward the hotel.

They drove in silence, both hypnotized by the darkness. The main building of the hotel appeared, inky black against a dark velvet sky peppered with stars, and he slowed down.

"Maybe it's not necessary," she said. "Maybe we shouldn't."

"It's necessary. I don't spend a night without wondering if he's really dead or just locked away."

"I think about it too."

"Then you know why I can't turn back." He turned into the driveway and drove up slowly, bringing the car to a stop near the side entrance. "There's a flashlight in the glove compartment," he said. When she handed it to him, they got out of the

car and went to the door of the hotel. They both
paused for a moment to listen and then entered.

"It's like we dreamed something," she said, "and
now we're returning to it."

"I know."

There *was* a dreamlike quality to everything. As
they entered the lobby, they felt as though they had
left reality. Each piece of furniture, each fixture,
every painting—all of it looked ethereal. As if a snap
of the fingers could make it disappear and they'd be
back in their own beds looking into the darkness of
their own rooms.

They headed for the basement stairway. Every
creak and echo in the building became threatening
and they drew closer and closer to each other,
practically moving as one body. They stopped at the
door. Marty's fingers were trembling as he raised his
hand to turn the knob, but he opened the door and
directed the flashlight down the steps. Again they
hesitated and listened. There were sounds in the
hotel, sounds they had heard before that somehow seemed terrifying now. Marty swallowed,
took a deep breath, and started down. Judy
held on to his arm as she followed very closely behind.

He found the first bulb cord at the bottom of the
stairway and pulled it. In its sickly yellowish glow
they saw a large rat squeeze past them into a hole
half its size. Judy gasped and clung tighter to Marty's
arm. He found the next light cord and pulled it as
well. A putrescent scent suddenly filled their nostrils. For a moment neither of them moved. Marty
directed the flashlight's beam farther in, on the
fieldstone wall.

"It's all right," Judy said quickly. "It hasn't been touched." She was trying to convince herself before he went to investigate.

She released him as he stepped forward. This was as far as she would go with him. He reached the stones and ran his hand over the spot Eric had chosen. There was a looseness there, but nothing appeared to have been moved.

Maybe now, he thought, his nightmares would stop. Maybe now it would be over.

"Marty?"

"It's all right. Nothing's changed; nothing's been touched."

"Let's go."

"Okay." He kept his hand against one of the stones for a moment and looked down in silent meditation. He felt a tremble in the rock and pulled his hand back quickly. But when he went to check again, nothing moved. It was his own body tremors, he thought. That's what it had to be.

"Marty."

"Okay, okay." He stepped back, ran the light over the wall one final time, and joined her. They turned the lights off along the basement corridor and moved up the stairway quickly. This time they didn't stop to look at anything.

It wasn't until they were in the car and Marty had started the engine that they began to breathe easier. Judy put the flashlight away and he backed the car up to turn around and drive down the driveway. Neither of them looked back as he turned onto the road and pulled away. Once again they rode in silence, but before they reached the house, she slid over on the seat to sit closer to him. He put his arm around her.

The darkness seemed to peel away from them as they drove on, and in this direction the night sky before them was filled with even more stars. No longer refugees of the night, they could gaze ahead and be dazzled.